Gathering Sara

A Novel

Jean M. Ponte

iUniverse, Inc.
Bloomington

Gathering Sara
A Novel

This is a work of fiction. All of the characters, names, incidents,
organizations, and dialogue in this novel are either the products
of the author's imagination or are used fictitiously.

iUniverse books may be ordered through booksellers or by contacting:

iUniverse
1663 Liberty Drive
Bloomington, IN 47403
www.iuniverse.com
1-800-Authors (1-800-288-4677)

ISBN: 978-1-4502-4881-5 (pbk)
ISBN: 978-1-4502-4883-9 (ebk)

Printed in the United States of America

iUniverse rev. date: 11/26/2012

TO MY HUSBAND

Joseph G. Ponte

CHAPTER ONE

S ara Mehan Kolenda tosses her jeans aside and hurries into the 1770's costume that she has been given to wear in her new summer job as a re-enactor at Fort Mac. She isn't eager for anyone to see her in her bra and underpants. Already they feel suspiciously snug. In her haste to keep from being caught undressed, she fumbles and mistakenly pulls out the drawstring in the skirt. "Oh blast," she mutters.

Quickly, in case someone actually does come into the cabin dressing room, Sara finishes trying on the costume by holding the skirt together at the waist with her hand. As she gazes into the long mirror, the dim ceiling light casts a shadow below her cheekbones and reinforces the fact that she appears sickly. That's exactly how she feels…sick. In contrast to her small white face, her nearly black hair gives her image a geisha girl appearance as though her face below the bangs carries a make-up of white flour with a feverish bloom of pink on her cheeks.

The log cabin in which she is dressing looks insignificant in height next to the twenty-foot walls of Fort Mac, a reconstruction of the British fort built back in the seventeen hundreds. Inside the rebuilt fort walls are replicas of row houses, soldiers' barracks, a blacksmith shop, church and many other buildings in which the interpretive programs take place.

Sara looks again into the mirror and sees herself as a young lass in a white cotton chemise and a dark skirt meant to gather at the waist but minus its drawstring. The homespun looking chemise is shirred

1

at both the neckline and the wrist-length sleeves. Sara watches her reflection slip arms through a blue and maroon striped bodice. The flag blue in the stripe is almost as dark as the blue of the skirt, but they don't match. The bodice has laces from the waist to just under her breasts. "It fits well, at least it does right now," she whispers. "I don't see how it can possibly fit by the end of summer. By then I'll be over six months pregnant."

Sara is well aware that her new job entails nothing more mentally complicated than simple acting and menial chores; her purpose is to re-interpret life as it was long ago at old Fort Mac, something any high school girl could handle with no college degree. She wants the job not so much for the money, though she does need money badly, but more as a temporary retreat; she wants to slip out of sight, take on the colors of her surroundings like a chameleon yet remain in contact with her mother and father, also Brian, her brother. But she fervently hopes that Larry, her former live-in boyfriend from Chicago, won't discover where she is.

She figures that the laces in the bodice of the costume can probably be loosened as she gains weight during her pregnancy, but even before that her breasts, which she already feels swelling as she imagines an activated seed might, will more than likely split the seams under the arms of the chemise. "Maybe," she mutters, "if I'm careful, I can avoid putting on weight too quickly, too noticeably." Right now the morning nausea keeps her from eating very much anyway. She guesses that she might lose a pound or two because of it, and then later gain it all back again. Firmly, she advises herself, a trace of her former stubborn nature rising up, "You'll just have to manage somehow."

❖ ❖ ❖

Sara had always managed her own life and done it competently, at least up until now. Her self-reliance was part of her upbringing, a confidence learned early because her parents had given her free reign to make many of her own decisions and mistakes...some of them tinged with embarrassment...to them as well as to Sara. She had been in uncomfortable circumstances before this one, and she had survived.

2

Yet, she had to admit, this new situation of having an unpredictable, rebellious body was totally different. She was no longer in charge. "Nature is holding a weapon over me. It's trying to flatten me; then fatten me." She flippantly attempts to sustain herself in a lighter frame of mind, but can't keep the good humor going for long. "I have a right to feel mutinous, haven't I?"

Typically she would have fought this situation of being pregnant exactly the way she had fought other adverse events in her life beginning way back in grade school. How she wished herself back there right now when she had had the aplomb to challenge all the rules. It had been so easy to feel confident back then, and even on into high school as well. "Oh yes, she reminds herself, "but none of those situations were anywhere near the challenge of this one...preparing for a new tiny life."

With her mind still cruising the past, she remembers when she and her high school friends had been temporarily expelled for blocking the office of the principal during a protest against assembly. It was school policy that all students must attend assembly. The policy had subsequently been changed but not, Sara suspected, because of their organized sit-in.

Her best friend, Emily, had asked her how she had dared to stage a sit-in when her father was a teacher in the same school system. "Mine," said Emily, "would still be yelling at me over the so-called crime, three years later. Didn't yours say anything?"

"Not much." But what her father *had* said about her flaunting the school rules had impressed Sara by its very softness, its sheer hopeful tone. In a subdued voice he had expressed a wish that she would put some of her natural drive into her studies. "Put that spunk to good use," he had urged. Sara hated the words *spunk* or *sassy*, which she heard time and time again from her mother, but enjoyed flaunting the "s" word that her brother, Brian, could get away with using. That word clearly expressed her feelings right now. "Shit," she whispered and then with a bit more gusto, "I feel shitty!" It rang true...absolutely genuine, and she felt a momentary outlet that didn't last more than two seconds.

Six years ago her mother had been more critical over the high school sit-in than her father. "Hold off till you find something more important to protest over instead of embarrassing your father over trivialities." Except for one occasion when Sara had helped her fellow students write a joint criticism of the dull assemblies they were forced to attend as part of their curricula, she had waited.

After her first youthful protests, based mostly on her stubborn dislike of the rules, any rules, which took away the freedoms that she thought she had a God-given right to—she had chosen her protests more carefully. During her senior university year at Urbana, she had gotten acquainted with a group of environmentalists who worked to clean up trash and garbage in poor neighborhoods. Then she and a few other girls in her social studies class had joined the sit-ins against abortion clinics.

A year later after getting her undergraduate degree, she had decided to move to Chicago in hopes of earning money toward a Masters at Northwestern.

"Mecca calls?" her friend Fay had shrugged sarcastically, projecting ahead and realizing that she was about to lose Sara's half of the rent money. "Wouldn't you be better off here? We have this apartment, but up there you'll have a hard time finding a place to live. Everything's too expensive."

"I'll stay at the YWCA until I find a place," she told Fay with great confidence. She packed her 1995 Suburu to the roof, made the transition, and even found a job the first week in Northwestern University's Admissions Office. She told Fay on the phone, "My biggest problem, so far, is finding a parking space."

None of the incidents in her past, Sara realizes, has been as daunting as this one…of being pregnant. There are no maps, no precedents, in her immediate life, to help cope with the situation. First, of course, it's far more serious than other things that have happened to her, and in no way does she feel any of that past confidence with which she is supposed to be so copiously endowed. "Where's your so-called "spunk?" she asks herself sarcastically. She doesn't feel in charge of this situation. Nature is in charge. She feels the way some of her father's older work shirts appear, floppy and lifeless from too much time in the drying cycle.

If I begin to look too suspiciously fat, she assures herself, as she quickly slips back into her own clothes, I'll still have the longer white kitchen apron to cover my stomach. She has learned from the historical information given to her regarding the 1770's period, that when a woman is cooking or cleaning, the shorter apron is worn outside her bodice and the rest of the time it's tied just under the bodice. But in addition, there is also a larger pinafore-type apron, which spreads from her shoulders down to the bottom of her skirt. That apron can hide almost anything.

Actually, it isn't absolutely crucial that she hide her pregnancy from her fellow re-enactors. It's her parents she wants to keep in ignorance of her condition, at least until later in the summer. Now that she has let them know where she is working this summer, they will doubtless be driving up from Oakland in the southern part of the state to visit her at some time or other. If they discover her secret and learn that she isn't planning to get married, they'll surely urge her to have an abortion. "I don't believe in abortions." She doesn't believe in marriage in this particular situation either. She intends to keep the baby, married or not.

Sara pulls the white mob cap over her hair. Only her dark bangs are left showing, leaving her long thin neck exposed like a colorless stalk. As always when viewing herself, she wishes she had inherited her Irish mother's curly hair along with her large velvety blue eyes. But no, her own eyes are only regulation size, gray but approaching green if she's wears blue colors, and her hair is straight as a plumb line and thicker than her Polish father's. Anyway, in a couple of weeks if she lets her hair grow longer, the mob cap will appear less like a mushroom perched on top of a bare stalk.

As part of the costume she has also been given a bonnet-type hat to be worn outdoors when working in the vegetable garden. She groans quietly. The very thought of bending over or doing any kind of strenuous work, leaves her feeling tired and washed-out. She supposes that such labor, bending and weeding and digging in the soil, won't harm the baby, but it may not feel too pleasant for her, the future Mom, especially until the morning sickness abates.

In years gone by, pregnant women often worked in gardens and fields right up until the birth of their baby, and probably still do in third world countries. Then after their baby is born, they carry it on their backs instead of in their wombs. In Sara's particular case it can't work that way. Besides, her own baby isn't due until two or three months after this summer job is finished in September.

❖ ❖ ❖

In the Northwest Row House kitchen, Ansel Holvorson got ready to lift the heavy iron kettle up onto the black wrought iron bar that swung out from the fieldstone fireplace. To accomplish this, it took both of her hands and widely spread, carefully balanced legs. Before swinging the bar back inwards over the hot fire, she tucked the front hem of her long curry colored skirt into her waistband to prevent it from catching sparks from the fireplace. Afterwards, she turned around and talked to a woman tourist who stood on the other side of the waist-high partition. The low wooden partition allowed tourists to observe what was taking place in the kitchen without actually interfering inside the working area.

"I just mixed up a corn and venison stew. The stew needs a good two hours to become savory even though the venison is already partially cooked and cut up into small chunks."

The tall thin woman in shorts sniffed, "It smells great already. But where on earth did you get the venison this time of year?"

"Oh, some local hunter probably felled it during the hunting season, froze it up and donated it to the Parks Department for use at one of the forts. If you have any other questions, I'll be glad to answer them." Ansel's brisk voice managed to cut off any further chit-chat.

"No. Thank you." The woman moved on and out the opposite door where Ansel heard her exclaim to someone waiting for her, "All those flies! They should have screens. Oh, I forgot," she giggled, "there probably weren't any screens back in those days."

Ansel had been told that the new interpreter, Sara something-or-other, was coming tomorrow to help with the work in the kitchen. "About time," she peeved, then turned to make sure no one had overheard her. "Let someone else answer all the silly repetitious questions," she scoffed. "With the new girl coming, I'll finally have time for something more interesting, more rewarding."

It wasn't that Ansel was unused to long work hours; she had been born into a family that took ten and twelve hours of work for granted because they ran the bakery in the village. Those on-your-feet work hours were exactly the reason why she didn't want to stay in the family bakery business. Vigorously, she exclaimed to herself for the umpteenth time, "No thanks!" She had taken her first opportunity to get out of the bakery and into something different even though it wasn't a year-round job. After all, this was a tourist town, and the only job opportunities to be expected were in gift shops, restaurants, or making beds in motels. Most of those closed up at the end of the season. This fort, like the summer gift shops, would also close in winter and reopen only for a few special occasions such as holidays and the sled-dog mush. In addition, some of the re-enactors would travel around to the schools in the state from time to time to supplement the school history lesson with some live history reenactments. She hoped to be included in that group.

Now she assures herself, "If the new girl turns out to be of any use at all, she'll free me up, and I can put my time into copying some of the old-time recipes I've collected over the last five years." Collecting old recipes had been a hobby of hers even before the Parks Department began considering printing a small paperback book of the same recipes she used here in the row house kitchen.

Having her cooking and baking ideas actually put into print will give her some of the gratification she craves, though she realizes the flimsy nature of paper is hardly the stuff to be considered an everlasting memorial. Still, the idea of seeing her name, Ansel Holverson, on the cover of a book and hearing people refer to her as an author sounds a great deal more important than cooking the same foods day after day in a kitchen.

So far, all she has to leave behind someday is a plethora of photos showing how she has gained weight year after year so that now at twenty eight she weighs one-fifty when she should only weight about one-twenty or less for her five foot height. It's exactly the same overweight story with her older sister. "What a shame," she laments out loud, "we both have fair, nearly white, soft hair and pale, freckle-free skin of which to be proud." The weight problem must be in the genes she decides, since their mother and father are both as heavy and square-cut as rustic picnic tables.

What if the new girl from Chicago has one of those stick-thin figures like the models she's seen on TV slinking across a stage with one hand on a bony protruding hip and cheeks sucked-in and shadowy from hunger? She warns herself not to be envious before she's even seen the new employee. This new girl may have a devastatingly lovely figure but possess a nose as pointy as Pinocchio or a chin that nature has almost eliminated.

"Anyway," she concludes with a shrug, "there's no obligation for me to be friendly with the new girl. She's being hired to reinterpret the gritty colonial life, and that includes keeping the wood box full and scrubbing the counters with lye soap as well."

CHAPTER TWO

*I*n the dressing room cabin, Sara has begun to zip up her blue jeans when she hears the squish-squeak of footsteps plowing through the sand outside the door. Quickly she grabs her T-shirt and dodges into a dark corner of the room. Whoever it is, passes on, probably going inside the fort through the Priest's Gate, which is very near to the dressing room where she now stands in the shadows. She knows from her past visits to the fort that the gate is called the 'Priest's Gate' because it had been positioned in the stockade wall right next to the priest's little house and once opened straight into his private garden. Only now there is no garden. Where once vegetables thrived, there is nothing but a gentle mound of sand spread with low choke cherry bushes and sharp-edged beach grasses.

Sara finishes dressing by quickly pulling the jersey T-shirt over her head. She notes how the waist of the jeans feels on the tight side, even though she is just now ending her first trimester. Perhaps the fat feeling is actually due to water retention. She has read something about it in the little paperback book, <u>Your Pregnancy</u>, which she keeps well hidden in a drawer under her bra and panties back in her rented room. With the costume over her arm, she steps outside and heads down to the shore for a lungful of clean watery air that she has missed back in Chicago. The Windy City is on the same body of water that laps against the shores up here in Mac Village, but the air down there gets mixed with big city odors, truck and car exhaust, leaving it without the pristine aerated aroma she savors so much.

Sara trudges through the deep sand, keeping close to the outside wall of the wooden stockade. She guesses that its weathered posts rise more than three and a half times her own height. She passes the Priest's Gate and a weathered picnic table and continues in the direction of the water. Here the sand is firmer and partially covered with tough beach grasses, jewelweed, and a few early harebells, blue, waving on their delicate stems.

As she approaches the corner of the fort, a loud boom echoes along the beach. The gulls, alarmed by the percussion sound, fly up and away from their rock perches, a slurry of white wings. The booming noise doesn't startle Sara. From previous visits to Fort Mac with her parents, she quickly surmises that a cannon demonstration is taking place. As she peers around the northwest corner of the stockade, she spots the cannon on a small wooden platform attended by three soldiers dressed in British outfits of red coat, white breeches and canvas gaiters. Nearby, a rope barrier holds back thirty or so tourists from getting too close to the cannon.

The soldier next to the cannon has to raise his voice to shouting level to be heard over a Jet Ski passing just off shore. "Get ready to cover your ears again." Sara watches as a second soldier holding the linstock, which in turn holds the slow match, reaches out to the hole in the breech and the cannon booms a second time followed by a puff of smoke rising straight up and then quickly dissipating. This second boom returns as a faint echo. The tourists then disperse and amble back through the Water Gate and into the stockade. Sara herself turns in the opposite direction, westerly, and walks up the beach a few yards and then sits down on a rock beside the water.

To her left just a hundred feet beyond the chain link fence that divides the park land from private property, she can see the first cottage in a long line of cottages that follow the crescent of the bay all the way to the next point of heavily wooded land. Then facing north straight across the body of water, she sees the upper peninsula attached to the lower peninsula by the long, five-mile suspension bridge. How fragile the cables look from here, like mere harp strings. Peering under the bridge in a northeasterly direction is the humped shape of Mackinac Island. Even some of the white cottages on the island bluff are visible on this clear day.

Today the whole panorama from west to east is a gorgeous sight. The water ever moving, each wave an original pattern of foam and bubbles, reflects the jewel tones of the sky. Nearby, over Sara's left shoulder, are some white pines, the sun glinting off their silvery-green needles; far off in the hazy distance across the water a dark shape appears on the horizon where there is no land. Sara presumes it's a freighter, its shape distorted by the curve of the earth. A few minutes later, observing the same shape again, she confirms it as a salty, an oceangoing ship.

Even the peaceful beauty of the scene in front of her can't assuage her nervousness concerning her uncertain future. Her mind anxiously slips back to the tiny life she is carrying. Though she is fairly certain that her parents will be unprejudiced enough to shelter her and the new babe through the coming event, she has yet to be honest about the situation. She has a lot of explaining to do about her six months in Chicago and her short association with Larry. Briefly, she thinks about those frightening days back in Chicago; then her mind is fairly yanked back to the present by a tinge of nausea. She places her hand on her stomach and swallows. The queasy sensation is increasing. She reaches in her pocket for a soda cracker, but her hand comes up empty. "I should have brought more crackers," she mutters to herself. Hastily she rises from the rock upon which she has been sitting and heads for her room at a trot.

This time as she passes the Priest's Gate, she sees a young man not much taller than herself, leaning against the stockade wall smoking a cigarette.

"You the new gal?" he asks with cheery welcome in his voice.

Sara doesn't want to be stuck in a conversation when she might throw-up at any minute so she nods and tries to hurry past, but the young man sticks out his arm as though to cordon her off.

"Hey, don't run away. I'm Skyler. We'll be working together you know. What's your name?"

"Sara. Sorry, I have to hurry…I have an appointment," she lies.

"Oh, then we'll get acquainted later."

Quickly, before he can stop her again, she veers off toward the back gate where employees usually enter and leave. On her left she passes a small pile of gravel and a truck loaded with black dirt. Next on her right are the the open garage doors of the Department of Natural Resources building, their offices, and according to the sign, the archaeological lab as well.

She walks straight on toward a second gate praying that she won't meet anyone else and have to lie again over her terrible hurry to reach the bathroom. Her pursed lips and slightly bent over posture will surely betray the terrible sickness she feels...the certainty that she will heave up the contents of her stomach at any minute. The street seems miles wide...the bathroom far, far away across a macadam desert.

In spite of the precarious feeling in her stomach and her anxiousness to reach her room, Sara stops and looks quickly in both directions before crossing the street. Yet she isn't in fear of being run down by a car; this road is seldom heavy with traffic. Maybe a few cars pass this way from the beach colony nearby or sometimes tourists coming off the bridge from the upper peninsula get their directions tangled and end up several blocks away from their intended route. Occasionally, cars belonging to the weekend re-enactors are parked along the side of the road. She knows this because her own parents have parked there in the past.

What keeps her on the lookout and on edge is the fear that any day, any hour, Larry might turn up. Like a mantra she repeats to herself, "I don't want him to find me. He must not know about the baby."

Though she has no proof that she is being followed or watched, there is also a chance that the FBI might be monitoring her, hoping she can lead a trail to Larry and his friend, Dars. The recurring worry makes her suspicious of every slow moving car or a car standing at the curb with men sitting in it pretending to be reading newspapers or snoozing.

Just across the street from where she now hesitates is a row of motel-type rooms. Each room has a wide window and a door with a plastic chair stationed beside it on the cement walk. The rooms had once been part of a commercial motel for tourists and later purchased by the Parks Department to house employees like herself. The motel pool has been filled-in and a new multipurpose building constructed over it and painted a soft, driftwood gray to match the motel section. Re-enactors like Sara are charged a minimum rate to live there, and the money is taken out of their paychecks.

Sara flings open the door of number five and rushes to the bathroom. In the tiny room she gets down on her knees and bends over the toilet for a few minutes with no results. "If only I could throw up…maybe I'd feel better," she groans, wiping the perspiration from her forehead with a damp washcloth. She grabs the box of crackers from the top of the dresser and plunks herself down on the bed.

The space in the room is just large enough for a bed, bedside table, and a long chest containing four drawers. There is no TV on top of the chest as there would be in a regular motel. The striped yellow and beige bedspread and matching curtains remind her of a girls' dorm. A few metal hangers clang like chimes against each other in the closet alcove whenever the outside door creates a draft. The room is freshly painted white and quite adequate except there are no bookcases. Sara's books, most of them history textbooks, remain on the floor in two boxes; a third box has already been sent back to her parent's house in Oakland for storage. Her one violet plant, more dead than alive, sits on the narrow windowsill facing south in the bathroom.

Though it's nearly lunchtime, the nausea persists. According to her little book on pregnancy, nausea usually dissipates by noontime. Why doesn't it? "Is there something wrong with me or the baby?" She quickly yanks two more crackers out of the box, works her shoes off with the toes of opposing feet, and then leans back against the spokes of the wooden headboard with a sigh. Slowly she munches the crackers. "As soon as I feel better," she decides, "I'll walk up town and find a place to eat…*if* I *ever* feel like eating again." She has read that walking is supposed to be good for ladies-in-waiting. She likes the old fashioned expression: Ladies-in-waiting.

❖ ❖ ❖

Pat, the office manager, gave her hair, a final touch to make sure it was neat; it was far too late to remedy the color. This time the treatment had been too strong and her hair had turned out to be more tow-colored than blond. She picked up a basket from her desk, closed and locked the office door, then leisurely walked across the street and through the back gates of the park, choosing the path closest to the outside of the wooden fort walls in the direction of the water. Across the sand dune she saw Linette Prother in her bride's costume sitting at the picnic table eating a sandwich from a paper bag. Then she spotted Ansel Holvorson's short apple-shaped form and Skyler's boxy figure coming through the nearby gate in the side of the stockade wall. Skyler was carrying an iron kettle, evidently quite heavy because he hurried to unburden it onto the picnic table. Pat laid down a paper cloth over the gull stains, then arranged the plastic bowls and plastic spoons she had brought from the office. Ansel began to ladle out the stew.

"Where's Steve and Cam?" Pat asked. "There's more than enough stew here for everyone."

"Cam had to stay on duty at the Soldier's Barracks and Steve was just heating a piece of iron over in the Blacksmith's Shop to make one of those twisted looking candle holders. Hillary was conducting games with the children on the parade ground." Skyler added, "I guess they'll all eat later,"

"I have to go back too," Ansel sighed. "There's no one around in the Northwest Row House kitchen to answer questions. I'll be so glad when that new girl begins work. Maybe then I'll get a chance to eat without interruptions." Ansel picked up the iron kettle, which was much lighter now, and headed back towards the gate in the fort wall.

"Gee, she didn't even offer second helpings." Skyler complained. "A guy like me needs more red meat to feed the muscles." He flexed one arm.

Ignoring Skyler's attempt to get attention, Linette asked Pat, "What's the new girl like?"

"Hmmmm, nice looking...dark hair." Terribly thin and pale, almost sickly, Pat added the last trait to herself.

Skyler nodded. "Yeah, she's a real looker." He wasn't going to admit that Sara had tried to ignore him earlier in the day by hurrying straight past, barely noticing him. "Where's she from?"

"Chicago."

"Originally?"

"Her parents live in some small town, Oakland, I think, if that's what you mean by 'originally.' Pat was keenly aware of her office position of trust and never revealed anything too private about anyone who worked at the fort. She had to admit to herself that it made her feel a step ahead of the others to know all the private things about each employee that others couldn't possibly know. It wasn't exactly a "power boost" thing with her though, and she had never abused the privilege by revealing anything too important. But just having the knowledge at her fingertips gave her, if not exactly popularity, well, status among the other employees.

At one time or another someone always wanted information about someone else on the payroll. Occasionally, as right now, it was just to satisfy normal curiosity. Except in this particular case she knew almost nothing about the new girl, because Sara had been interviewed by someone in the Park Commissions' Office over on Mackinac Island and not here.

Most of the re-enactors were in their teens and twenties while Pat was a seasoned thirty-three, which left her feeling like a mother duck. Holverson and Van Hecker were the exceptions. Both were closer to Pat's age. Van Hecker was new this year. She suspected that he was using this job only as a fill-in since he was so over-qualified. Everyone knew about the big "layoffs" at the car factories, and Van Hecker had a degree in engineering with a minor degree in history.

Pat had often dispensed band aids to the young re-enactors, literally and figuratively. Sometimes Van Hecker got his dander up over a program or walking tour that fell way behind schedule and then chewed-out one of the re-enactors leaving Pat to smooth the ruffled feathers. It had happened more than once already this summer.

Oh yes, she thought again, "mother duck" that's my unofficial title, no doubt about it.

"Great stew or do they call it sagamity?" Again Skyler scraped his spoon loudly around the bowl.

"This has venison in it so I believe it's called stew. Sagamity is parched corn with fish or pork...or maybe it's venison as well. I don't know for sure," Pat confessed. "Better ask Ansel. She knows far more about early American foods than I do. I've got to get back to the office. Two commissioners are coming over from the island this afternoon to look at the new exhibit in the Soldiers' Barracks." Pat tossed her half-eaten sandwich back into her brown bag, and collected her empty can of soda. "Don't forget to clear off the table and leave no messes, except those already here. Pat was referring to the white gull stains. See you all later."

❖ ❖ ❖

Ansel found no tourists waiting to nag her with questions back in the Northwest Row House, so she ladled out some of the leftover stew into a bowl for herself and sat down at the gate-leg table to eat. The old rough-hewn table was situated near a corner cupboard containing brass candlesticks, a teapot, and a few creamware cups and plates.

As she sat there Ansel planned the next day's work. She decided that tomorrow she would need to roll out dough for two pies. She could have easily brought along some frozen dough from her parents' bakery, but she had been told not to take short cuts like that. Everything she baked or cooked was supposed to be made from scratch using only ingredients that the women had available in the 1770's. Later in the season when more people would be milling about and things got too hectic to bake and talk at the same time, she might, just might, sneak in some frozen dough.

Remembering that the wood box must be almost empty, she rose from her chair and lifted the cover. Time to replenish. She shrugged, "Why bother. I can get the new girl to carry the firewood from now on." The cords of firewood were stacked nearby; some were piled behind the Guard House and another pile leaned against the wall of the Soldiers' Barracks. Neither pile was that far away, so she needn't feel guilty about pushing the job onto someone else. She went back to her bowl of stew before it got any colder.

She had taken just four more bites of the rich dark stew when a family of mother, father, and two girls came strolling through on the other side of the low counter, which divided the kitchen from the narrow hallway. Ansel set her spoon down once again and rose from her chair. After a brief glance around to observe the colonial kitchen, the two girls and their father walked straight on through the room and out the opposite door, but the woman lingered and asked, "Where did they get their water for drinking back in the seventeen hundreds?"

Ansel was supposed to answer questions by staying in character, but this time she sensed that the woman really wanted to know if the water was sanitary, so she answered as a contemporary person. "There used to be a well right over there under the Commander's house and also one near the parade ground. Now we have city water here at the fort and that's what I use for my cooking. If you're thirsty, there's a water fountain just inside and to the left of the Land Gate."

"Oh no, not thirsty, just curious. When is the next cannon demonstration?"

"At two o'clock, I believe. Weren't you handed a schedule as you entered through the gift shop?"

"Oh yes. I forgot. Here it is." The woman fumbled around inside her shoulder bag, pulled the schedule out, and then walked out the opposite door to join her children and husband who were restlessly standing about waiting for her.

Hurriedly, Ansel began spooning more stew into her mouth in case a second group of tourists should appear and interrupt her. Too bad the new girl couldn't start the job right this minute. When she does come, Ansel told herself, I'll be able to join my friends out at the picnic table for a normal half-hour lunch. The new person, Sara or whatever her name was, could stay right here in the kitchen during the whole lunch period to answer questions and feed the fire.

Skyler had proclaimed the new girl "a real looker." Ansel stopped eating and huffed sarcastically, "Well, so am I…from the neck up. There's got to be a diet somewhere that will work for people like me." She dumped the last of the stew out of her bowl into the tin garbage pail and moved over to the corner cupboard again where, after checking the doorways for approaching tourists, she moved the teapot and lifted a chocolate power bar from its hiding place on the shelf.

CHAPTER THREE

When her stomach feels more secure, Sara unplugs her laptop, which has been sitting on the floor connected to an outlet to rejuvenate its battery. Reclining again on the bed, she places the computer across her lap and begins to boot-up to send an E-mail to her parents. Then she remembers, "I have no server up here in Mac Village." She slaps down the cover in disgust at the uselessness of her older computer and shifts it off her lap. She begins digging into her briefcase, groping for a tablet and a pen. Maybe next time she can send an E-mail from the bookstore up town if the price isn't too steep.

Hopefully, this letter will appease her parents about her safe arrival in Mac Village from Chicago and, even more importantly, forestall them from driving up here to see her too soon. If she can thwart them from coming and learning about her pregnancy until the end of August, it will positively be too late for them to advocate an abortion if they should have any such ideas.

Dear Mom and Dad,

I start on this new job tomorrow as one of the interpreters at the fort. In the meantime I have a raft of papers to read...history, etc. Tonight there's to be an orientation meeting...sort-of like the rehearsals I used to have for one of Western Michigan's theatricals. I'm suppose to act the part of a soldier's wife in the 1770's and 80's who also does the cooking for the commander of the fort. It involves working in the Northwest Row House cooking sagamity or venison stew and making hearth bread, sometimes pies as well, at least that's what I've been told. As I cook or bake, I'm supposed to be friendly and talk to the tourists at random about the long hard days of surviving in a frontier fort. Well, you get the general idea since you've been to Fort Mac several times.

Actually, she had done something similar to this interpreting previously when she had accompanied her parents to different encampments during the summer. Reliving history was her father's hobby, so he, a high school history teacher nine months of the school year, usually took the family to different northern Michigan, Minnesota and Wisconsin historic forts where Sara and her brother, Brian, lived in tents and learned to cook over an open campfire.

Occasionally, Brian still traveled with Sara's parents, but she herself had gone with them only intermittently, stopping entirely for a few years. When she was eight years old, she had been traumatized by being trapped in a large box by two young boys at one of the encampments. The entire incident was now pretty hazy in her mind. With the help of time, she had managed to blot out most of the details so successfully that she isn't even sure where the boys had cornered her. Probably though, it had been in a tunnel or in a long hallway at one of the encampments. She does remember that she had managed to bite the thumb of one boy in retaliation before they slammed down the lid.

After that occurrence and her resultant terror, she had stayed with her grandmother Lacey in Vicksburg during the following summers. Later, when she was around twelve, she once again resumed traveling with the family to various forts during the summer. At that time, however, she and her mother usually stayed in nearby motels while Brian and her father slept in the tent. Once or twice it had been this very same motel where she now sits on the bed eating crackers and intermittently brushing crumbs off her letter.

❖ ❖ ❖

Yesterday I was taken out to see Old Mill Creek. You remember it? Well, it's changed a lot since I saw it. Now it's called Discovery Park. I guess that the outing was meant to give us, we new re-enactors, a better idea of how the logs were cut and floated over to Mackinac Island in the 1780's, after which Fort Mac was moved over there by the British. Or maybe the purpose was for us to pass on information to the tourists about other attractions for them to visit in the area.

I have a costume to wear for my part as a soldier's wife. Mom, I want to tell you that it's not as well-sewn as the one you made for me years ago to wear at various encampments.

Her mother had sewn most of the costumes that they wore at the summer encampments. Her father's and Brian's hunting tunics were made from a pattern ordered through a catalog with the strange title, Smoke and Fire Co., which specialized in historical patterns, costumes, and other paraphernalia. For herself and Sara, her mother had sewn gathered skirts and bodices very similar to the one she is going to wear for her new job this summer.

Sometimes, when she was just a child, people would stop by and take photos of her in her flowered dress and mob cap while she stood at the open fire stirring the meat stew in the iron pot hanging there.

"Stop the reminiscing," she orders herself out loud. Should she mention anything in her letter about Larry, she wonders? Surely her folks will expect her to explain what happened between herself and Larry that has prompted her to run away from him and a perfectly decent job to this strictly temporary one. "I'll face that later," she tells herself. She nearly finishes the letter when there is a light tap on the door.

Quickly, Sara rises from the bed, brushes off the cracker crumbs, and chucks the soda cracker box inside the top drawer of the dresser. No sense in giving people ideas, she thinks as she opens the door.

"Hi, remember me...Pat Hurley from the office?" Sara nods and opens the door wider. "There's one more official paper I forgot to have you sign before I can make out your first paycheck...so to expedite matters, here it is." Pat thrusts the printed sheet and a pen out to Sara. With her other hand she tries to hold down the fine strands of her short, rolled-under hairdo. "Windy today," she exclaims.

"Yes. Come inside out of the wind if you like."

"Just for a second. I'm supposed to meet two of the commissioners from Mackinac Island in just a few minutes." Pat's tall figure slips quickly inside the door. She seems apologetic over the intrusion.

"Who are the commissioners?"

"Oh, the Parks Department Commissioners help to make decisions regarding this fort and the other state parks up here. There are seven commissioners, most of them from Mackinac Island and one from here. She lifts her softly rounded chin and sniffs. It smells like...food in here."

"Yes, crackers," Sara admits, but makes no attempt to elucidate. She signs the printed sheet and adds her social security number in the blank space provided.

"Don't forget about the meeting tonight. Seven o'clock, right after the fort closes."

Sara follows Pat out the doorway and watches her as she enters the back door of the office, which is just across the narrow paved alley from Sara's room. Afterwards she goes to the window and raises it high. Next time she gorges herself on crackers she'll leave a window open, though she doubts anyone can put "two and two" together and come up with any suspicions over her pregnant condition.

By four o'clock Sara's stomach feels more stable, and she decides to take a walk to town to mail her letter before the post office closes. But first, she remembers to add a postscript to her letter.

Sorry Dad, you didn't get chosen for that exchange teaching job in England. I know how much you deserve a sabbatical. Love, Sara

How disappointed he must feel that the other history teacher, Mr. Patterson, has been selected just because he's been in the school system longer than her father, though only by a year or so. Sara addresses the envelope and sticks it in her pocket. She can buy a stamp up town.

❖ ❖ ❖

Slowly and reluctantly, because the walk to town and back has tired her far more than she had anticipated, Sara made herself ready for tonight's meeting, actually a rehearsal to determine if she is familiar with the character she is expected to portray as the interpreter in the Northwest Row House.

She took the few steps from her room over to the back door of the office and stepped inside. Unexpectedly, the office itself was empty, but she could hear voices emanating from the room behind so she tapped lightly on the edge of the open doorway.

"Come right in." Pat called out when she saw Sara standing there waiting. Pat quickly introduced her to Dr. Reidel who stood up and held out his hand to her.

"We use first names around here so please call me Jonathan or just Jon."

Pat explained, "Jon, Dr. Reidel, is curator for the park here, the park on the island, and also Discovery Park. He was visiting the fort today to check on one of the new exhibits and decided to join us."

Immediately, Sara's attention became focused on Dr. Reidel's melodious voice. She recognized its ability to sooth the irate wrangling at a protest meeting or one of her father's school board meetings with which she was also familiar. She noted Dr. Reidel's shock of dark brown hair, lighter than her own, but just as straight...Indian straight. Could he be Indian? His skin was no darker than her own. Later, she watched as he slipped a pair of dark rimmed glasses over his nose when Pat handed over some notes for him to read.

"This is Sara Kolenda, everyone."

Sara noticed that most people were dressed casually in jeans except Pat who wore the same skirt and white blouse she had been wearing during the day. Even Dr. Reidel was casually dressed in khaki pants and a dark maroon sport shirt.

As Pat introduced Sara to the other re-enactors, she explained: Gary and Cameron play the roles of French voyageurs in a sequence where they supposedly land on the beach in a thirty-five foot birch bark canoe at the Water Gate and tell the tourists about their perilous trip paddling along the Lake Superior shore to the Grand Portage region to buy furs from the Indians and bring them back here to the fort.

"Skyler Wilks," Pat gestured towards the young man whom Sara immediately recognized as the fellow she had tried to ignore this morning in her haste to reach her room before her stomach upheaved, "plays the part of a soldier and usually conducts the musket demonstration out on the parade ground."

"And I," the young girl, Hillary, with the ponytail, spoke up, "I have charge of the children's outdoor games."

"Yes," Pat confirmed, "and she also tells the children old time stories when they gather in the garret of the Southwest Row House. Hillary and Cam are brother and sister. Sometimes Hillary will also fill-in for Linette Prother as the bride in the French marriage sequence that takes place in the church. Neither Linette nor the young man, an exchange student from Lyon, France, who plays the role of the Jesuit Priest, could be here tonight. Sara, you might also be called upon to play the part of the bride sometime in the future, so watch the wedding re-enactment whenever you get the opportunity."

"Wasn't Ansel Holvorson supposed to be here tonight?" Dr Reidel asked. "It was my understanding that Sara was to be working closely with her. Am I right?"

"Yes, but she said she couldn't come...a birthday party or some family celebration."

Sara nodded cordially at all of them in the circle of chairs and headed for the empty folding chair next to Dr. Reidel. His relaxed manner and pleasant voice drew her interest. She decided to sit next to him, but Pat quickly laid some papers on the chair seat as though to reserve it for herself, so Sara settled in a chair across the room next to Hillary whose smile welcomed her.

"Tonight, Sara," Pat began, "to give you a little practice in speaking to tourists, we are each going to fire questions at you. Remember, try to answer the questions as if you were actually a soldier's wife who cooks for the commandant at the fort in the Northwest Row House. Hillary, you start out."

Hillary thought a minute then asked, "Do you work in the kitchen all day?"

Sara answered mechanically, as though she found it hard to warm to her role: No, I also have to wash clothes for my husband who is a soldier here at the fort. Sometimes I also work in the garden over near the Southwest Row House."

Next, Cameron, Hillary's brother, fired a question at her, "Who cuts the firewood?"

"The soldiers have wood cutting detail. It takes a lot of wood to keep all the fireplaces in all the row houses going, especially in winter. That's why at one time the land became barren for seven miles around."

"Oh? But now I see lots of trees around the fort," Skyler interrupted her in his role as a tourist.

Sara turned to face Skyler, but found his blue eyes so intensely glued to her breasts that she had to look down before answering. "The trees you see now are all second and third generation trees."

"How do you make sagamity?" This was another question from Hillary.

"We learned how to make sagamity from the Indians. Usually it's parched corn and some kind of meat or fish. Whatever kind of meat our soldiers can hunt or fish for; most often the Indians used fish. Whitefish and trout are abundant here…so are passenger pigeons."

The next question came from Pat. "I believe I've lost that little map or layout of the fort that was given to me at the entrance. Where do I find the archaeological diggings?"

Sara had to think carefully about that question for a moment before answering. "First go back to the parade ground, that big open area where the musket demonstrations take place, then head towards the Land Gate. Just after you pass the parade ground on your left, you'll see a roped-off area where the archaeologists are working. There should be someone there to answer any questions you might have."

Finally, Gary spoke up shyly. "What kinds of vegetables did folks grow in their gardens back in the seventeen hundreds?"

"Oh, corn, beans, and squash are our staples; onions and beets are also grown plus kale; we have a separate herb garden for seasonings... but we don't grow tomatoes. Tomatoes are poisonous. A lot more corn than we grow is needed to feed the garrison here as well as send as a dried staple with the voyageurs on their treks into the wilderness. Therefore, some corn has to be bought or traded with the neighboring Indian tribes in order to have enough to feed everyone." Sara heaved a weary sigh after her long verbal answer.

"Do you make pies just the way the colonials used to?" Pat asked.

"Yes, we try to. We use lard as they did and flour that hasn't been bleached." Sara's head was beginning to feel blowsy from tiredness, but the session seemed to go on and on until eight-thirty when to her relief, Pat called a halt.

"That should be enough for tonight. What do you think, Dr. Reidel?" Pat asked deferentially.

"I have just one more suggestion to make, Sara. Don't forget if someone asks about archaeology to also mention the exhibit: The Sands of Time that is just next door to the kitchen where you'll be working. It's down some stairs directly under the British Trader's House."

Sara nodded, yes. It seemed like her head would "nod" right off her neck if she couldn't lay it down on a pillow soon.

"All right," Pat concluded, "Let's call it a wrap as they say in the movie business." Sara rose from her chair, anxious to leave.

As the others slowly dispersed, Dr. Reidel touched her arm, a friendly gesture to get her attention. He lowered his voice so that others in the room couldn't hear, "You appear to know your part very well, though you seem a bit uninspired. Perhaps you might try to put a little more enthusiasm and energy into your part as the soldier's wife."

She felt her face turn pink as a burst of resentment rose up. It was all she could do to keep from spurting out, *If you had spent half the day fighting nausea, you'd sound floppy as a dishrag too!* The spunky retort, so ready on her tongue, died. She wanted this job. After a brief hesitation, she got enough of a leash on her tongue to mutter, "I'll try."

Skyler stopped Sara in the doorway. "How's about joining Gary and me for a beer uptown?"

The very thought of the sour smell of beer wafting around her nose made Sara feel nauseous. She gulped before abruptly answering, "Thanks, perhaps some other time."

As she left the room, Sara made brief character notes in her mind regarding each person in the room so that she could remember them later: Cameron, Hillary's brother, seemed a gentle sort; both he and his sister had very similar features, though Cam's face was tanned from spending so much of his day outdoors, and Hillary's face still retained some of its baby fat. Skyler Wilks was a bit on the cocky side, definitely a "loud mouth" type. Gary, like Skyler, had also let his hair grow long, suitable for his voyageur role, but unlike Skyler, his behavior was less swaggering, more mannerly.

Jonathan, Dr. Reidel, a man probably in his thirties, had irked her, though his voice had sent a chill up her spine just as Vaughn Monroe's slightly nasal voice had done when she played an old record belonging to her mother. Dr. Reidel's baritone voice must be the envy of every speech coach. If she weren't so tired, she might have enjoyed debating with him over her seeming lack of energy. Tonight she simply longed for everyone to disperse rapidly so that she could slip away without causing undue attention.

Back in her little room for the night, Sara plops down on the bed. "Why does this baby seem to sap all my strength?" she asks the empty room. The little book on pregnancy claims that pregnant women usually appear glowingly healthy. "Perhaps that stage will come later? Well, the sooner the better," she grumbles. "I can't go on feeling half alive like this and keep a job." Everyone, not just Dr. Reidel, had probably noticed her lackadaisical manner.

This lack of pep is so atypical of her. When she was growing up, her mother had often sighed and called her, "...my little jumping bean." It has seemed, until recently, as though she possessed boundless energy. Now this same Sara, a physically changed one, rises up from the bed and stands in front of the bathroom mirror to brush her teeth and intermittently complain to herself, "Life has become impossible. Can't run too hard, can't drink, can't even make male attachments if I should find someone nice to date." And at last she wails, "Where am I going to get money to pay the hospital for the birthing?"

Well yes, she snaps back at her mirror image, aren't those the very same problems that other unmarried, pregnant women have to face? She stabs the toothbrush at her mirror image. "So, smarty, how does it feel now that you're walking down the same bumpy road? This predicament you're in is *exactly* why those women preferred to get abortions. Remember how you chanted at them in a loud sing-song derogatory voice during those anti-abortion protests in front of the clinics? Most of those women deserved your sympathy, instead of the mean shouts."

Sara shakes her head at the ugly crying image in the mirror. "Now you're beginning to understand why those pregnant women took the chance of walking straight past a hooting crowd screaming obscenities and into a clinic that might, just might, be planted with a bomb."

"Oh!" she verbally points a finger at herself, "you're starting to wobble on both sides of the issue." That had never been her problem before...seeing another side to the abortion argument.

But, since she's become pregnant herself, isn't it only natural to have a clearer view on the other side, both sides? Maybe. "Indecision has never been one of my faults before." She wipes her drooling chin in disgust. "I'll always believe the fetus is a living human being."

Sometimes now, she even feels remorse over the fact that she has made life so miserable for those poor women going into the abortion clinics. "But my personal beliefs haven't changed," she staunchly assures her mirror image. "I'm not going to have an abortion, though I may be sorely tempted if my stomach doesn't get back to normal."

No, she hadn't joined the anti-abortion groups lightly as one might join a country club. She had first done some solid thinking. Back then she had absolutely no *on the fence* attitude. And now? She's still sure that life and death belong to the province of God, not man. But until lately, she freely admits, she had seen only one side...the side proclaiming that abortion kills.

Right now, Sara realizes, that she is feeling only the tip of the isolation that a lot of young girls must feel when they face the first shock of finding themselves in a pregnant state and more or less alone in the world. No wonder they take the abortion route. Some of those girls don't have understanding parents or any parents at all. "I do," she firmly reiterates and wishfully adds: If only I could tell them.

CHAPTER FOUR

*A*s Pat was locking up the office after the rehearsal that evening, Jonathan asked her for the key to room number three. Instead of taking the last boat back to Mackinac Island, he made a decision to stay here for the night since he still had work to finish up in the morning. For instance, in the Soldiers' Barracks, he hadn't taken pictures of the unusual bunk that was wide enough to sleep at least six or seven men at one time; it seemed a bit cozy by today's standards, but at least the men, by sharing their warmth, would have kept from freezing to death in the cold northern winters. He needed to continue taking photographs and check out the historical accuracy of the display cards.

He had often stayed here in one or another of the nondescript motel-type rooms, yet always preferring to be home in his own book-lined room in his mother's cottage on the island. Maybe at age thirty-two he had already become like the stereotypical character so often depicted in literature, a comfortable bachelor happily ensconced in his own moldy books. All those shelves of books in his room gave him the impression of walls lined with ideas and solutions instead of wallpaper. Many of the books had been his late father's medical journals, several obsolete, but most still useful. Also there was his collection on anthropology, history, and a few on photography. Jonathan could pick out any book, open it, and quickly immerse himself.

The island cottage, really his mother's house, on a quiet lane next to the water, had no relationship to the huge, expensive cottages up on the bluff with their scenic views looking down on the harbor and far out over the translucent water. His mother's much older cottage had a bay window facing the lane instead of a water view. He supposed that back in the late eighteen hundreds when it was built, the idea was to conserve fuel, specifically logs, and so a wide bay window facing the water would have been unthinkable, causing a huge loss of heat in winter. There were four fireplaces: one in the parlor, one in the combined kitchen dining room, and one in each of the two largest bedrooms. But there was also a wood-burning stove, which he used in winter, when he came up to the cottage to ski.

His mother's colorful garden of roses, larkspur, and dahlias lined the walk in front of the bay window; more of the same and a few vegetables filled a small kitchen garden that was not much larger than twelve by fifteen. There was one large lilac bush, its blossoms of the deepest hue, nearly purple-black, which his mother babied because it had been planted about the time the house was originally built in eighteen-seventy.

Unlike many of the other people on the island who rented bedrooms to tourists during the summer, his mother had kept her little summer home free of commercial atmosphere. The house was down a lane just a block from the street that circled the nine-mile island. One could hear only the faint clomp of horses and the whirring of bicycle wheels during the day. Other than those noises and the soothing wash of nearby water, the cottage was quiet. Jonathan thought happily of the days when the water roared and spilled up over the pilings and consequently muted all the other sounds. At those times, and in winter, he felt as though he were truly isolated, far from a village. Even so, his personal choice in cottages would have been one located in a remote cove surrounded only by woods on three sides and, of course, water on the fourth side.

Behind his mother's cottage in a shed, once his father's workshop, he found the freedom to repair the old pieces of furniture that he discovered in junk shops or tossed out on the street. His mother often disagreed over the value of the pieces, much less the need to restore them. "Are you trying to resurrect them? With a chuckle she'd add,

"You'd have a better chance of saving them if you took them to a church service." But that was the whole point to Jonathan. He *liked* the feeling of saving a thing from being misused or thrown out. Saving furniture of style and dignity, as well as genuine historical artifacts, gave him a sense of achievement. His ultimate goal, however, was a tireless unraveling of history.

Jonathan guessed that his propensity for collecting orphan furniture and sometimes even orphan people was beginning to test his mother's patience. Though when she spoke of "orphan people," she was mostly teasing him, referring to that time at age twelve when he had brought home, unannounced, a young couple to dinner. They had lost their wallets and all their credentials while cycling around the island. As a young boy, there had been plenty of occasions when he had brought home the more usual types of orphans, such as cats and dogs and once a baby rabbit whose mother had been smashed under the huge foot of a dray horse.

"You've got twelve rooms and a basement down there in that house in Kalamazoo all to yourself," his mother complained not too patiently, "all the space you need for storing these odds and ends of scrap furniture. Have I mentioned this before? Would about twenty times be accurate?"

"Now Mother, it's not all scrap. There's a fine 19th Century wash stand here that only needs refinishing."

"Yes, but you seldom have time to work on it. Anyway, you know what I mean." He did. Her cottage on Mackinac Island was small, and his habit of collecting had made space tight for her. Sometimes he had collected pieces indiscriminately because he hated to see things go to waste if there was the slimmest chance of saving them. It was more or less how he felt about everything…especially people.

Last week his mother had also begged him to take some of his wooden ship models down to his house in lower Michigan so that she would no longer have to dust the delicate spars and miniature lifeboats. He never had spare time to spend on model ship building anymore. Mostly, he was too busy checking out the state park exhibits to make sure they were historically accurate to even notice how quickly the season had progressed. Before he knew it, the summer would be over and he would be back to teaching history at Western Michigan University in Kalamazoo.

In bits and pieces he was transferring his notes to the computer for the new manuscript on <u>Colonial History of Mackinac Island</u> that he was preparing for the Parks Department. That was another reason he needed to stay here in Mac Village overnight. The local library, though small, had an excellent selection of history books and papers relating to this particular area of Northern Michigan. He needed them for reference along with the information he gleaned from the web, which wasn't always accurate and needed to be double-checked.

Jonathan unlocked the door of room number three and went inside, dropped his briefcase, and placed his laptop computer on the dresser. There just didn't seem to be enough hours in the day to do everything that he wanted to do. He ran his fingers through his straight, thick hair in frustration. Tomorrow he needed to drive to Cheboygan for a haircut if he could fit it into his schedule.

He thought about the new employee, Sara, whom he had met tonight. She was attractive, very attractive, with a certain relaxed...no, he corrected himself, with a too passive demeanor. No one expected the interpreters to be seasoned actors or actresses, but this new girl appeared lethargic, almost sickly. Yet, the sharp, snappy look from her green eyes...green or gray...when he criticized her, was enough to burn out a fuse in one's brain, so there had to be a spark of energy in there somewhere. Maybe she wouldn't work out, and the Parks Department would be forced to find someone else to take her place. He decided to talk it over with Pat tomorrow and see what she thought.

Tonight, though these cabin rooms were only a short distance away from the water, he would miss the sound of the slurping and sucking against the sea wall just a few yards from his mother's cottage on Mackinac Island.

CHAPTER FIVE

"You want me to get water from the faucet just outside the Priest's Gate?" Sara asked.

"Yes, and it's not called a faucet," Ansel Holvorson corrected her sharply. "It's a spigot." Ansel showed her how to carry water in two small barrels, ten pounds each, by hanging them on a wooden bar that rested across her shoulders; when Sara was out of Ansel's sight, she lowered the barrels and carried each one individually.

Without even a welcome get-acquainted chat this morning, Ansel had immediately asked Sara to fill the wood chest. The firewood was stacked high and piled in three rows against the Soldiers' Barracks, about sixty feet from the Northwest Row House. Sara could carry only four or five of the very small logs at one time or only two of the larger ones. It took her six trips to the woodpile to satisfy Ansel who afterwards explained in detail that someone must fill the wood chest two and a half times to bake just one pie or a loaf of bread.

Of course, when Sara had visited the fort with her parents nearly five years ago, she had seen the kitchen where she was to work but had forgotten how narrow it was. That was because space had to be taken out of it in order to make an aisle from which the tourists could watch the interpreters at work. There was a cobblestone fireplace, blackened by use, and a huge box for wood. The low rafters, which made the room feel mellow and dark, were festooned with dried onions, Indian corn, and bunches of dried herbs. The small alcove in the north corner of the kitchen under a window contained a table for mixing food, several shelves, and a dry sink. At the other end of the room stood the cabinet for dishes and a worn gate-leg table near a tall window that opened inward in two halves like wings.

When she had first met Ansel in the kitchen of the Northwest Row House, Sara likened her ample form and her apparently laid-back personality to an inviting comfortable chair, the kind you could relax into and slough off layer after layer of concerns, letting all the secret things that were eating away inside to wash away. She was quickly disabused of that notion.

After fetching the wood, Ansel started her on scrubbing down the worktable with lye soap. That's when Sara made her first big mistake. Without thinking, she asked Ansel, "Are there any rubber gloves available?" Naturally, she assumed lye could damage the skin on her hands.

Ansel snapped, "Do you think women back in the 1770's had rubber gloves?"

Sara, showing a trace of her former spunky manner, retorted, "That's no reason why someone in the twenty-first century has to suffer." Ansel's rebuff was a disgusted look.

When lunchtime came, Ansel disappeared after warning Sara to keep the heat up in the fireplace so that the Dutch oven sitting on the coals could bake the bread properly. "When the wood ashes begin to cool on the cover section of the oven don't forget to replenish them with fresh hot coals."

After Ansel leaves, Sara looks around. There is absolutely no food anywhere in the kitchen for Sara to eat for her lunch. The sagamity isn't quite cooked thoroughly enough yet, and the bread has another hour to bake. Not that she craves food; she doesn't, but she does have to have something in her stomach to keep the nausea down. Even the smell coming from the sagamity sets her stomach roiling like the hot bubbles rising to the top of the iron pot. No tourists are passing through the room so she allows herself a low groan of misery.

This morning while dressing, she had stuffed the little cloth pocket, which was tied with a cord around her waist as part of her costume, with crackers. Now she nibbles on these as she sits on one of the ladder-back chairs. At the same time she listens carefully for footsteps that will warn her of Ansel's return, or that a large group of tourists is about to flow through the row house kitchen like waves washing up on the beach nearby.

A half hour later when Ansel does return and dismisses her so that she can go and eat her own lunch, Sara hurries back to her room and gorges herself on more crackers. Too bad she hadn't thought of buying lunch materials when she passed the grocery store last evening after dinner at the restaurant. Somehow she will have to stock-up on bread, cheese or peanut butter so that she can make a sandwich each day at noon. There is a community kitchen near her room that has been set up especially for the convenience of the employees. Supposedly it includes two stoves and three refrigerators, or is it three stoves and two refrigerators? She can't remember exactly what Pat has told her.

In the afternoon, Ansel sits at the gate leg table copying down recipes in a notebook. In two large tin basins, Sara washes and rinses the bowls and other utensils that Ansel has used to mix up and roll out pie crust. The clean dishes are set on a towel to drain. The rest of the time when Sara isn't talking to tourists as they pass through the room, she perches uncomfortably on a backless stool next to the dry sink and swats futilely at the flies. After an hour or so, Ansel closes her notebook and tells Sara that she will show her how to weed the vegetable garden during this lull in the afternoon's stream of tourists.

"Did you bring your bonnet with you?"

"No, I didn't know if I would need it today or not."

"Oh yes," Ansel affirmed. "You'll need it almost every day. But maybe by now the sun isn't hitting the garden as directly as it does in the morning. Come on." Sara followed Ansel past the blacksmith shop and the church to the east end of the Southwest Row House where the little garden was located next to the Saw Pit, an area partly shaded by the Southwest Row House itself. Yet the garden still remained in full sun.

"There's the hoe leaning against the fence," Ansel pointed. "Just use it to loosen the dirt so that the weeds get uprooted. Then go back with this basket and drop the loose weeds into it. It's still early in the season so nothing is ripe yet, but you can see the yellow squash blossom buds. I'll leave you to it and get back to the kitchen in case some tourists come through. If people stop to watch you, try to engage them in conversation. Just tell them that this is more or less typical of the little kitchen gardens that used to grow behind each section of a row house like those over there." Ansel gestured towards one of the fenced off areas, now full of tall weeds.

"What are those other green plants?"

"Those are green beans. Don't you know anything about gardens?"

"Only flower gardens." Sara admitted, and Ansel shook her head in disdain, then hurried away.

"Wait!" Sara wanted to ask her how long she should stay here in the garden, but Ansel had already disappeared around the end of the wooden church. Sara picked up the hoe and noticed that the squash plants had already spread out so much that the row was no longer a clear-cut line of plants. Half-heartedly, she jabbed the hoe to loosen the dirt around each plant wherever she could. As she bent over to pick up the basket to collect the weeds, her left heel dug into an onion set in the row behind. She kneeled and tried to prop the onion back up by mounding dirt around it, yet the onion still flopped over in sad retribution. She doubted that it would live. The sun was hot, making her feel logy, even more phlegmatic than she already felt. Leaning on the handle of the hoe, she stopped to rest and watch the sawing demonstration.

The sawing area consisted of a wooden platform holding a long saw with wooden handles. Sara guessed that the saw must be about six feet in length. Underneath the platform a pit had been dug in the sandy soil just large enough for a man to stand and wield the other end of the saw. Sara watched Gary climb to the top of the wooden structure and take one end of the saw. A board had already been secured across the top. A tourist volunteer stood in the pit ready to push upwards on the saw. Sara heard Gary make a great point of offering a cap to the man in the pit, but he refused, foolishly waving the cap aside. As Gary pushed the saw downwards from the top of the structure, the hatless pitman below pushed upwards on the saw and at the same time tried futilely to protect his head from the sawdust falling from above like a sudden amber snowstorm. The tourists watching nearby enjoyed this little joke on the volunteer pitman and clapped heartily.

❖ ❖ ❖

Shortly after the sawing demonstration, Sara notices several people hesitating at the garden and then walking on. She knows that she is supposed to be friendly and engage them in conversation, but she really doesn't feel up to the effort this afternoon. The sun beats down fiercely on her hatless head and she longs for a cool drink. She bends to pick up the weeds and toss them into the basket, then straightens up again to rest her back. Nearby, a young boy asks, "What are those plants with the little yellow blossoms?"

"Those are squash," Sara answers feeling thankful that she even knows the answer. "And see over there? Those are onions. They were purposely set out between the rows of squash and beets to keep the aphids away." She had read that bit of information somewhere in the vast amount of material she'd been given concerning the fort.

"Yuck," the boy laughs, "Onions would keep me away, too."

The boy's mother smiles and explains, "He hates onions."

"But I'll bet you would like this Indian corn." Sara picks up a sample of the dried Indian corn from the ground and holds it up to show the boy. "Isn't it colorful? Each cob is..." Sara doesn't finish the sentence. The sun and the heat are making her dizzy. Rather than fall flat on her face in a faint, she sits down right there in the middle of the young corn plants and lowers her head into her voluminous skirt to keep from passing out.

"Hey, we need some help here!" The mother of the boy waves frantically at a passing soldier in a red coat. "She looks sick." The soldier turns out to be Skyler who is on his way to start the flintlock demonstration on the nearby parade ground. He crouches down to look into Sara's face.

"Are you all right? I'm Skyler, remember me?"

"No. . .yes."

"I'll get some water." He rushes off to get a cup from the row house nearest to the garden, grabs a pewter mug from the counter of the trader's store, and runs to the drinking fountain at the Land Gate where he roughly pushes a child aside. "Sorry, this is an emergency." By the time he returns, several more people are hovering around watching, and Dr. Reidel is bending over Sara. Her head is still lowered into her blue skirt, which billows out like a misplaced flower in a vegetable garden.

"Here," Skyler thrusts the cup under Sara's nose. "Maybe this will help."

"Thanks." She gulps several swallows of the cooling water; then Dr. Reidel dips his hand in the remainder and pats it onto Sara's forehead and her wrists. That's when he first notices that her fingernails are bitten down to the pad of flesh just underneath the nail.

"I'm so sorry," Sara says, raising her head. "It must have been the hot sun or going without lunch. I'm so embarrassed."

Dr. Reidel pats her hand. "I'm sure you couldn't help it. Skyler, isn't this close to the time when you usually have the Brown Bess demonstration? You had better go ahead to the parade ground and get started or all the other activities will be off schedule. I'll take care of Sara."

Jonathan helps Sara to her feet and guides her just around the corner into the trader's store away from the group of curious people who have suddenly gathered. He sits her down on a tall stool. "Feeling better now?"

"Yes. I shouldn't have gone without lunch."

"Are you sure that's the problem? Maybe you should see a doctor."

"I'll be fine, Dr. Reidel."

"Call me Jonathan, remember? Here, I often carry one of these trail bars around in my pocket. They're awfully dry but might give you some energy." He unwraps the bar and offers it to Sara.

"Thanks." She nibbles cautiously, hoping the roughage won't upset her stomach and create even more embarrassment by making her up-chuck. "I should get back to the kitchen. Ansel will wonder what has happened to me."

"You sit here a little longer. I'll go and tell Ansel where you are."

Through the door Sara watches as Dr. Reidel walks into the church and out the opposite door. It's a shortcut, one that she herself has recently discovered, to reach the Northwest Row House.

A few minutes later, Dr. Reidel returns and tells Sara that Ansel can get along without her until four o'clock. "Come on, I'll walk you back to your room. I assume you are staying over there in the cabins. I'm on my way to the parking lot anyhow. Do you have these fainting spells often?"

"No, never before. You sound like a doctor."

"Almost went in that direction, same as my father, but changed my mind during my junior year. Here, let's go this way through the Priest's Gate and along the outside of the stockade wall. That way we'll avoid the curious." He took Sara's arm and guided her through the church to the gate. "Well, now that I've spilled my youthful ambition of becoming a doctor, what's yours?"

Sara guesses that Dr. Reidel is trying to engage her in conversation to keep her mind off the embarrassment of her fainting. "Anthropology or History, like my father. He's a high school history teacher. I had planned to start my Masters Degree this coming fall, but I'm not sure now if I'll be able to..." She lets the sentence peter out.

"Where?"

"Possibly Western Michigan."

"That's where I teach." By this time they have reached the street. Dr. Reidel still has a hand on her elbow. What room are you in?

"Number five. I'm really fine now. I don't need to delay you."

"It's no bother since I am going your way anyhow." After they have crossed the street, he said, "You rest now before going back to work."

"Yes, thank you for your help."

"Take care." Jonathan waves and then walks off in the direction of the office instead of going straight to the parking lot.

Quickly Sara shuts her room door, removes her shoes and skirt, and sinks down on the bed. Then reaching under her pillow, she brings out her book on pregnancy. She partially reads the chapter titled, <u>Nutrition During Pregnancy</u> and grows sleepy. Her last clear thought before falling asleep is about food. She will have to find something to eat…something her stomach can tolerate…perhaps something mild like tomato-rice soup or at the very least a dish of ice cream from one of the nearby gift shops. Fuzzily, she muses, "Maybe I should consider stocking up on a few of those snack bars like the one Dr. Reidel gave me."

It seems only minutes later when a tapping on the door wakes her up. She looks at her clock. Three-forty. She has been sleeping for over an hour. "Coming," she calls to whomever is at the door. She steps hurriedly into the full skirt and ties the string at the waist before opening the door. Pat is standing there.

"Sorry to have to wake you. Jonathan said you were going back to work at four o'clock so I brought you a sandwich and something to drink. He mentioned that you hadn't eaten any lunch and maybe that's what made you feel faint."

Sara is so astounded at Pat's kindness that for a few seconds she doesn't know quite how to respond. "That's so thoughtful of you. Please come inside; I'll get my purse and reimburse you."

"Oh, no. You don't owe me a thing. This food was already in the community kitchen. I have to get back to the office. See you later. There's a picnic table around the corner if you should want to eat outside. We're plagued with ants here." Pat looks briefly around the room as though expecting to see a trail of ants, and then her eyes appear to linger on the large black print across the top of a book half lying under the bed.

"Pat, thanks again. I wouldn't have had time to go and buy something to eat since I slept too long." Sara closes the door and removes the plastic from the sandwich before sitting down on the edge of the bed to eat. She fairly gobbles the cheese sandwich. The drink is a small can of cranberry juice with a tab on the top. Pat has thought of everything.

"Kind folks," she remarks out loud. Not telling them about my pregnancy makes me feel like a sneak. Guiltily she takes another bite out of the sandwich and glances over to the edge of the bed where she had earlier dropped her book on the floor when she fell asleep. The large black letters of the book title ending in NANCY peek out from under the bedspread where it touches the book.

"Oh drat!" she groans out loud. Could Pat have seen the book? Of course Pat hadn't actually stepped very far into the room, but the bold black lettering on the paper cover would be hard to miss. That was the very reason she herself had spotted it so easily on the rack in the Quick Shop where she bought it in Urbana before traveling here.

"What a dunce I am!" Will Pat spread the news immediately, or will she come back to the room later and ask me pointed questions before informing others at the fort or getting me fired?

She wasn't terribly worried about other people knowing about her condition unless it also cost her the new job. "Maybe I should talk to Pat and try to persuade her to keep the information quiet until later in the summer. But how can I do that unless I'm absolutely sure Pat has definitely seen the book?" What a dilemma. She squeezes her eyes shut, crimping the tears that have already begun. It seems like the simplest little bump in the road starts her tears flowing all over again.

A look at the clock on her nightstand reminds her that this is no time for self-recriminations. She is already late in getting back to work. Ansel will be pricklier than ever because of her absence this afternoon.

CHAPTER SIX

*P*at stood outside of room five, Sara's room, for a few seconds wondering what to think, if anything, about her suspicions. Sara's fainting spell plus the book she had just spotted on the floor didn't prove anything by themselves, but still, everything together... well, they added up, didn't they? Was Sara pregnant? She had no time to think about it further because she heard the phone jangling, so she hurried across to the back entrance of the office. The caller, Dr Reidel, was phoning from the boat pier uptown. Pat always found it soothing to hear his deep resonant voice. Somehow, Jonathan always managed to make her feel as though he himself gained great pleasure from speaking to her and to her alone. No, she corrected herself, he gave everyone that impression...as though they were somebody special. She was still hopeful that the personal attention he had shown her just this spring during the Voyageur Festival on Mackinac Island, barely two months ago, might develop into something more intimate. Wasn't their shared companionship during the festival a good sign that he was becoming interested in her personally, not just as a fellow worker because he needed her office assistance from time to time?

"Do you have the resume on the new girl, Sara... I've forgotten her last name?"

"Kolenda. No, I never had the complete file on Sara since it was someone on Mackinac Island who interviewed her back in late May. They'll probably send her file over to me soon because most of the employee records are to be kept over here in the future. Pat glanced around at the new, half-filled filing cabinets. If there's something you need to know, I can get the information quickly to you by E-mail."

"Oh, don't bother. I'm on the way back over to the island right now and I can get it myself. Thanks Pat. I'll probably return to the mainland the day after tomorrow to take more pictures of the new exhibit if these prints fail to turn out well." He hung up, and Pat immediately wondered if Dr. Reidel also had some suspicions concerning the new employee because of the fainting spell, or could it be something of a more personal nature? What man wouldn't be attracted to a dainty girl of five-two with dark hair, high cheek bones, and so obviously in need of protection. Pat sighed, wishing she didn't stand five-eight and appear quite so proficient at caring for herself and everyone else. Well, if Jonathan learned that Sara was pregnant, he would surely lose interest in her fast enough.

Pat had already perceived that Jonathan had what some might term a soft spot for the underdog, so naturally this new girl might appeal to that part of his nature. According to his mother, Edith, whom Pat communicated with once or twice a summer, this same character trait of Jonathan's extended to saving orphaned pieces of furniture, which were filling her island cottage to its limits. Jonathan's compassionate nature towards people was certainly something Pat could empathize with. They had that much in common, but not ratty old furniture. That was going a bit overboard, which is where old furniture ought to go. She sympathized with Jonathan's mother, and shivered at the thought of a house full of smelly old secondhand furniture. It put her sense of neatness all out of kilter.

This last spring, she and Jonathan, whom she had known for well over a year now, had accidentally crossed paths on Mackinac Island during the Voyageur Festival, one of the big events of the season. They had watched the flotilla of canoes and sailing vessels come into the harbor laden with furs just as the voyageurs had done in ages past. Afterwards they had decided to team-up for the rest of the day.

Since photography was one of Jonathan's hobbies, he had planned to take pictures of the whole Voyageur Festival for his own benefit. But as Curator of History for the Parks Department, he had been obligated to record the event on their camcorder. Though he could make copies of the camcorder pictures, he still wanted to take photos with his digital camera. He couldn't handle both cameras at once so when Pat volunteered to assist him, he accepted her offer. She had held his camera handy so that he could switch quickly back and forth from the camcorder to the digital as the need arose and sometimes, when time allowed, she had taken pictures with her own camera.

Together they had dined at an outdoor café on Hoban Street just off of Market. During lunch Jonathan had told her some interesting historical tidbits that she had never heard before. One was about the Indian girls who married the French voyageurs by a mere exchange of rum or blankets to the girl's Indian parents. "Some French traders even brought their Indian wives into the forts to live...forts like St. Joseph and Mac Fort."

Pat had never been particularly enthralled with the subject of history, but it was the manner in which Jonathan related the details that pulled history out of the bleary past and suddenly gave it color and interest much like an old black and white movie updated into Technicolor. At the end of their day together on Mackinac Island, she had been left with the happy impression that Jonathan had shown more than a general interest in her. Now she was waiting to see if he would follow up on their friendship this summer. She expected that Jonathan might invite her to attend one of the Associate Members' functions such as the special candlelight dinner that occurred once a year at the fort on the island. But he hadn't. She was keenly disappointed, but remained hopeful.

Leaning forward in her office chair, Pat absently straightened the blotter and realigned her pen set until it was exactly parallel to her stapler. Again, she thought about Sara. Clearly the book lying on the floor in Sara's room had been written for a specialized audience. With a subtitle of nutrition and exercise, it could have been suitable for general readers, but the title letters that she was able to recognize were probably the last letters of the word, "pregnancy." Sara wasn't married...or had she lied on the employment form? She clearly recalled that Sara had put an x in the little box designated "single" on the withholding tax form.

Pat tried to think of alternative scenarios for Sara's situation. Sara could have been married previously, she supposed, and then divorced before discovering that she was pregnant. If true, what a nasty trick nature had pulled. But things like that did happen. Several times Pat struck the pencil hard against the pad of paper on her desk, making holes in the top sheets. Sometimes it was so completely unfair being a woman.

Now if she went straight ahead and reported her suspicions about Sara directly to the Personnel Office on Mackinac Island, it might turn out that she would be ratting on a girl who was in a difficult situation and truly needed to earn her livelihood from this job. After all, it was just a summer position. Even if Sara were pregnant, the baby probably wouldn't be obvious to others until the end of August, so what harm could it do to keep mum on the subject and let Sara remain? She would have to mull it over before deciding what to do about it, if anything. There was no need to be hasty.

In the meantime, she told herself, I'll just keep my eyes open. If I am correct about Sara being pregnant, it certainly would explain one thing: why she keeled over in the garden earlier today. Maybe Dr. Reidel was also thinking along those same lines, and that's why just a few minutes ago he called on his cell phone to ask about Sara's personnel file. "I'm reluctant to be a whistle blower, and I doubt if Jonathan would think well of me if I were."

❖ ❖ ❖

Soon after seven o'clock when the stockade closed, Sara walked back to her room accompanied by Hillary and Cam. Hillary was explaining to her about their hometown, Munising, and its location up on Lake Superior.

"A bit far for commuting," Cameron smiled in his slow, calm manner. Besides, it's good to get away from the home environment."

"You can say that again!" Hillary let out a long sigh.

Sara noted that there was more than a touch of impatience in Hillary's tone of voice. She, herself, recalled how anxious she had been to get away from home when she was a teenager. Life at home had seemed so impossibly dull. Now the urge had passed, and she wished fervently that she could literally scoot for home and fall into her mother's arms.

"By the way, I'm in room seven and Cam is in number eight." Hillary added with a laugh, "We're right next to each other so I can keep an eye on my little brother."

With a quizzical look, Sara turned to Cam, "I thought you were older than Hillary and attending engineering college in Houghton?"

"He is...does," Hillary teased, "but I kind-of act as a big sister fly swatter anyway. I keep the girls like Linette Prother from buzzing around his head and landing on him."

"Oh, very funny." Cam gave his sister a disgusted look, unlocked the door of number eight, went inside, and slammed it shut. Hillary laughed in childish delight at having succeeded in riling Cam. To Sara it seemed as though Hillary often acted far younger than her eighteen years.

"Didn't you say you had a brother, too?" Hillary asked.

"Yes, Brian. Why? Are you on the prowl?" Sara teased.

"No, but if he's as nice as you, I wouldn't mind meeting him."

"He's quite a bit older than you, thirty this coming fall."

"Oh, yeah, terribly old." Hillary twirled a little dancing step, making her long full-skirted costume fly out like an open umbrella. "By-the-by, Cam and I are going out for pizza tonight for dinner. Want to join us?"

Sara thought a minute and decided that her stomach felt pretty stable. "Sure. What time are you going?"

"Fifteen minutes or twenty minutes? I'll knock on your door."

Sara nodded. "See you."

❖　❖　❖

47

Inside her room, Sara quickly strips off her costume, washes her face, and struggles back into her jeans. She puts on a clean blue cotton shirt and begins to pull a jacket off the hanger from the closet, then decides that a sweater will be more appropriate. It's doubtful if anyone dresses up much in a tourist town like this, especially in a pizza-type restaurant.

Before leaving, she looks around the room, a final check, to make sure her pregnancy book is well out of sight. Hiding things is probably futile since Pat must certainly have a spare key for each and every room and can easily get inside if she has the inclination to do some snooping. Already, it feels like she and Pat have a mutual liking for each other, so Sara is reluctant to think of her as the meddling type. Hillary and Cam are the other fort employees with whom she has felt comfortable right from the first meeting at the orientation. Hillary has brown eyes so sparkling with fun, and a ponytail as bouncy as her personality; Cam is just the opposite, quiet and earnest. Sara tells herself how nice it is to have friends again, as long as those friends aren't too nosey. "I have things to keep hidden a little longer."

One of those things was her association with her past boyfriend, Larry Weidercot. Sara recalled how they had become drawn to each other because of their mutual interests, primarily their beliefs regarding the abortion issue. They had met during an anti-abortion rally in Urbana while she was still attending the University of Illinois and then again several months later at a sit-in across the street from an abortion clinic in South Chicago. They were both against the idea of destroying life. Larry had quoted from Barnabas, 14:11, "Thou shalt not destroy thy conceptions before they are brought forth; nor kill them after they are born." Being around Larry had helped to firm up her growing belief that a fetus, though still in the womb, was a living being endowed with a spirit.

Over a latte in a Starbucks Coffee Shop, Larry had shown her the photos of the sweet delicate fingers of a thirteen-week-old fetus and how at twenty-one weeks its sturdy little legs could kick in the womb. For her, it would never be possible to believe that the tiny being wasn't already a human, not just a specimen floating around in amniotic fluid.

Bringing herself back to the present, she asks herself, what if Pat with her precisely rolled-under coif and her neat office garb, so unexpected in a relaxed tourist town like this, is indicative of an uncompromising nature? If so, she might consider my pregnancy an out and out sin. During the many abortion sit-ins Sara has attended, there were always a few people in the group who were narrow-minded in the extreme…judgmental, ready to blame the woman for the trouble she got herself into…seldom the man.

There were also those Christian fundamentalists at the abortion rallies. Their thinking ran like this: a pregnant woman would never have gotten pregnant in the first place if she had been a good Christian and read the scriptures. Their attitude was, 'let those girls live and learn from their mistakes.' Indeed, she herself was going to live and learn quite a lot more than she planned to, because of her own carelessness.

CHAPTER SEVEN

O nly a tinge of nausea upsets Sara when she wakes on the following morning. She sighs with pleasure at the relief, though coffee does produce a slight discomfort. The evening before on her way home from the pizza parlor, she bought eggs, cereal, milk, bread, peanut butter, cheese and yogurt. So now in the community kitchen, she quickly slaps together a sandwich to take with her over to the fort for lunch plus a container of yogurt.

When she leaves her room and heads towards the street, Sara notes that the usual traffic sounds emanating from the ramp leading to the bridge are a little less audible this morning. "Wind must be strong from the west and sending the noise and fumes to the east," she mutters to herself after looking up at a nearby white pine tree and noting in which direction the green tips are being swayed by the wind.

The improvement in her stomach is allowing her mind to dwell on other things again, and she wonders if some environmental group like Sierra is active in the area. There is no reason for her to let the whole summer go to waste and not put in a good word for Mother Nature if she can find an environmental group to join.

Before she crosses the street to enter through the back gate of the park complex, she checks apprehensively in both directions. No Larry. "Sometime or other he will track me down. I'm almost positive." Where is he now? Part of her hopes she'll never see him again, yet in the back of her mind she retains a nodule of concern for his safety.

Basically, Larry is a caring being, unselfish; how can she dismiss his past kindnesses from her mind so unfeelingly?

She remembers, when she met Larry for the second time at one of the anti-abortion meetings, that she had been living at the YWCA for women on the near north side for several weeks. Life there was depressing. All those women in the dining room eating alone and living in tiny rooms and waiting for a break in their jobs or their relationships...waiting for the exciting lives they had imagined, or had seen on some TV drama, to begin, but which seldom did. Her own room at the Y had been one of those long narrow spaces, approximately eight by ten, with one window at the end and a sink at the other.

Knowing how Sara hated the YWCA, Larry had offered the couch in his apartment. "It's a shabby place," he had admitted humbly as he made the offer, "...all I could find near the Evanston Campus, but you're welcome to share until you find something better."

Most of the available rental apartments in Evanston were far too expensive, so Sara took Larry up on his offer of the sofa bed, thinking that she would soon find a place of her own in spite of the expense. Moving into Larry's apartment greatly simplified things for her. "Anything," she decides, "will be easier than taking that early morning train to reach my job on time." Driving her car up to the campus from the YWCA was certainly possible, but finding a parking space upon returning to her room in the late afternoon after five was nearly impossible.

Her escape from the henhouse atmosphere of the YWCA made her feel once again that kick-your-heels freedom she had felt when first leaving home as a teenager. Though it wasn't at all logical, moving closer to the university campus gave her the feeling of gaining ground on her goal of returning to college. She had absolutely no idea if her scholarship would come through in time or not, and she had yet to fill out the grant form. Still, she registered for the following fall semester. In the meantime, she had a job in the admissions office.

When she first moved into Larry's shabby third-floor apartment, he had begun by treating her with the reserve a shy person usually exhibits when plunging cold into a new friendship. Then, after an incident at one of the group protests in front of an abortion clinic where she had been roughly handled by the police, her relationship with Larry changed.

She had been told by the protest organizers to completely relax and remain limp if she should be arrested. When she was actually arrested for the first time, a policeman holding her limp body had tried to hoist her into the police van so roughly that her knee had jammed against the metal door. She had begun to cry, not so much for the hurt knee but for the embarrassment of being arrested like a criminal even though she had been warned ahead of time to expect that sort of thing to happen.

The young policeman, who was attempting to lift her into the police van, had muttered, "Oh shit," when he realized what he had done. As she was gritting her teeth from the pain of gouging her knee, he had whispered into her ear, "I know you're supposed to go all limp as part of your protest rules, but if you don't help me get you inside, I may accidentally drop you on the cement." She had nodded and grabbed the edges of the door to help him boost her inside.

Later, sitting in the crowded cell, she had felt a twinge of conscience, especially after Larry had been so solicitous over her bloody knee. By helping the policeman guide her into the van, she had failed to fulfill her part of the sit-in. Hopefully, no one had noticed during the melee.

Larry had not been arrested, so he was free to demand that someone look at her damaged knee, which was bleeding profusely all over the cell floor. It had taken twenty stitches to pull the skin of the knee together. After that incident and Larry's obvious concern for her, their relationship had evolved into a closer one. The first step seemed innocent enough: Larry gallantly insisted that she use his firmer mattress in the bedroom while her knee was healing. He slept on the sofa bed where she had previously been sleeping.

Larry's face reminded one of a youthful Jimmy Stewart, brimming with wholesomeness. The likeness didn't extend to the hair. Larry's hair had recently been buzzed so short that it took several weeks for

Sara to discover that he wasn't bald at all. Finally, she was able to note a soft fuzz appearing, and she realized he was actually blond. Larry completely fulfilled her idea of the "perfect brother" minus the teasing of her own brother, Brian, who still enjoyed getting a rise out of her.

Even though Larry was busy researching for a bioengineering professor in the McCormick School of Engineering, he managed to do both his and her share of grocery shopping, so when she returned to the apartment in the late afternoon, she hobbled up the stairs, because her knee still hurt, accompanied by the aroma of cooking food. She repaid his generosity by providing some curtains from Walmart for his bare windows and she gave him the only three bath towels she owned. The sofa needed a new slipcover to disguise the holes caused by a former smoker's carelessness, but she couldn't afford that luxury. After a few paychecks, she did manage to replace one of the very dingy, yellow lampshades.

Larry was always questioning her about her preferences. "What's your favorite," he would ask, "green beans or asparagus?"

Of course she never said "asparagus" knowing how expensive it was. "Do you like the Anne Perry or the P.D. James novels best? Roses or mixed flowers?" Sara became careful of her answers because the question about flowers brought roses and the one about authors brought a new James novel that she doubted he could afford on his research salary.

A short time later, Larry had proclaimed his love for her, and they began sharing the same bed. At the time it seemed like a natural sequence, though she in no way voiced a commitment similar to Larry's.

"Darling," he urged, "together we can make such a difference. Our love will be an example for others."

It was easy to convince herself that eventually she would feel the same urges as Larry. His lovemaking had been thoughtful of her needs, but it never stoked any fiery responses in her. Having someone constantly at her side seeing to her wants and comforts was an easy habit into which to slide. Not long afterwards, Larry had begun to behave as though their attachment was certain to be permanent. "After all," he said, "our strong beliefs over the abortion issue affords us great influence on others." Sara continued to stall over making their attachment legal.

Sara wrested her mind back to the present as she passes through the outer fence of the park complex. She lowers her head in shame after mentally going over her past. Her present thinking is now totally at odds, totally reversed, enlightened by time and distance. Thank goodness no one here at the fort knew how weak and dependent her nature had become while living with Larry...or that she lived with him at all.

She had been chagrined to learn, by overhearing Larry's conversation over the phone to his friend, Dars, that he actually considered her as his *common law wife*, a term she considered demeaning; yet when Larry asked her to marry him, she continued to stall. This was a wake-up call reminding her how carelessly she had accepted everything from Larry as though he would be her caretaker forever.

Larry was smart...had earned a research scholarship at Northwestern. He was a bit shy, yes, and even droll at times, and always there was that guileless Jimmy Stewart face. He was a sweet man. Sara doubted that she would ever find anyone as caring as Larry. "Why not commit? Didn't they make a well-balanced couple?"

Besides the abortion issue, she and Larry had other things in common. His enjoyment of hiking and camping had fit in nicely with her own past experiences, which included camping out with her own family. During spring break, she and Larry had gone kayaking off the Keweenaw Peninsula in Michigan. They had rented a double kayak and followed the rugged shore for miles, almost making it halfway down to Eagle Harbor. Larry was adept, just as her father was, at wilderness living. She admired his skills just as she had always admired her father's.

Then in January, a week after one of the major sit-ins at an abortion clinic in Detroit, which she didn't attend, Larry and his friend, Dars Neilson, simply disappeared. Things began to unravel quickly after that. The professor for whom Larry worked told her that an FBI agent had come around asking him questions about Larry.

To escape being questioned by the authorities and to preserve her dwindling savings, Sara moved out of Larry's apartment, back into the YWCA for one night, and then back to Urbana to stay with her friend, Fay, until she could decide what to do next.

❖ ❖ ❖

"I'm pregnant," she confessed to Fay after a week of feeling as though she had the flu or some strange Asian bug caught from someone at a protest meeting. But it wasn't the flu. "Damn the luck."

"Sometimes it takes two to make rotten luck." Fay knew enough about Sara's views on the importance of preserving life to realize it would be an affront to suggest an abortion.

"I know it's more my fault." Sara admitted to Fay. "I missed taking my pills a few times."

"Or maybe the pills weren't foolproof." Fay commiserated, hoping to comfort her.

"My fault anyway." Sara knew her usual keen senses had become dulled, as though she had smoked a long joint while cohabitating with Larry. She hadn't smoked; instead, she had become weak, spoiled. Defenses down, she had been happy to indulge herself by letting Larry take care of her and sleep with her. She was appalled by this picture of herself...someone who had literally exchanged bed for breakfast. How easily she had lost her direction, yes, even the compass, and succumbed to letting someone else be her care-giver instead of taking care of herself. Where had her touted *independence and spunk* disappeared?

"You're welcome to stay here," Fay offered.

"Thanks, you're a brick, but I'd better move on. Larry would find me here too easily or some of the officials who are obviously trying to track him down. I don't want to see him again." Neither did she want to rat on him.

"But isn't he the father? He would probably marry you and make the baby legal."

"Yes, he's the father."

"As they say, *in a storm take cover.*"

"Hey," Sara retorted with a trace of her old wit, "This is no storm...it's a baby."

That conversation with Fay had been just weeks ago, yet it seemed like a year. Sara sighed and stopped to check her watch as she leaned against the fence at the animal pens. She still had time to go down to the shore before facing her discouraging day with Ansel.

Now, standing near the water by the shore, she found it hard to keep her mind from replaying further sequences from her recent past life, especially the overly cheerful telephone call she had made to her father during her last stay with her friend, Fay, in Urbana.

"Are you all right?" her father had asked when Sara first telephoned her parents. "What made you quit your job in Chicago?"

"I'm quite all right," she answered his first question and managed to exude her usual confidence and spread a screen of partial truth over her sudden departure from Chicago. In fact, outside of her bitter disappointment in Larry's character and her worry that he or the FBI might track her down, she really was "quite all right." That phone call occurred a few days before she discovered her pregnancy.

"They were downsizing personnel in the offices. Anyway, I never did like big city life." *Downsizing* was a term she had read about in reference to some large corporate firms who were divesting themselves of employees to save money.

"That doesn't sound like something a university would do," her father countered doubtfully, "and certainly not without more notice. Why don't you come home? You know we'd like that."

"I'm fine here for a while." She made an effort to sound confident.

"You sound like your old spunky self."

Sara sighed at the hated word. At a very young age Sara had been tagged with the name, *spunky,* by her father, who probably should have tagged her with harsher terms such as *sassy* or *disobedient.* At school she had earned a reputation for fudging the rules and sometimes not following them at all. Her failure to comply had gotten her into trouble even as far back as grade school. For instance, in her particular school, it had been a long-standing regulation that all the children line up, as though they were convicts lining up for chow, before being allowed inside the classroom each morning. Sara thought it was degrading.

"More like slaves!" she had stood up in class and challenged the third grade teacher. She had been eight years old at the time. The white-haired elderly teacher, who adhered to regulations and a strict daily regimen in her own life, felt that Sara was a bit too rambunctious and maybe even headed out of control, and, as she told Sara's parents, "needs a strong hand." She sent Sara to the principal for a nice little talk. Sitting there across from the principal's desk, Sara nodded docilely as he kindly discussed the need for rules and regulations.

During recess that day on the playground Sara had persuaded two other girls and one boy into standing outside the school classroom the next morning with signs that she herself made out of cardboards slipped from her father's dress shirts. In her haste to escape her parents' bedroom before being discovered, she had left the newly laundered shirts in a rumpled pile. Sara carried the signs in her red backpack to school. The next morning all three children stood in the school hallway holding the signs stating: LINE UP HERE, SLAVES. Unfortunately, Sara had misspelled the word, Slaves, and the signs read: LINE UP HERE, SLAVS. Her signs hadn't changed the school rules, and her continued unruly spirit made her future teachers wary. The hated nickname, "spunky," had stuck. Sara grimaced and shook her head at the memory.

Just one week later after her phone call from Urbana to her parents, she discovers that she isn't *quite all right. She is pregnant.*

She could feel herself sinking into depression during her bouts with morning sickness. Yet eventually it was that so-called *fighting spirit* that pulled her through the morning trips to the bathroom to throw up in the toilet. Most of the time she wished she could never wake up at all. Since she didn't believe in abortion nor leaving a newborn on a doorstep or in a trash bin, the alternative was to carry through with the pregnancy and keep the baby. She was determined to manage somehow.

And now? "At least I have a job…one where Larry or some government official isn't likely to find me so easily." She shook her mind out of the past and checked her watch. It was just a few minutes past the time when she should be at the kitchen. Ansel would likely have some snide remark to make about her lateness.

CHAPTER EIGHT

*T*he wind is a bit chillier this morning, and Sara shivers on her way to work. Out beyond the low sand dunes she can see the waves tussling with each other like children playing too roughly, then running up on the shore as though to escape each other. To her right are the Scots Guards standing at the Land Gate to greet the tourists as they enter the stockade. Later on in the day she will probably see them marching across the dusty parade ground, a splendid sight in red and black plaid kilts keeping step to the sorrowful cry of the leaky sounding bagpipes.

When Sara arrives at the Northwest Row House, Ansel is already rolling out the pie dough that she had mixed yesterday. "You're late. Watch how I do this since I'm supposed to be training you...evidently not very well since you're late. You'll probably never have to make pie or bread unless I'm sick or something." Ansel's voice sounds quite confident that such a dreadful weakness in her character, as that of being sick, will never occur.

It's on the tip of Sara's tongue to inform Ansel that she already knows how to make pies, but she decides not to challenge what Ansel presumes to be her, and only her, expertise. Sara knows that she could probably make bread as well.

Time after time she has watched her mother kneading and slapping the bread dough by hand. Her mother's hands are strong just from this weekly practice. Many times those same muscular hands have easily hauled Sara off to her room to enforce a "time out" after she has misbehaved. Then there have been the other times when her mother's hands, those same strong hands, have rubbed her aching back and made her feel more comfortable when she was ill. If only her mother could do that right now...be with her, hold her head when she is nauseous, and tell her that everything will "be all right." Sara feels a river of moisture flowing into her eyes. Fortunately, Ansel is so absorbed in shaping the pie crust to the tin plate that she doesn't look up and notice.

"There," Ansel brushes her flour-covered hands across her apron, "I'm through with these things so you can start to wash up. Heat the dishwater in that larger teakettle, then cool it down with cold water. You'll have to go and fetch two more barrels of cold water from the spigot outside the stockade."

Sara picks up the barrels and goes to fetch the water and nearly collides with Skyler who is hurrying past the Priest's House. "Sorry," she smiles at him.

"Hey now, I don't mind bumping into you." Skyler puts his arm around her. She doesn't protest. Her unusually light bout of nausea this morning has filled her with hope that the mornings to come will be completely free of sickness; she feels more cheerful than she has since arriving in Mac Village. She smiles again at Skyler. "Beautiful day, isn't it."

Skyler grabs the barrels from her hands and fills them. "Not too full," she protests, " or I won't be able to carry them."

"I'll carry them. No more fainting, I hope?" She can feel his green eyes checking her face for reactions. She shakes her head, implying "no." He walks back with her through the gate and starts to deposit the barrels in the kitchen by stepping through the open window instead of using the door. Ansel looks up from the pastry table and gives him a smirk. "Aren't you the little helper this morning."

"Always ready to oblige."

Just as Ansel steps towards the fireplace, Skyler catches his right toe on the window sill and sends one whole barrel of water cascading across Ansel's legs, soaking the bottom of her skirt, and putting out the hot coals in the front edge of the fireplace.

"Out!" Ansel yells, pointing at Skyler. Sara turns her back for a few seconds to control the giggle forcing its way up from her stomach to her mouth. There have been times when she would also have liked to throw icy cold water on the Queen of the Kitchen or push her into the fire as in the Hansel and Gretal fairy tale.

Skyler goes, leaving an unremorseful grin behind to anger Ansel even further. Sara picks up the empty barrel and mops up the water. Then she goes back for more water. When she returns, Ansel tells her in a commanding voice, "We'll need more wood to build up the fire again where Mr. Clumsy spilled water." Sara obediently starts to carry logs back and forth, stacking them inside the wood chest. She is on her third trip to the woodpile when Skyler spots her from the Blacksmith's shop where he is complaining to Steve about Ansel.

"Hey, Sara, doesn't Ansel ever let you rest?"

"Oh, everybody has to take their turn at fetching and carrying. Now Ansel's busy making cherry filling for a pie."

"Ummm, sounds great. I'll be over when it's baked. Here, let me." Skyler picks up twice as many logs as Sara is able to hold in her arms and carries them back to the kitchen. In defiance of Ansel, he once again steps straight through the long open window and drops his load with much flexing of muscles into the wood box. "Call me next time you need help."

"Looks like you have an admirer." Ansel glances disdainfully after Skyler's form before continuing to spoon the cherry filling into the pie crust. "Watch out, though. Skyler doesn't do favors without expecting something in return."

"Oh?" Sara replies and wonders how Ansel knows. She doubts that it's from first hand experience. She has it on the tip of her tongue to ask with a touch of sarcasm, "You've had experience?" but decides that *keeping the peace* is more important. Instead, she places her hand on the teakettle. "Not hot enough yet."

"Rake out a place in the fire to set the Dutch oven and give me a hand." Together they lift the oven onto the hot nest of coals that Sara has just arranged. A second shallow tin plate is set on top of the oven, and Sara drops hot coals into the plate with a small black shovel. "How long will it take to bake?"

"From an hour to an hour and a half. Depends on whether you keep the fire underneath hot and change the wood coals in the top tin plate as they grow cold. I think the water in your kettle is warm enough now so you can start to wash up the dishes. I'm taking a break." As Sara watches, Ansel rinses her hands in the dishpan of clean water and leaves the kitchen.

"So much for sanitary conditions," Sara mutters. She has no sooner started washing up the dishes than Skyler returns, coming through the door this time.

"Tonight's a good night for me to take you out," he states without preamble. Sara notes that his invitation isn't a question. It's an assumption. "You're new around here, but I know some great places. There are some nice sunset views you wouldn't want to miss."

"Like where?" Actually Sara has no intention of going out on a date with Skyler or anyone else, but she is curious to know what sort of places he has in mind. Inwardly she smirks and thinks his choices will likely be remote areas where he can feel-up a girl.

"Well, there's the swimming beach. It's got nice clean sand dunes to sit on or hide between, and there's a small lake nearby all surrounded by woods, French Farm Lake. One might even hear a loon out there, if the mosquitoes aren't too bad. Or we could drive over the bridge to the town on the other side. I live over there you know."

"Sounds nice, but I don't think so. Maybe sometime when there's a whole gang of people going…a camp fire or picnic…something like that."

"Aw come-on! How else are we going to get acquainted? I'd like to know more about you. I'll bet we have a lot in common. I already know you're not married. I can see your pocket is worn where it shows, on the outside of your apron."

"Oh, that's right. I'd forgotten. Married women back in the 1770's and earlier wore the pocket hidden, didn't they?"

Skyler nods. "Got any boyfriends?"

The question takes Sara by surprise. If she says "no," he will keep on nagging her to go out, and she doesn't want to get involved with him or anyone else. In fact, she must not even consider getting involved with anyone because of the baby. In answer to his question, she decides to fib, just to get Skyler off her back. "Yes, I do have a boyfriend. Thanks for the invitation anyway."

"Oh," he snaps and walks away muttering something that she can't decipher clearly except for the two words, "teasing cunt."

❖ ❖ ❖

Hillary had just finished conducting the children's play program and was now gathering up the large hoops that the children have been rolling around on the parade ground just as they might have done ages ago in the early fort years. Hillary stashed the hoops in a huge cardboard box leaning against the porch of the Commanding Officer's house located at the north edge of the parade ground. Her honey colored hair, having broken loose from its ponytail after her vigorous activities, hung straight and thick halfway down her back.

From her vantage point on the porch, Hillary saw the Scots Guards as they began to march in front of the tourists who were sitting on backless wooden benches on the opposite side of the parade ground from where she was watching. The bagpipes cried like the mewing of gulls or the wail of poor trapped animals in constant pain. She felt tears coming to her eyes. In spite of the sunny weather and the bright plaid kilts and flags flapping in the strong wind, the sadness of the music made her swallow hard to hold back a sob. It was a glorious moment.

Out of the corner of her right eye, she also watched Skyler Wilks. He too looked splendid when a few minutes later, dressed in his British costume of red coat and white britches, he strode confidently across the parade ground behind Terry, the drummer, to start the musket demonstration. Faintly, because the wind carried some of his words in another direction, Hillary could hear Skyler expounding to the audience, on the workings of the long musket.

Skyler lifted the heavy musket to his shoulder and squeezed the trigger. Nothing happened. He then explained to the tourists nearby how unreliable the flintlock guns could be in damp weather. He tried again with the second musket. First he opened the packet of gun powder with his teeth, sprinkled some powder in the pan to prime the gun, and then poured the remainder into the end of the gun and tamped it down. Skyler continued with his spiel: "If this weren't just a demonstration, the gun would also contain a lead ball. No man would be recruited as a soldier unless he had at least four front teeth, because he needed those teeth to rip open the gun powder packet." Once again he reminded the audience to cover their ears against the pending blast.

This time the musket fired. The sharp sound reverberated as it hit the walls of the stockade. Skyler thanked the audience, and then he and the drummer marched smartly away. In front of the Commanding Officer's House where Hillary stood, he stopped. "Whew. Two more demos to go."

Hillary sympathized. "By August we'll all be tired of the routine. I just finished my third children's program today. Three more to go unless there aren't enough children attending with their parents."

"Yeah? You're still a kid yourself, kiddo, and prettier than most. Phil is going to do the demos for me tomorrow. I get my two days off."

"Lucky you!" She's been wondering how she could draw Skyler's interest onto herself. There's something animalistic about Skyler. He stares you straight in the eye as though he's seeing your innermost weaknesses or your naked body like an x-ray machine and when he does that, Hillary quivers, enthralled all the way down to her ... well, her folks would definitely not approve of that word.

Her brother, Cam, talks about Skyler with disdain and claims his charm is mere surface veneer with plenty of polish from his long experience at chasing after girls. In spite of Cam's negative opinion, she can't thwart the excitement she feels inside when she's close to Skyler. It's sort-of fizzy, like the bubbles rising from carbonated water. Also there's a feeling of anticipation, similar to the excitement attached to a hoped-for Christmas gift. She longs to learn more about Skyler. Maybe now is her chance if she can rivet his attention on her long enough.

"My day off too," Hillary says. "Got any plans?"

"Nope. Stay home I guess and just fool around."

"I think we'll go swimming at the town beach. You don't have any nice beaches like that over there on the other side of the bridge, do you?"

"Oh, a small one. Who is 'we'?"

"Probably Sara and Cam. Why don't you come along?"

"I might join you. What time are you going?"

"In the afternoon around...two o'clock probably. I have to run now. I'm filling in for Linette in the French Wedding."

Hillary does run, literally. She barely has time to get to the changing cabin outside the Priest's Gate when the church bell begins to ring and she hears Gary's voice announcing, "Hear ye, hear ye. The French Colonial wedding and dance will take place next."

Hillary scrambles to get out of her plainer costume and into the two petticoats and the brocade blue dress with sleeves just below the elbows. The three inches of lace sewn on the sleeves hangs like a waterfall of soft white bubbles. It's a good thing that she and Linette can wear the same costume. Though they are both thin, Hillary thinks proudly how she fills out the bust line a little better than Linette.

Sometime or other Sara will have to take the role of the bride in the wedding sequence and what then? Hillary doesn't believe the dress will fit. Sara is only five-two or three and more busty than either Linette or herself. But the blue of the dress will look lovely next to Sara's light-colored eyes and against the contrast of her dark hair. "Oh, my hair!" But there isn't time to fuss with her hair. She places the lace handkerchief on her head, sticks in a bobby pin to hold it in place and runs for the church, humming, "get me to the church on time," from her favorite old movie starring Audrey Hepburn.

CHAPTER NINE

Sara and Hillary have quickly become great friends, and also Cam to a lesser extent, since he is often with Hillary as they walk back and forth from the fort to their rooms. All three of them usually get together in the community room for dinner or in a restaurant in the village. Hillary's cheery outlook on life is particularly appreciated right now; her fun-filled dark brown eyes light up with good humor. Her personality, like a child constantly skipping, is spirit-lifting. It makes Sara smile. Then at other times she feels more relaxed in the company of Cam's slower, but more contemplative manner. In fact, Cam often reminds her of Larry, or the Larry she first became acquainted with…an introspective person. Only Larry, of course, was tall and lanky whereas Cam is shorter, not much above Hillary's height.

Soon, Cam and Hillary begin to seem like family to Sara. Their presence keeps her from dwelling on herself and her problems. When she is off by herself, too many worries spring uninvited to her mind and she finds herself succumbing to "what ifs?" What if the baby is damaged…what if Larry comes back and tries to claim it? What if her parents learn about the baby too soon and try to persuade her to have it aborted?

Once in a while Steve, the blacksmith, joins the three of them when they go to dine in the village. He, like Skyler, is from St. Ignace, the town at the other end of the bridge that connects the upper and lower peninsulas of the state. More often he goes home in the evening just as Skyler does. Ansel, of course, is from right here in town and simply goes home to where her parents live in a white house near the bakery. Linette Prother drives fourteen miles from her home in the town of Cheboygan and at the end of the day drives the same fourteen miles home again.

"Prother keeps to herself," Hillary explained. "She worked here last summer, but Cam says he never got to know her very well. I'm sure he'd like to." Hillary raises her eyebrows implying that Cam is infatuated with Linette.

"Tell me more about yourself," Hillary demands. This isn't the first time she's made the attempt to ferret out the facts of Sara's past life, thinking there must be some juicy mysterious reason for Sara to exchange her exciting life in Chicago for this tourist town. "I guess, since you've been here before doing re-enactments with your folks, you feel more comfortable working here. Is that why?"

Sara nods. "Yes, probably. But historical re-enactments are things my dad likes to do, and my brother Brian, much more so than mother and I."

"Your brother's married?"

"Now Hill, take that look off your face."

"What look?"

"Like your eyes have just spotted chocolates in a store window." Sara laughs.

"I'm not on the prowl, just curious." All the same, Hillary blushes. "Will your folks be coming up here this summer to see you?"

"Maybe," Sara answers. She prays not…at least not until late in August. One can never be too sure about her brother Brian, though. He is apt to turn up anywhere, at any time. It all depends upon his caseload at the law firm.

"Did you say you had a boyfriend in Chicago?" Hillary probes anew.

"No, I didn't say, did I?"

"Cagey. Teaser!"

"Well, all right; I did have one, but no longer. He was against abortion…" She starts to reveal more about Larry, but decides not to.

Instead, she changes the subject. "How do you stand on the abortion issue?"

"Oh. I guess there are times when one is necessary, but our church is definitely against it even if the baby might harm the health of the mother. I'm not sure I agree...oh, that's a slippery question. I know a girl who was planning to marry a nice guy and then she was raped by another fellow six months before the wedding. She became pregnant. Under those circumstances, I'd want one too, wouldn't you?"

"Possibly." Sara realizes that she isn't as fired-up over the abortion issue as she once was and certainly not eager to argue the subject any further. The urge to counter Hillary's beliefs with pro-life statements hasn't overtaken her with the strong zeal it usually does.

"If I knew my baby might be impaired and consequently lead a terrible life, I don't know how I would decide. The thought of killing a human being, a potential one, is terrible."

"*All fetuses* are human beings, living, not just potential humans."

"Well yes, I suppose that's the way anti-abortionists think, but isn't that the part that is still unknown? I mean, no one knows for sure when a fetus gains a spirit."

Sara decides that it's time to drop the subject. She wants and needs Hillary as a friend, not as an adversary. "Where shall we eat tonight?"

"Let's go to Burger King. I'm low on funds, but I'm also sick of frozen dinners and canned stew. I'll ask Cam what he wants to do. He said something about a carnival down in Pellston. It's a small carnival, but hotdogs with mustard and lots of pickles sounds great to me, also cheap."

Immediately, Sara begins to think about making excuses. How can she get out of going with them? She will be afraid to go on any stomach-dropping rides for fear of regurgitating the hot dogs and mustard. Just thinking about the Ferris wheel as it swoops upwards and then forces her to look straight down again riles her stomach. But what excuse can she give Hillary? "I think I'll pass on the carnival."

"Hey, it could be fun even though it's just a small town thing."

There seems to be no way of getting out of it gracefully so Sara decides on a partial truth. "My stomach has been a little upset lately."

"Sorry. Anything I can do? I could get you some Pepto Bismol."

"Thanks, but I just need to take it easy and eat plain food for a day or so...no chili, mustard, or anything like that."

"O.K. But you don't mind if I go with Cam instead of eating here with you, do you?"

"Of course not! Go. Have a good time. I'll see you later, and you can tell me all about it." Sara gives Hillary a wave of her hand as she unlocks her room door and disappears inside.

❖ ❖ ❖

Sara's day off is tomorrow and she decides, if her morning sickness isn't too bad, to take the boat to Mackinac Island...maybe even rent a bicycle, but again that depends upon how energetic she feels when she wakes up. A bit of guilt lingers in her mind for not first telling Hillary who has already talked about going to the island with her.

"Anyway, I could wake up feeling terrible. Then what excuse could I give her? I've overused every one of my sick headache excuses, and just yesterday I added an upset stomach to the list." But more importantly, she doubts that the attractions she wants to see on the island are of much interest to Hillary. She wants to be free to linger and absorb the historical exhibits. "Also, I need to sit down frequently. Hillary wouldn't understand why I'm such a weakling."

❖ ❖ ❖

Monday morning turns out to be a winner in two ways. A look at the cloudless sky convinces Sara that the weather appears to be great, and a check on her stomach finds the nausea slight. She slips a friendly note under Hillary's room door to tell her that she won't be going to the beach as planned, then takes a sweater, visor cap, scarf, and drives off to the village. At the boat dock the fresh early morning air fuses with smells of churned-up water slightly tainted with fishiness.

Sara has previously discovered that the faster, cruiser type boats to the island run every twenty minutes this time of the morning so she knows she won't have to wait long. After purchasing her ticket she buys a cup of coffee and a doughnut and sits down under the blue and white awning at a café table to wait. Already a few people are lined up on the wharf even though the boat itself hasn't arrived back from Mackinac Island yet. Still, Sara doesn't hurry to join them. Past experience tells her there will be plenty of seats on the boat this early in the day, especially on the top deck where it's usually too windy for most people. The top deck is where Sara feels in rhythm with the boat. It's her favorite spot...or has been in the past. She hopes the up and down boat motion won't affect her stomach now that she's pregnant.

The white cruiser blasts its horn as it swings around the breakwater. Already, it has slowed to the harbor speed of four miles per hour. The captain makes a clever U-turn in limited space, just missing the boats moored in slips at the marina close behind.

First the bicycles and luggage are off-loaded from the boat, and next the passengers are allowed to disembark. Sara counts only ten people coming back from Mackinac Island this early in the day. She watches as a blonde young man in navy colored shorts and white T-shirt checks the rows of seats for lost belongings and litter, then she and the others are allowed to go on board. Sara heads for the top deck, slides onto one of the bench-type seats near the bow, and secures her scarf over her beige visor cap by tying it firmly under her chin.

After the boat leaves the breakwater and heads north, it picks up speed, the bow rises, and they cruise along smoothly. Later when the heading changes to a more northeasterly one, an occasional light mist of water sprays Sara's face. It feels wonderfully cool, feathery and light as one might imagine the dainty touch of fairy fingers. The hum of the boat, an extremely loud one due to the twin screws, obliterates all nearby human voices and mesmerizes Sara; the sun off to the east, though still not very high in the sky, forces her to close her eyes in spite of her sunglasses. Behind her closed eyes pictures dance, and she smiles at the soothing scenes.

What Sara pictures is a different boat drawn as a backdrop for a stage performance in grade school. Actually, she is the one who painted the misshapen boat on a huge roll of brown wrapping paper. The play had been about the Pilgrims with herself as Pricilla and a young boy, a classmate, as John Alden. The script, geared to children of her age, was stilted...very serious stuff back then, but now almost funny in the reminiscing. She recalls how important she had felt standing up on a stage pretending to be someone else. Perhaps acting the part of a different character from her own, just as she is doing here at the fort, allows her to slough off her own problems at least temporarily. Just another form of escapism? But no, she absolves herself, I'm just taking mental refuge, not trying to escape motherhood. Larry, if he shows up, may be another matter.

Behind her closed eyes the school scene dissolves, and her past with Larry begins to resurrect itself. How had she missed the fact that Larry had become more and more fanatical over abortion, possibly as warped as those cedar post in the animal pens at the fort. She had ignored the change in Larry to the point of disaster...the disaster that had eventually occurred in Detroit. She had swept aside every suspicion in her mind until the consequences were literally shoved in front of her face. Why had she ignored the truth so long? Because it had been easier to push her anxieties into a back corner and permit her life to proceed in the easy, comfortable manner to which she had become accustomed while living with Larry.

Were there other signs she had missed as well? She tried to think back. Dimly, she now recalled something about his sister, Amanda. Hadn't he once said, "I'll never speak to her again, no matter if she is family, not after she had that fallopian tube thing done." Had he meant a tube tying operation? Unlike his usual calm, methodical manner, he had fairly spit out the words: Baby Killer! Sara had chalked-up his animosity towards his sister as something he would eventually get over as time moved on. Surely he would forgive her, his own sister.

Larry was very adept at quoting passages from the Bible that he interpreted, sometimes even twisted, as God speaking against killing the unborn. Yet his hate against his sister and of abortionists was totally out of character because he didn't believe in killing anybody or anything. He wouldn't even kill a big-eyed little mouse that got inside the apartment. He trapped it and took it over to the Northwestern Campus and let it escape in the bushes. He never wanted to hurt anything. So how had he felt about that terrible incident that occurred in Detroit? He must have been deeply appalled...and sick.

Now she opens her eyes widely, purposely, as the boat approaches Mackinac Island. It's time to thwart any further intrusions of past memories.

CHAPTER TEN

*A*ll day today, she tells herself, I can relax. I won't have to worry about accidentally revealing my pregnancy by some slip of the tongue since absolutely no one knows me over there on Mackinac Island. She sighs with pleasure and tucks a strand of dark hair back under her scarf. Her hair has grown at least a quarter-inch in the past several weeks, and she thinks her neck looks less bare, less pathetically vulnerable.

After disembarking, Sara walks up the main street and turns left to reach Market Street where she visits the Comfort Station. There might not be another restroom available until she climbs to the fort on the hill. Might as well get that necessary thing over with, she tells herself, then I can take my time at the historical sites and looking in the shops. She had read in her book on pregnancy that later on in about the eighth month, she might be stopping often at such facilities. Well, thank goodness, she sighs, I'm not at that stage quite yet.

On Market Street she ambles past an English China shop, a small gallery full of pictures by a local artist, and several other shops, all intriguingly arranged with unique gifts. She glances into three more stores and then sits down on a bench in front of the last shop to rest and watch a line of plodding saddle horses go past and on up the hill to the middle island trails. She herself had ridden just such a hired horse in the past. Her horse had stopped to nibble leaves on every available bough hanging over the path and refused to move any further along the trail. When she turned him back towards the stable, he was more than willing to trot along at a lively pace.

Sara decides to climb the long gradual hill past the Grand Hotel; a round-about way to the fort. Half way up the hill she grows tired again and wishes she had taken the shorter but steeper route. At the outdoor restaurant next to the golf course, she orders a lemonade, and sits down again to rest. Why does being pregnant make me feel so tired, she wonders? Maybe I need vitamins; she decides to purchase some the next time she drives to Cheboygan. As she sips her lemonade, she glances across the street at Grand Hotel and notices since her last visit, and that's been quite awhile, the shrubbery has been artfully pruned into animal shapes. She watches as the elegant carriages are drawn up to the center steps of the long porch to let passengers alight.

After resting, she takes a shortcut across the rough golf course green to the road, which leads behind the governor's white cottage, and on up a gradual hill to the back entrance of the fort. She shows her free entry card at the gate, enters, and watches from this higher entrance level as four men dressed in dark blue American Military Uniforms of the 1860's parade down below and then shoot off their rifles.

After viewing Hill House Quarters she enters at the lower level of the two-story Soldiers' Barracks that contains an exhibit depicting the history of the island and the British-American Fort. Her father had seen the exhibit last summer and remarked on its comprehensiveness. He was a stickler for authenticity, so it was rare for him to be so complimentary. Doubtless he would enjoy discussing the exhibit with Dr. Reidel if the opportunity ever arose.

Sara is just finishing the section which tells about the trapping of beaver when the sound of a familiar voice breaks into her concentration. There is no mistaking the soothing cadence and the well-enunciated words. She glances around and spots Jonathan in one corner of the large room talking to a workman who seems to be repairing one of the hinges on the flip-up exhibits. On the wall in front of Jonathan is printed a historical question. Then to learn the correct answer to the question, the viewer has only to lift the flap of wood just below. Kids loved that kind of puzzle and so did most grownups. She decides not to disturb Jonathan since he is obviously working. She walks quietly in the opposite direction to the next display area, which shows the process of making hats from beaver pelts. Anyway, she suddenly realizes that she needs to get off her feet and rest. She doesn't see any benches in this section of the exhibit so she moves quickly on to the next room and then the next. The whole exhibit covers several rooms and more than one floor of the building. It isn't until she is nearly finished that she finds a large carpet-covered bench in the center of one of the last rooms on the upper level and sits down to rest. She looks at her watch. One-thirty and way past lunch time. No wonder she feels so lethargic.

On her way back to the main street, she stops at the Yankee Tavern for a cup of potato soup and half a corned beef sandwich. She feels so much better after eating that she decides to walk easterly a short distance along the shore towards Sainte Anne's Church. Several horse-drawn carriages and bicycles pass her as she approaches the church. Wasn't Sainte Anne's Church supposed to be the same church that was taken apart piece by piece from the fort at Mac Village and slid over here on the ice and then reconstructed? "There must be some mistake," she murmurs. Surely the earlier church could not have been this grand. She stands there for several minutes on the opposite sidewalk admiring the beauty of the stained glass windows and trying to figure out why this church is far larger than the little replica church back on the mainland in that fort.

Sara heads back to the boat dock and literally weaves her way like the shuttle of a loom through the heavy throng of tourists on the main street. Out on the dock she joins a long line of people waiting for the next boat back to the mainland. It's only three o'clock, but she feels quite limp and tired.

A few minutes later Sara is checking her watch again when she feels a hand touch her arm. She jerks aside in apprehension. Her first panicky thought is: Larry! She almost blurts out his name before someone behind her says, "Sorry. Didn't mean to startle you."

Sara recovers, realizing as soon as the melodious voice penetrates her brain that it isn't Larry. She turns and smiles at Dr. Reidel hoping to make amends for her unfriendly reaction.

"You always seem very nervous. Are you hiding something besides those chewed up finger nails?"

Sara quickly hides her hands behind her back and shakes her head in denial.

"We'll have to treat you like a thumb sucker and put disgusting tasting medicine on your fingers. Either that or delve into the source of your tension."

"You have no bad habits?" she challenges.

"One or two, but mine don't show. Let's see. I can confess to knock knees, one ingrown toenail, a cowlick, and sometimes I don't mind my own business."

Sara laughs. "You really are in a bad way. I won't exchange my chewed finger nails for any of those faults...especially the knock knees."

"If I'd known you were coming over here to Mackinac Island, I'd have given you a personal tour through the fort."

"Thanks. I've been here before, several times, but I hadn't seen all the newer exhibits." She doesn't mention seeing him earlier in the Soldiers' Barracks. "There is something I'd like to ask you." He nods to show that he is listening, and she continues, "That church, Ste Anne's. It's too elegant to be the same one that once stood inside the fort at Mac Village."

"It's not the same one. The one the British took apart and shipped across the water or slid across the ice, was reconstructed in the downtown area over here on the island. Later it was moved out to the site where you see a church now. But it was torn down and the new church, the one you just saw, was built."

"Oh, that explains it."

"You're looking much better, not so white and peaked," he states after carefully inspecting her face.

"There's the 'doctor' persona showing up again. Want to take my pulse? I think you ended up in the wrong profession."

"No, I'm quite satisfied with burrowing into history instead of guts, but my past interest in medicine keeps me alert to nuances like skin color and also the way people behave...well, like your jumpiness."

"Oh, I really have nerves of steel," she jokes, but immediately reacts with a spasmodic jerk when a whistle blows as their return boat pulls near the dock.

"I don't think so." He carefully scrutinizes her face.

"Oh good," Sara changes the subject and gestures towards the end of the dock, "looks like we're boarding at last"

"Want to sit up on top?"

"Sure." Sarah begins to tie the scarf over her cap, and Jonathan puts his arms through the blue nylon windbreaker he has been carrying over his arm.

"This is one of the perks of my job. I love riding back and forth across the water. Sometimes I even take the slower boat just for the joy of the longer, more leisurely ride. Also it gives me a chance to think through my manuscripts and decide upon new exhibit ideas that I might not have time for otherwise."

"My brother and I," Sara begins, then pauses wondering why she feels so free to confide in this stranger, "used to ride the tubby, slower boat when the water was rough because it rolled so easily and gave us a thrill."

"You would like being here in the fall then. That's when the weather gets brisk and mean. Do you know that we have some skiing here on the island in winter? Over there on the island," he corrects himself since the boat is already passing the harbor lighthouse. "Do you ski?"

"A bit. I'm barely past the beginner's slope."

"Our hills on the island aren't that steep. You'd do fine, and you don't live that far away either. Kalamazoo, didn't you say?"

"Oakland, just south." Sara immediately groans to herself, no skiing for me this winter or even next probably. She adds vaguely, "I don't know for sure where I'll be this winter. Anyway, there are closer places to ski." Just last winter she had been to Boyne Mountain, a ski area near Petoskey, with a busload of skiers from Chicago.

"Whoa. Looks like we're in for some of that rough fall weather right now."

The boat begins to plow over the rising waves and then wallow from side to side, first to the port and then to the starboard. Sara has never been sea sick in her life, but since the baby has begun growing, she reacts more sensitively to everything: foods, hot sun and too much standing on her feet. Right now she feels a growing apprehension over the way the boat is pitching about. She must not, she tells herself, be sick in front of Jonathan. She slumps down in her seat to escape the wind.

"I can feel you shivering next to me. We could go down below or… here, snuggle closer so I can wrap my windbreaker partly around you. Jonathan takes off his windbreaker and begins to tuck it across Sara. "If we hunker down closer together, I think it will protect both of us though it will leave our backs exposed."

"Thanks." Sara tells herself to switch her mind onto something else besides the wallowing boat. With grim determination to overcome her queasy feeling, she presses her lips firmly together. With Jonathan's body warmth penetrating her body, it's hard to take her mind off either him or her stomach. Enjoying his proximity is forbidden territory, yet a strand of his hair is tickling her ear, and it's a most enjoyable sensation. She is aware of his dark eyes tracking her face every now and then to see how she is reacting to the rocking boat.

Getting cozy with Jonathan for bodily warmth is exactly what she should be avoiding. She has absolutely no right to have close associations with any man even with the lame excuse of needing warmth. She knows intuitively that a relationship with Jonathan could be as easy as skiing down a slope and just as exciting. She keeps chanting inside her head, mustn't…mustn't.

"We're almost there now."

With relief she feels the wave action easing as the boat slows and approaches the breakwater at Mac Village. Reluctantly, she unwraps herself from Jonathan's windbreaker. The rough ride is over and she hasn't lost her soup and sandwich. Her head is giddy, and a bit of a sour taste rises in her throat. "Home at last," she shivers and sighs as they disembark. "I have my car here if you'd like a ride over to Fort Mac."

"Yes, thanks."

When they arrive back at the rooms, Sara stops her car in front of the office to drop Jonathan off before parking in the lot just around the corner.

"How about having dinner with me tonight?" he asks still standing beside the car with the door open.

"Oh, thanks, but I'm a bit tired." It's the truth. Dinner with him would have been pleasant, but once again she firmly tells herself, *hands off.* Sometime though, she wants to question him about classes at Western Michigan University in Kalamazoo. It just might turn out that she could squeeze in a class or two and still take care of the baby. "Maybe some other time," she finally answers, knowing full well that she should cut this relationship off cleanly and leave no rough edges.

"I'll give you a rain check. I'll be coming back here on Friday. How about dinner then?"

"Perhaps," she demurs.

"I'll take that as 'yes' and ignore the 'perhaps.'"

"Goodbye, and thanks for sharing your windbreaker on the boat." By Friday she will be able to think of some excuse to cancel Jonathan's offer of a dinner date. She can either tell him that her folks are coming to visit or…that she and Hillary are going on an out-of-town jaunt or…well, something. She's getting tired of always having to dodge the truth.

CHAPTER ELEVEN

From her office window Pat had seen the car door open and Jonathan step out and then immediately lean back inside the car again as though to ask Sara something. She saw Sara hesitate and then nod her head, the car door closed, and Sara drove away. She wondered if Jonathan had met Sara by accident or if it had been a planned outing.

Pat had expected Jonathan to come this afternoon, though not so late in the day. Her patient waiting had finally been rewarded only to see him arrive with Sara. It was a disappointment, but probably had a logical explanation. Perhaps the two of them had accidentally met up in the village. Jonathan was making what he considered to be a routine visit to the fort and would naturally see Pat, the "office Pat." He didn't know as yet that on this particular occasion he was going to see Pat, the homemaker. She planned to conduct a little experiment... an attempt to discover just how he did think about her. Was her place in his mind only that of a buddy-buddy Parks Department employee or possibly something more? Naturally, she hoped she occupied a more important place in his mind.

Last night in her apartment on Muster Street, she had made a Penne Pasta casserole and this morning brought it over to the community kitchen refrigerator with the intention of asking Jonathan to stay and eat dinner with her. She wanted the invitation to sound very casual, as though she had just thought of inviting him at the last minute. If Jonathan accepted her invitation, she would quickly reheat the casserole in the microwave over in the community kitchen. If he didn't, she would take the meal home again.

After mulling it over, she decided that serving the meal in the community kitchen would defeat her purpose. There would surely be several other employees hanging around, and they might distract Jonathan from focusing on her. Instead, she could serve the meal in the room behind the office where there was no one to interrupt them. When Jonathan finally did show up, she was greatly relieved, but the fact that he arrived in Sara's company was a letdown. Immediately, she suspected that the two of them had already formed a close relationship.

Pat kept a supply of tablemats and napkins and even candles in her desk drawer. Well, candles, she warned herself, might be going a bit too far. If she made too much of a fuss over this dinner or tried to be stagey by having a candlelight atmosphere, it might scare Jonathan off, unless he already had a very strong interest in her. That was exactly what she was hoping to find out. "Perhaps," she thinks, "he never has seriously considered me as a possible girl friend, just an office convenience."

While she waits for him to appear through the office door, Pat reminds herself that part of the purpose of this first dinner—she hopes there will be others later—is to make him aware of how much they have in common. They are both compatible as far as age, and surely her organizational skills will nicely highlight his scholarly ones. After all, aren't they both deeply involved in making the parks a success?

When Jonathan opened the office door and entered the hallway prior to getting his room key, Pat stepped forward.

"Pat? I thought everyone would be gone this late. How has your day been?" He sounded cheery.

"Oh, lots of extra work to do." It isn't a pretext. She has always had more work than she could handle and was hoping to be given some office help soon. "Since I had to stay later than usual, I planned to eat here tonight...even brought a casserole for my meal." She tried

to make her invitation sound completely casual. "Why not join me...
if you don't have other plans?"

"Well, sure. But is there enough food for two?"

"Oh yes. No problem. I always make extra. I'll heat it up, and we
can eat in the other room. It's less noisy than the kitchen. Be back
in a jiffy."

"Thanks. I'll wash up first." Jonathan uses the back office door
and crosses the driveway to number three cabin. Pat is a thoughtful
woman, he muses, as he unlocks his room door. She works hard, is
well organized and always appears attractive. In fact, that overused
expression, "never a hair out of place," suits Pat perfectly. He is willing
to wager that her housekeeping is as systematized as her office desk.

When Jonathan returned to the office and stepped into the
room beyond, he spotted a small table set with china and brightly
colored napkins. In the center of the table stood a bowl of mixed
salad...a huge bowl. It began to dawn on him that Pat had planned
on company. His? That was certainly the way it appeared to him. She
had known yesterday that he was coming over from Mackinac Island
this afternoon, so perhaps she had purposely made the dinner well
ahead of time. Five minutes later he watched her hurry into the room
holding a hot casserole in her oven-mitt hands. "Coffee or tea?"

"Tea, please" From a nearby table she poured iced tea with a
lemon wedge. He also noted a plate of brownies for dessert.

"Anything interesting happen over here today?" he asked politely
as they sit down to eat.

Pat shrugged, "Nothing special. The employment records and
references for the new girl, Sara, have finally been sent over." Again,
she was tempted to tell Jonathan about her suspicions.

"Anything unusual in it?"

"She has a good recommendation. It states clearly that Sara
herself terminated her job at Northwestern. It was a perfectly good
job, which paid a much higher salary than the one she now has here
at the fort. Besides, this is only a temporary job...summer only. A
little strange don't you think?"

"Maybe she didn't really like the other job. . .or found that it was too expensive to live in Chicago."

Pat shook her head doubtfully. "Or maybe she had a boyfriend and the relationship went sour."

"Possibly." He recalled how white and pale Sara had looked upon first arriving. Even her enormous gray-green eyes had looked heavy from lack of sleep or possibly crying. There had been the fainting episode, as well. It wasn't the first time he'd wondered about the fainting, but today Sara appeared much healthier, her face fuller, pinker, and her manner cheerful. "Anything in her papers about having an illness?"

"You mean a terminal illness or perhaps pregnancy?" Purposely she allowed a pause. "Nothing." There ... that's as far as she intends to tattle, but at least she had left Jonathan with something to think about.

"This is very good." Jonathan indicated the casserole. It had Italian flavoring including plenty of garlic. . .maybe just a mite too much garlic, but in general his tastes were very eclectic.

"Thanks. It's from the Moosewood Cookbook: soybean, brown rice, eggs, but with some of my own added seasonings. More tea?" He indicated yes, and Pat refilled his glass and replaced the salad bowl with the plate of brownies.

"By the way," Pat continued, "I've been wanting to ask you to recommend a book that covers the fort's historical period. It's difficult to choose with so many available over in the Park gift shop."

"Depends. Do you mean the British period of this fort or the American period on Mackinac Island?"

"This fort primarily."

"Why not borrow a book from me instead. If you like it, you'll know what to buy before wasting your money. I'll bring one over from the island on my next trip."

"Thanks, I'd appreciate it."

After they had finished eating he helped Pat bus the dirty dishes back to the community kitchen. The room was completely empty of people by this time in the evening. He also lent a hand with the washing up—good manners his mother had instilled in him. "Maybe you'll join me again sometime?" Pat asked.

"Sure." He felt compelled to answer in the positive. After drying the last dish he told her, "I have some work to do on my manuscript, so if you'll excuse me, I'll leave you to finish up. It was a very good dinner. Thanks again, Pat. Goodnight."

After Jonathan left, Pat felt an anticlimax, a let down. Actually she wasn't sure if her dinner had proved anything at all. Had Jonathan shown her any particular deference that he wouldn't have shown anyone else? He had been friendly enough, but he was always sociable...good mannered. He would probably be just as polite to a complete stranger, or maybe even a chimp. She had hoped he would ask her for a date. He hadn't.

❖ ❖ ❖

After returning from the island, dropping Jonathan at the office, and parking her car, Sara stops in the community kitchen to open a can of soup. It's all her stomach wants after all the rocking back and forth on the return boat trip. She finds Hillary in the kitchen heating canned chili and humming. Apparently she has already made and devoured a turkey sandwich but is still not satiated.

"Hey! I missed you today. Did you have a good time on the Island?"

"Sure, though I didn't do anything too exciting...mostly just walked around in and out of stores and then looked at the exhibits at the American Fort."

"No bike ride? Let's go again and ride bikes. All right?"

Sara hesitates before answering. "Sure, let's. What did you do today?"

"Went swimming. Cam took a long hike up the beach. He must have been gone almost an hour, so mostly I sunned myself."

Sara notices a very satisfied smile, almost a smirk, on Hillary's face. "Something special happened, didn't it."

"Well, sort-of. Skyler came to the beach with us. At first he seemed pissed off. You see, I'd told him just the day before that you'd be coming with us. Afterwards he thawed a bit, and we went swimming and..."

"Yes? Tell all."

"We got acquainted."

"In what way "acquainted?""

"We fooled around a bit out on the second sandbar."

"Oh? Sounds like he really thawed a lot." Sara makes little effort to keep the sarcasm out of her voice.

"See, there weren't many people out there at the beach, but there were one or two so we were pretty discrete."

"How far did you...?"

"Oh, he pulled down my bathing suit straps so I could feel the deliciously cool water on my breasts. That's about all."

"And Skyler? Did he let the deliciously cool water run over his bare private parts?" She sees the answer on Hillary's face. "Hillary, I wouldn't trust Skyler."

"Ummm, I doubt he'd go too far."

"Will you?"

"My bible-toting church has put plenty of fear into me. But I can't help liking Skyler. He's, well, like his green eyes...always a "go" light and upbeat...and there's this animal attraction."

Probably it *is* the animal attraction that has tripped-up Hillary. But surely she, Sara, is not the one to preach sexual abstinence to Hillary. Un-saintly Sara is hardly a virtuous model to follow. Look at the trouble her own sexual laxity has gotten her into. She wants to caution Hillary, yet she of all people has no right to put on a prudish, sisterly act. She decides to say nothing more on the subject for now.

"Here, have some chili with me." Hillary hands Sara a cup.

"Thanks, but I've already fixed soup." Just the smell of Hillary's chili is riling up Sara's stomach.

❖   ❖   ❖

After dinner, Jonathan wanders past Sara's room on his way to his own. No light shines from inside. He glances at his watch and notes that it is just a bit past nine-thirty, about sunset time. When he looks towards the beach, he can just see a glimpse of the lowering sun peeking from behind the trees. Where is Sara, he wonders? Why, he reprimands himself, are you assuming that it's your responsibility to check up on her? Then he recalls her saying that she was tired. That had been her excuse for turning down his invitation to dinner. Maybe she really has gone to bed, and that's the reason her room window appears to be dark.

It's too beautiful an evening to waste inside a stuffy little room so he walks across the street, through the gates, and ambles down to the shore. Maybe he will be in time to see the sun set. The paper work can wait a bit longer.

As he tops the low sand dune, he can see someone sitting on a rock down by the water's edge. Eagerly, hoping it is Sara, he walks closer but still isn't sure of the person's identity. Several interpreters and archaeologists are living in the rooms and cabins across the street so it could be anybody. Since the rub-and-slip of his shoes in the sand can't be heard over the sloshing and receding sounds of the lake water, he takes the person by surprise.

"Hello. It's a pretty evening, isn't it," he says. The figure turns. It is, as he has already guessed, Sara after all.

"Yes. I'm waiting for the sun to drop down into the water. Have you ever heard people say that just after the sun disappears, one can often see a greenish glow rise up?"

"Yes, I have. I suppose there's a scientific explanation, but I rather like the mysterious aspect of the phenomenon."

"Me too." She likes his answer. She can tell that he has imagination. In a way, asking people what they see as the sun sets is a kind of test, though there is no specific reason for her to test Jonathan. She has mentioned the green after-glow to other men and their reactions have always been one of two things: a simple huff of disbelief or "it's because we look at the red of the sun so intensely that after it's gone, we see the opposite color which is green." Those were the usual prosaic answers.

"There it goes." They watch as the sun appears to get swallowed up by the deep inky water off in the far west.

"No green," Sara whispers, as though disappointed.

"Not this time. Maybe next time. Sara..." he begins, but hasn't quite formulated what he is planning to say, so he starts again. "Sara, if you have any problems while you are working here at Mac Fort, will you call on me?"

"You mean about the job?

"That and any other problems that might crop up."

For an unsettling moment she doesn't know what to think or how to respond. Has he put two and two together and guessed at her pregnancy, or has Pat already reported what she suspects after seeing the book lying on the floor of her room?

"It's nice of you to offer, but I'm just fine. Everything is fine." She realizes immediately after the forced upward lilt in her voice, that she has sounded very unconvincing, more like a child denying she has stolen a cookie, or that overused phrase: "me thinks you protest too much." She rises from the sand, purposely not looking at Jonathan, and says politely like a well-taught child, "Goodnight." Then she quickly heads back towards the gate, the road, and her room.

"Goodnight," he calls after her. He feels "classroom dismissed" though obviously she is the one to leave.

CHAPTER TWELVE

*A*s usual when Sara wakes up, she puts herself into *testing mode*. She lies in bed for several minutes not moving, listening for the complaints from her stomach. The nausea has disappeared, but she still half expects it to make a comeback. It doesn't, and she feels a great surge of relief flowing over her. Except for the sensation of fatness, which is similar to the feeling of stuffing one's body into a girdle far too small, she almost feels like springing, antelope style, out of bed. Instead, she reaches over for her Walkman and listens to music for ten minutes or so before getting up.

Yesterday, between her work shifts, she had driven the fourteen miles to Cheboygan for her appointment with the obstetrician. "Everything looks fine," Dr. Eldrich had told her. "Buy the vitamins and get more calcium into your diet," he suggested. "Later, we may take a sonogram, but only if necessary." She realizes that she probably owes Larry a thanks for her good health. He had always insisted that they have a salad or fresh vegetables for every evening's meal. He himself had been a broccoli fan, so she knew that at least for a time she had been getting plenty of folic acid.

Afterwards, on her way back down the main street of Cheboygan, she notices a second hand shop run by the Salvation Army, so she stops to check it out. Inside are rows and rows of clothing. The combined odor of all those old clothes, though supposedly washed, hits her nose, and she nearly turns around and straight back out the door again. She overcomes her distaste and stays long enough to look at larger-sized jeans. She doesn't want to spend much money on something she might never wear again after the baby arrives. She buys a size ten in jeans, tan ones, one whole size larger than her usual eight, and from the boys' rack, two oxford cloth shirts that won't need ironing. Both shirts are more ample than the ones she now wears. The total purchase cost her only five dollars.

Nearly everyone dresses casually, even sloppily, in a tourist area like this one so probably people won't notice that now she wears her shirts outside her jeans instead of neatly tucked in or that she no longer wears T-shirts at all. The knit shirts are beginning to over-emphasize the blossoming of her breasts. Also, for fifty cents, she finds an old straw hat that she can wear when she works in the garden at the fort. Naturally it isn't a 1780's style bonnet, but it does have a flat shaped crown and maybe with a few ribbons, it will look old fashioned enough. Her attempt to buy a secondhand bookcase is unsuccessful. Her favorite novels by Ann Tyler, Kurt Vonnegut, and Fitzgerald plus her numerous history books, will have to remain in cartons on the floor of her room. When she gets back inside her car, she sniffs at the jeans and shirts and decides to leave them out of the plastic bag to air on the way back to Mac Village.

Sara barely makes it back in time for her afternoon shift in the row house kitchen. She hurries into her costume, noting how snug it feels. Already, she has let out the laces on the bodice twice. Today, the drawstring in the blue gathered skirt also has to be loosened a bit more.

Just before closing time, seven o'clock, Sara decides to take a quick look at the archaeological exhibit under the British Trader's House, which is just another section of the long weathered row house in which she and Ansel work. All she has to do is step outside of one door and then step inside the next door on her left and take the stairs down to the underground display area, which is kept at the correct temperature and humidity to protect the artifacts.

At the bottom of the stairs Sara finds a door leading to the exhibits. She pushes the door open and immediately notices the large glassed-in, ceiling to floor display to her right where there are two very lifelike manikins. One manikin is kneeling with a dental pick in its hand apparently to extricate an artifact. A whisk broom and spatula lay nearby. The second manikin, stands behind a tripod holding a camera. Signs explain how the ground is first marked off in five by five foot plots before the digging begins.

Sara starts to pass the exhibit when a movement catches her eye. She shivers and stops. Has she caught a brief glimpse into a fourth dimension? Weird! But yes, she has definitely caught a manikin coming to life. Then she realizes that it's really Jonathan, a very much alive person, standing inside the exhibit behind the camera, preparing to take a picture. With a sigh of relief, she waves to him and turns to the opposite side of the passage to look at the smaller displays behind glass.

Some exhibits are to explain how the archaeologists proceed by sifting the dirt through small sieves, and then hosing down the remaining materials on a larger table-size sieve. Other exhibits display the numerous artifacts that have actually been dug up and identified. Further along on the same side are miniature models of the fort depicting how the stockade's walls have gone through various stages of reconstruction over the years starting with its earliest beginnings, 1714, when it belonged to the French, and was more of a trading post than a fort.

At the end of the passage just before the hall makes a u-turn into a parallel hallway, there is a small alcove, separated from the hallway and the other exhibits, which contains a much larger display behind glass. The alcove is kept in semi-darkness unless the display button is pushed by a visitor. Sara pushes the button, and the scene behind glass lights up and shows what the fort looks like in the 1780's before the British moves it to Mackinac Island and then burned the remaining buildings. Immediately afterwards, the display shows the viewer how the strewn ground appears after the burning. Sara has just watched the complete sequence, and now the exhibit and the alcove are almost in complete darkness again.

"Gotcha!" a voice claims, wrenching her arms behind her.

Sara screams and sinks down to the floor. Her breath comes in short spurts. She hears running feet and then a familiar voice, Jonathan's. "Sara? What happened?"

"It was only a joke." Skyler throws out his arms in sheer puzzlement. "I don't know why she got so upset?"

Jonathan squats down beside Sara. "Did Skyler do something?"

Gulping air, Sara stammers, "It's just that…that…in the dark he grabbed my arms, and I panicked."

Jonathan looks at Skyler suspiciously. "Skyler, you go along. I'll sort this out." Jonathan tries to calm Sara. He can see that she is shaking badly. "Skyler has gone now. Breathe deeply, slowly." He waits for her to gain control and breathe normally again.

"Once when I was eight years old, I was kidnapped by two or three boys. It was all meant as a joke. But…the boys trapped me in a passageway, almost like this one, I think." She gestures at the hallway. "Then they locked me in a large chest for a couple of hours. I don't remember the details. I shouldn't have come down here at all."

"Maybe you should have come down here far sooner to help you get over the bad memory. Next time come down here when there are lots of people around to keep you company. There's safety in numbers even if it's just psychological. Skyler seems to have a strange sense of humor, although I doubt if he meant any physical harm. Come-on, let's get you out into the open air. Sometimes underground passages will give anyone a trapped feeling."

"You're always rescuing me." Sara smiles guiltily.

"Right," he jokes. "If things like this keep happening, you and I will have to be connected at the hip permanently so that I can always be handy. Perhaps I should tie a string around your waist and attach it to my wrist."

"Oh," Sara answers very seriously, "I promise to stay free of trouble for the rest of the summer."

"Do you realize that the summer season is nearly one-third over and we still haven't gotten around to that dinner we talked about?" Jonathan holds Sara's arm as they leave the exhibit and ascend the stairs. When they emerged into the open air and sunshine, Sara notices with relief that Skyler has disappeared.

"Now," Jonathan orders, "take a lungful of air and let it out slowly. It will help to calm your nerves." After she has taken several deep breaths, he asks, "How about that dinner?"

"Perhaps, soon," Sara evades Jonathan's eyes. She wants to have dinner with him, of course she does. Jonathan is so thoughtful...has been so solicitous of her welfare. Here is someone with whom she can easily relate. Yes, all too easily. He is intelligent and apparently caring of other human beings. She likes his sense of humor and feels the easy familiarity, as though they have known each other a very long time. Yet those ideas don't quite capture all of her feelings either. When she thinks about Jonathan, it's with a tinge of excitement...an element of something unknown waiting just around the corner.

Standing opposite each other at the exit doorway, Sara forces herself to look squarely into Jonathan's face. A warm molten liquid causes her legs to almost fail her, and she puts her hand out against the rough logs to steady herself and thinks, *I'll have to put a stop to this sensation immediately.* Quickly, to switch off her own imaginative yearnings, she changes the subject. "My brother, Brian, is coming to visit on July 4th, tomorrow."

"I'd like to meet him, but I'm planning to spend the Fourth with my mother who lives on the island. Where's your brother from?"

"Indianapolis. He's a corporate lawyer. Thanks again for the rescue. I need to go now and check-in or rather check-out with Ansel."

"And I need to go back down and collect my camera before one of those wide-eyed manikins steals it." He watches with pleasure as Sara lets loose with a hearty giggle over his silliness. "I'll see you after the Fourth."

That same evening Sara heads for the Boyeo Restaurant to eat. It's a habit she has gotten into when she's not joining Hillary and Cam or some of the other re-enactors. She likes the salad bar, which offers an extensive but not too expensive variety. Right now she is trying very diligently to eat the proper foods for the sake of the baby as well as feed her own growing appetite, which has taken a bizarre turn for foods she usually avoids.

Lately she seems hungry most of the time. Yesterday her hunger prompted her to venture into the field of crime by digging up some young carrots from the garden before they were mature. If anyone had caught her in the act, she was going to claim, "Just checking to see if they're ready for digging up yet."

Tonight she decides to eat first and then afterwards take her washing to the Laundromat just a block away from her room. Already, the town is filling up with tourists for the Fourth. People come from all parts of the state and the nearby states of Illinois, Indiana, and Ohio. Apparently many of them plan to spend a whole week in the area because she has seen cars over-loaded with camping equipment, bumpers almost touching the pavement, and a solid line of RV's and cars filling the parking spaces along the main street. On the day after the Fourth, the Laundromat will be overrun with business, so it's best to get her clothes washed and completely out of the way tonight.

At the Boyeo Restaurant, Sara has first been shown to a table in a corner near the hostess's desk. She has never felt at ease away from the light cast by the windows. She supposes it has something to do with her fear of closed-in spaces like that tunnel underneath the row house. When she asks for another table, the waitress cheerfully moves her ice water to a table beside a window and tells her to help herself to the salad bar whenever she is ready. Sara has just dipped out her tomato-rice soup when out of the corner of her eye she spots Jonathan being shown to a booth. She pretends not to notice him, but he sees her immediately when she returns to her own booth nearby.

"Sara are you alone?" He registered her nod. "Do you mind sharing a table with me?"

She tells herself not to feel so pleased over the chance encounter, but finds it impossible to keep the lilt out of her voice when she answers, "Of course not."

"I'll also have the salad bar," he tells the waitress, "and coffee. He glances at Sara's glass of milk. Immediately he leaves their table to dip out his choice of cabbage soup, and a handful of wrapped crackers.

He breaks the crackers up while still in their plastic wrapper, then opens the wrapper and pours the crumbs neatly into his soup.

Sara smiles to herself. Crackers-in-the-soup is definitely one thing they do not have in common.

Jonathan has finished half of his soup before he speaks again. "You didn't care for your job in Chicago?"

Sara's mouth would have dropped open in surprise at this direct sally except that her mouth was already open and waiting for another spoonful of the pickled green bean salad, which seems to appeal to her so much lately. Jonathan has stopped eating, looks up, and waits for her answer.

Sara looks away and hedges the truth. "Summers in Chicago are terribly hot, and anyway I'm hoping to return to the university in Kalamazoo in the fall." Finally she looks at him to see if he buys her answer.

"Oh yes. Now I remember. You mentioned Western Michigan."

"Possibly."

"My territory."

"I assume they do have graduate studies in history or anthropology?"

He nods. "But it wouldn't be as prestigious as Michigan State or Northwestern. What kind of marks did you graduate with at… Urbana?

Evidently he has scanned her employment form. "A three-point-four."

"Then you should have no problem getting accepted into any one of the three, except it's getting almost too late to register formally for the coming session. You could take a few classes and apply them later towards your degree."

"Yes, that's what I thought, except…" She pauses wondering if she should be so frank about her finances with Jonathan, "…to attend Northwestern or Michigan State I would need a grant. If I live at home in Oakland, which is not far from the campus at Western Michigan, I could save quite a bit of money."

He nods that he understands. "You would probably have to take a graduate class from me. I'd be tough on you." He smiles, negating all the implied threat of toughness.

Now that their conversation is again in safe waters, Sara can relax. "So, you're a holy terror in the classroom?"

"Absolutely. It makes my day to call on the unprepared students." He tries to look severe but ends up looking beatific. "Would you like to borrow my school catalog? I can bring it next time I come over from the island."

"Yes, I would, if it isn't too much trouble. Thank you."

"You know, if you really wanted to earn enough money for college, that other job, the one you left in Chicago, paid much better than this one at the fort. I'm wondering why you switched jobs."

My God, she thinks, he's going to succeed in cornering me yet. She has assumed, incorrectly, that he had been satisfied with her reasons for leaving the Chicago job. She doesn't want to fib to him anymore than she has to, so she says nothing.

"Perhaps you were ill or had other personal reasons?"

"Well, yes, something of that sort." At least that answer isn't a lie. She really had caught the flu last winter.

"Shouldn't I know? We are friends aren't we? Almost connected at the hip. Remember?"

Sara feels a giggle rising. There is a long pause before she controls the giggle and answers, "It's nothing catching." The idea that being pregnant could be catching sounds so ludicrous that she starts to laugh.

"Glad to hear that." Jonathan isn't smiling.

Hoping that the meal can continue on an impersonal basis, Sara tries to give the conversation a completely new spin by inquiring about Jonathan's mother and also some details about his teaching career. Mostly she is successful until the very end of the meal, which culminates in Sara wolfing down an overly rich piece of chocolate cake.

"Sara, I still feel you are holding out on me, but I suppose from your point of view I'm probing into something that's none of my business. I like you and..."

"Please," Sara interrupts, serious pleading in her voice. She wonders if she looks as distressed as she feels. Surely now he is about to bring up the subject Pat has no doubt hinted at. Just then Hillary and her brother stop to say "hello" on their way to a nearby booth. It's one of those timely and providential interruptions that makes Sara believe there must be a benevolent spirit looking out for her.

"Will I see you later?" Hillary asks Sara.

"After I do my laundry, and I'd better get right to it." Quickly, she scoops up her check and slides out of the booth. To Jonathan she says, "You won't forget about the catalog?"

"I won't forget. Leave your check. This one is on me."

"Oh no, but thanks anyway."

Jonathan watches Sara sway gracefully down the aisle between the booths and through to the gift shop where the cash register is located. So, he decides, Pat has no doubt made a wise guess. Sara has probably broken off from a relationship and wants to get as far away as possible from Chicago. Furthermore, she doesn't want to talk about it. Then he remembers how Pat had hinted that an illness might be involved in Sara's choice. Maybe in this case "illness" is just a euphemism. Just Pat's way of stating how psychologically ill Sara might be over an aborted relationship with her boyfriend. Yes, he decides, that may have been the problem because just minutes ago, Sara herself had laughed and claimed, *it's nothing catching.*

CHAPTER THIRTEEN

The Fourth of July is not a holiday for the interpreters or the Rogers' Rangers who have camped on a grassy half-acre between the gift shop and the fort. Sara ambles past their tents pitched under the tall shady pine trees. She is heading from the stockade to the park gift shop to buy her friend, Fay, a thank-you gift for having let her stay for the week in the Urbana apartment free of rent.

The Rogers' Rangers group have started their morning cooking fires in front of the tents, and Sara's nose takes in the wonderful aroma of frying sausage and bacon as she passes. Some of the men are using a folding type grill over their fires exactly like the one her father uses when they go camping together as a family.

The tents of the Rogers Rangers are light beige military wedges with their headquarters stationed in a more imposing marquee type. Many of the men wear green tunics and leather britches. Historically, they mostly dressed in the type of clothing that camouflaged their presence when they were waging combat or reconnaissance in the woods. Though it isn't that cool this morning, a few men appear in a capote, a coat made from a colorful red and white blanket. Probably, Sara thinks, they wore them all night in their tents to keep warm as her brother Brian used to do. The nights have been cool lately, though from now on during July, the nights will be comfortably warm even when camping this close to the water.

The capote reminds her of the wool camp blankets her family brought with them on camping outings. The blankets weren't purchased from any of the colonial catalogs or from a regular store either. "Those blankets are far too expensive," her mother had stated firmly. Instead, she had bought brown wool blankets from a paper mill that had gone out of business. At the mill the wool blankets had been used to roll the water out of the pulp in the process of making paper. The blankets were then washed and reused or sold at an inexpensive price.

At the gift shop Sara becomes uncertain over what to buy for her friend. There are so many interesting things, at least they're interesting to her, but would Fay, a sophisticate who always wears black, black, and more black, care for prints of wild ducks or flowered stationery or toy fifes? Sara doubts it. She ends up purchasing a CD of water and wind sounds, soothing as a mantra or so the label says. For herself, she would have liked to buy the new edition covering <u>Mackinac Island History</u>, but she can't afford it even with her employee discount.

Instead of returning the same way she has come, Sara leaves the shop through the wide doors leading to the parking lot, which is located right beneath the road ramp leading to the bridge. It's the dry land portion of the bridge. Above her a loud rumble begins, and knowing that a truck is about to pass above her, she covers her ears from the grinding noise of the truck downshifting off the bridge. Leaving the parking lot, Sara walks past a garden containing a huge wooden carved statue of an Indian, past three gift shops, a large fountain, not in operation this early in the morning, and then walks the remaining block and a half back to her room.

Today her work shift is from eleven to eight in the evening. Since it's a holiday, the stockade is to remain open an extra hour. In the evening after dark, which at this time of year will be close to ten o'clock, there will be fireworks in the city park. Hillary and Cam have already asked her to join them at the band concert and the fireworks to follow, but usually she feels overcome with fatigue by that time, having spent most of the day on her feet. "Maybe," she tells them, "if I'm not too sleepy."

"Hey! The Fourth comes just once a year. Can't you stay awake that long?" Hillary can't figure out why her friend always seems to be fagged-out so early in the evening. "Maybe you need vitamins or something. Sometimes you behave like my Mom and Dad, and they're fifty years old. They conk out at nine o'clock every evening."

Sara laughs outright at the comparison.

"What? Did I say something funny?"

Sara changes the subject by musing, "I wonder when my brother will show up? Probably not until late afternoon or early evening."

"You promise to introduce us?"

"Sure," she smiles, "unless you're conducting a group of children, Pied Piper style." Brian had phoned her yesterday during work hours, and Pat had taped his message on the door of her room. Sara felt more than a little apprehensive over Brian's visit. He could be quite intuitive, sometimes almost reading her mind. More than once in the past he had guessed at some thoughts and motives she would rather have kept secret.

Brian might interrogate her about her decision, as Jonathan has already done, over giving up a perfectly good, better-paying, job to come up here for the summer. But Brian, the lawyer, will do it in a much more scrutinizing courtroom style. Sara isn't sure she can bear up under Brian's questioning and refrain from confessing. Likely she will crack like a criminal and tell all. On the other hand, she thinks how soothing, how relieving, it might feel to unload all her anxieties onto someone about the baby's care and her lack of money. But no, of course, she mustn't. She must be careful. Brian might feel an obligation to turn right around and tell her mother and father. It will be more prudent to stay mum on the subject of her pregnancy for a while longer.

❖ ❖ ❖

The office was to be closed on the afternoon of July Fourth, so Pat had promised to bring a cake and some soda as a holiday celebration around one o'clock for the interpreters such as Ansel, Hillary, Steve, or whomever wasn't conducting a walking tour or a presentation at the time. The huge chocolate cake with white frosting sat on the picnic table under a tent-shaped net to keep off the flies. The picnic table was the same gull-stained one just outside the Priest's Gate where the interpreters often met for lunch, only this time Pat had covered the table with a gay red, white, and blue paper tablecloth.

The day was considered hot for this area, eighty-five degrees, and the sky was an intense blue except where it appeared to touch the land across the water. There, the usual clear view had a smudged-thumb appearance caused by the air over the cold water pushing against the hot air of the land. Pat looked up at the sky wishing for shade over the picnic table so that the frosting on the cake wouldn't get soft and gooey so quickly. Maybe, she thought, I should have served the cake inside the locker room. But no, those dim light bulbs in the locker room would quickly spoil any feeling of festivity.

"Happy Fourth!" Ansel called as she and Steve approached the picnic table.

"Same," Pat said, smiling. She quickly sliced off two pieces from the cake revealing a thick lemon sauce between layers and slid them onto paper plates; then she stuck a tiny paper American Flag into the thick moist frosting. "Where are the others?"

"Hillary is just finishing with the kids' games and Sara is staying in the kitchen until I return." Ansel glanced down at her watch. "Linette has the French wedding coming up next, so she probably won't get here at all."

"Mind if I take my cake back to the blacksmith's shop?" Steve asked. "I have to keep feeding the fire and using the bellows so it will stay hot enough for a demonstration at two o'clock. You girls want any leg irons or chastity belts?"

"No thanks," Pat laughs and waves her knife at Steve as he walks away. "So far there hasn't been a waiting line to seduce me." She thinks about her failure to prompt any further interest from Jonathan since her casserole supper. "So, Ansel, how has your new co-worker been working out?"

"Fair. Never complains. You know, she does all the chores: washes dishes, carries wood, when Skyler doesn't." Ansel shrugs after mentioning Skyler's name. "I haven't been near the garden to do any weeding since she started working here."

"Not overdoing the grand lady bit, are you?" Pat has a suspicion that Ansel is "queening" it over Sara and giving her all the menial work. "No more fainting?"

Ansel shook her head. "Why?"

"Well, she certainly did look peaked when she first arrived. Awfully thin, too."

"Not any longer. You don't think maybe?" Ansel's hand made a circle implying "round tummy". She had leaped to a conclusion.

Pat shrugged. "I see Skyler coming."

Ansel whispered quickly before Skyler drew too near, "I'll have to keep more of an eye on her."

"On who?" Skyler arrived at the table just in time to hear the last words."

"On Sara."

"You want to know who's really keeping an eye on her?" Both women looked up at Skyler waiting for him to continue. "Dr. Reidel. Whenever he's over here from Mackinac Island, he keeps close tabs on her." He retold the incident that occurred in the alcove exhibit under the British Trader's section of the row house. "It was yesterday afternoon just before closing time. Boy! He was at her side in a flash."

"And what were *you* doing down there?" Ansel smirked. "Keeping tabs also?"

"Sure. I'd like to get her off on a lonely beach somewhere and do some discovery... like matching pubic hairs."

"Don't be disgusting." Ansel made a face.

"Have some cake." Pat sliced a piece of the cake with a vengeance, then added a tiny flag, inadvertently poking it deep into the cake.

"Hey! I'm a patriot, but I don't eat flags with my frosting." Skyler laughed at his own clever retort.

"Oh, sorry." Pat looked at the embedded flag. She hadn't meant to take out her frustrations regarding Jonathan on anyone else. She lowered her head to hide her disappointed expression and sat down again to finish her own cake.

Skyler checked his watch and picked up the last chunk of cake in his fingers to cram into his mouth. "Flintlock demo is coming up in a minute. Gotta go. Great cake, Pat. Thanks."

After Skyler was out of hearing range, Ansel resumed their interrupted conversation regarding Sara. "If she's pregnant, she sure doesn't act like it."

"No," Pat agreed.

"It doesn't show much yet, but she sure isn't ultra skinny any longer."

Pat nodded.

"You could snoop in her room and find out. You have all the duplicate keys."

Pat's mouth worked into a straight line, a prim grimace of distaste. "No, I couldn't do that. It isn't ethical."

"Then why not ask her straight out?"

"Go ahead, " Pat challenged.

"I'll think about it." Ansel brushed the crumbs off her striped skirt. "I have to get back. Should I send Sara out here for cake?"

"Sure, if it's within the next fifteen minutes. The frosting is getting soft sitting here in the hot sun."

❖ ❖ ❖

When Ansel returned to the row house kitchen, Sara was standing just outside the door embracing a good-looking man with curly black hair. Immediately, Ansel could see the resemblance between Sara and the man and drew the conclusion that he was the brother she had talked about. It wasn't just the thick dark hair that resembled Sara's, it was also the shape of the cheekbones and the slightly turned-up eyes, though his, Ansel noted, were a strong blue and Sara's were closer to gray-green. Nearby stood an attractive blonde girl in white shorts, seemingly waiting to be introduced. Ansel heard the man say, "Hey! Usually I don't rate such a huge welcome hug."

Brian smiled at Sara in surprise and pleasure and gave back an additional hug. Sara realized she was still clutching at his hand as though he were a lifesaving ring and she about to go under for the third time. Finally, she released his hand and turned to be introduced to the woman who had arrived with him.

"This is Francine."

"Hello, Francine."

Ansel stepped through the window since the doorway was blocked and went over to the dry sink to put away the dishes that Sara had previously washed. From that corner of the kitchen Ansel could see and even hear most of the conversation.

"Your face is fuller, and I think you've finally put on some weight," Brian was saying, carefully studying Sara up and down. "Must be..."

"Oh, it's all this fresh air," Sara chimed in, then realized how much it sounded like a prepared speech. "It makes me hungry."

So, Ansel thought, even her brother noticed the change. Then Ansel couldn't hear any more of the conversation because the three of them, Sara, her brother, and the girl had moved further away from the open door. With the pretense of clearing off the gate-leg table, Ansel wandered closer to the window but still couldn't decipher what they were discussing, so she gave up.

Sara was disappointed that Brian had brought a friend with him. She and Brian had lots of news to catch up on since they haven't seen each other for over six months. On the other hand, with Francine around, her secret about the baby was more secure. The presence of a stranger precluded any chance of Brian probing too deeply into her reasons for leaving Chicago and trading a permanent job for this temporary one.

"You heard the disappointing news about Dad and the exchange program to England?" Brian asked.

Sara nodded. "The School Board chose someone else." Oh, she thought, what would I have done if he had been chosen? She felt sorry for her dad because he deserved the opportunity, but under the circumstances the relief to her was immense. Where else, except at home, could she afford to go and have her baby?

"Francine and I are traveling on to Munising tonight; tomorrow we'll going to take the scenic boat ride to see Pictured Rocks."

"Oh, good idea," Sara agreed, "but take the boat ride in the afternoon while the sun is behind the boat. Otherwise, it's hard to take good pictures."

"Thanks for the tip, and speaking about pictures, Mom wants me to take a photo of you in your costume." Brian hauled out his Olympus digital camera from the carrier slung over one shoulder. "How about inside in front of the fireplace?"

All three stepped inside the kitchen and Brian backed up as far as he could against the wall on the tourist side of the counter and took a flash picture of Sara. "It's terribly dark in here, and besides, I couldn't get a full length shot of you. Let me take one more shot out in the sunshine so I can get a full view of your costume."

"Oh, must you?" Sara knows her weight gain will be much more obvious out in the full light and especially to her parents who remember her as overly thin.

"Yes, Sissy, we must. Outside with you. It will take only a minute." After the picture taking, Brian told Sara that he and Francine wanted to look around the fort briefly and then get back on the road. "What do you recommend?"

"You've seen most of this place already when you were camping here with Mom and Dad a few years ago, but the Soldiers' Barracks exhibit would be new to you. That just opened last year." Sara pointed off across the dirt path in the direction of the barracks, which was visible near the Guard House. "There's also the archaeological exhibit down under the British Trader's house just next door and that's quite interesting. It's in this same row house, but just the next door over."

"That tunnel exhibit has been here for ages, Sara. Surely you couldn't forget how those kids ambushed you down there when you were eight or nine years old? They shut you up in some kind of box and you were hysterical and never wanted to go with us to any of the encampments after that…at least not for a long time."

"That happened right here in this place?" She saw Brian nod and a shiver rippled down her spine. "But I'm sure that it must have been a different exhibit. I vaguely remember that other tunnel as being dark and damp with a cement floor. This one is all carpeted and well-lighted except for one special alcove." Thinking back over the recent incident with Skyler, she again felt embarrassment over her childish screaming and the need to be rescued by Jonathan.

"I recall that the tunnel was beneath an empty building located about where you pointed out the new exhibit." Brian gestured towards the Soldiers' Barracks. "Maybe it was under that one, the one that's been newly completed. We'll take a look. Bye for now. If there's time on our way back through town, we'll stop and have dinner with you." Brian gave Sara a tight squeeze. He whispered in her ear, "You certainly have put on weight, but it's becoming." Then in his normal voice he queried, "I thought you were obsessed with those sit-ins at abortion clinics? There aren't any clinics up here are there?"

Sara shook her head. "I haven't any idea. "Francine smiled briefly and then she and Brian disappeared through the door of the British Trader's House. Again Sara imagined to herself how nice it would have been if just she and Brian could have had a bit of time together. Yet, she supposed that it was much safer this way. He might have asked some embarrassing questions, and she would have had as much of a problem fibbing to Brian as she did prevaricating to Jonathan.

As Sara turns back to the kitchen, she catches Ansel studying her through the open door. What exactly has Ansel overheard? If it is so obvious to Brian that she has put on weight, surely it must be just as obvious to Ansel and everyone else here at Mac Fort. More and more each day she feels as though she is losing ground at keeping her pregnancy a secret. But then she rationalizes, so what if other people know. In just seven or eight weeks the job will be nearly over anyway, so it really doesn't matter who knows...except for Jonathan.

What if someone hints to Jonathan about her pregnancy? Please, not that, she almost prays. I don't want him to find out that way. Even standing here in the hot sun, a chill of apprehension dampens her back. Her hands and fingers grow tense as she thinks about him. The urge to bite her fingernails is insurmountable. She begins to nibble, then recalls how Jonathan had immediately noticed her blighted nails and surely would again.

If Jonathan must know about the baby, I want to be the one to tell him...to explain the situation. But to explain what? There are no mitigating circumstances, no way to excuse her behavior of casually bedding down with Larry other than that she had rushed to judgment. She had believed Larry was a smart choice, the logical choice, with whom to spend her life. He was both intelligent and thoughtful.

But why had her moronic brain been so willing to *settle* for him even though she had felt no overwhelming sexual urges? Sometimes, though, comfortable urges were safer ones. Maybe she subconsciously believed he was a solution to her future, a fitting destiny. He would get a professorship somewhere, and she would go back to school. So convenient. Now, when she thinks about it, it also seems coldly calculating...or coldly miscalculating.

Yes, she throws blame like a knife at herself: I let it happen because I grew lazy and spoiled, as though my past independence had been muted by too much care and attention and ease. "Then Larry changed. He disappeared, and that finally jolted me awake."

If Jonathan should discover the truth about my past, my lax nature in succumbing to Larry's comfortable bed, there is no way for me to keep him as a friend. Friend? "You're deluding yourself, my girl!" In a sudden epiphany, she admits that she wants more than a watered-down relationship with Jonathan. "You little ninny...you know perfectly well the weak-legged effect he has on you." Friendship would never be sufficient.

CHAPTER FOURTEEN

The strong wind fills Sara's long, striped skirt with air and tries to whisk it up to her knees. She wonders why full skirts didn't have weights at the bottom of the hem, like draperies. Maybe they did once. Suddenly an unexpected gust from the northwest pushes her sideways against the stockade walls, exactly as the white gulls are being swept sideways out over the water. Only the gulls are taking advantage of the wind, allowing it to push them in an easterly glide a short distance before their wings take over again as they inspect the water below for signs of food. "I'm not gliding gracefully," she laughs out loud as the wind again pushes her up against the rough gray walls of the stockade.

In places there are still patches of blue left in the sky, but the clouds over the opposite shore just five miles away are beginning to morph into menacing cloud figures straight out of a fantasy nightmare. Occasionally from the blackest clouds, sharp licks of lightning fork straight down into the water. The wind and waves seem to be tuning up for a concert, a raucous one, growing louder all the time. The coming storm gives Sara shivers of foreboding and maybe does the same to the old swaybacked horse over in the corral because it lets out several excited whinnies.

White caps on the water no longer arrive on shore in a leisurely controlled manner, but follow each other closely, big and mean like trucks tailgating on the highway. On this side of the Straits where the sun still shines, the spume after hitting a rock, takes on delicate prism tints before it drops back into the water.

When Sara slips through the side gate, the roar of the waves continues, but the wind loses its power to move her bodily. She can see off to her right a glimpse of the open parade ground where the wind has freer reign. It sweeps tails of sand and dirt up off the ground and twists them into miniature tornados. She passes the Priest's little house with its red-checked curtains and walks on toward the row house kitchen. Suddenly she feels a hand clamp down on her shoulder. She responds with a jerk.

"It's only me." Hillary whispers.

"Oh, sorry. I was afraid it was Skyler." Sara notes the anxious expression on Hillary's face and waits for her to explain.

"I need to talk to you...not around here though," Hillary's eyes dart quickly from side to side. "Could we meet some place...where my brother or anyone else can't overhear us?"

"Sure. My room? Or we could take a walk together. I need the exercise...if it doesn't rain, that is." Sara is curious about Hillary's behavior lately. The outgoing, smiling teen has become quieter, more secretive, not her naturally garrulous self.

"A walk then, at six-fifteen? The fort closes earlier now."

"Make it six-thirty."

After changing out of her costume, Sara knows she will have to grab an apple or something to eat before taking exercise. She always becomes very faint from hunger about that time of day. Lately she finds that she needs sustenance every two hours or so, which leads her into robbing more carrots from the garden. At the moment, several are tucked under her laced bodice to eat later when Ansel is out of the kitchen. At the time of her uprooting crime, she remembers smiling to herself, surmising which small innocent animal Ansel might blame for the missing carrots, that is, if she ever deigns to go anywhere near the garden again. Fortunately, several rabbits as well as skunks and raccoons have made the garden their dinner table as well as mine.

Just minutes before the rain begins to pour down heavily around four o'clock, Sara watches from under the roof near the garden as the archeologists hurriedly cover their digging site with tarps. Then they collect all their tools and brown paper bags full of artifacts and the pails of dirt still to be sifted; they stash everything in wheelbarrows to be hauled away to a dry shed near the Natural Resource's Garage. Only a few tourists are in the stockade during this rainy episode, and most of them hover in doorways trying to stay dry.

By five o'clock the wind abated, and the shower finished laying the fine dust on the parade ground. Obviously, the town across the water on the other side of the bridge had felt the full brunt of the storm that this side of the Straits had escaped.

❖ ❖ ❖

A few minutes after the fort closed, Sara hurried back across the street to her room and changed into her jeans, the larger ones that she had purchased second hand, and a loose shirt. She was munching on an apple when Hillary knocked on her door.

"All set to go?" Hillary asked in a tight, nervous voice. Sara noticed how she glanced surreptitiously over at Cam who was dodging around puddles in order to practice basketball shots into a hoop just a few doors away.

They took the sidewalk to the main street of town but headed west, away from the gift shops and restaurants. "There's sidewalk as far as the library on this side of the street, then we can loop back," Sara suggested.

"Whatever."

What had caused Hillary's sunny, vivacious temperament to disappear? Sara hadn't witnessed much of it in the last couple of days. She waited until they had finished walking past the first block of small white houses before she asked, "You had something on your mind? Give."

"Yeah, but it's hard to get started." They walked another block before Hillary burst out, "Skyler and I have been spending a lot of time at the beach...mostly at night."

"Oh, Hillary!"

"I'm pregnant."

Abruptly Sara stopped walking. "How do you know? Did you take one of those home tests?" Hillary nodded, tears already flooding her eyes.

"Those home tests aren't always accurate you know."

"I'm sure. I tested twice…two different brands." Hillary began to sob. Sara put her arm around her quivering shoulders and gave her a hug. "I'm sorry…so sorry. Do you think Skyler might want to do the right thing?"

Hillary shook her head. "Not me either. Cam would kill Skyler if he knew. He dislikes him anyway."

"That makes two of us. I wouldn't wish him on you either except as a temporary solution to your problem." Then immediately she remembered her own situation and asked herself: Would I have accepted Larry as a temporary solution to my problem? Probably, if he hadn't gone missing. "I thought you were deeply enamored with Skyler."

"Not any more," Hillary sniffed. "What can I do?" Her eyes pleaded with Sara as though she might have the proverbial magic wand to wave. "I'll need an abortion, and I doubt there are any clinics near here. So what excuse do I give Cam or people here at the fort if I suddenly disappear to go down state to visit an abortion clinic?"

Hillary had come to Sara for help and advice, but all Sara could think about at the moment was why-oh-why did she have to confide in me of all people? To herself she lamented…anyone except me!

Sara stopped on the sidewalk next to a vacant lot full of Queen Anne's Lace and made Hillary turn to face her. "You know a fetus is a living human being. Rather than kill it, lots of girls go through with a pregnancy and then let the child be adopted or even bring it up themselves." She almost added, but didn't, "as I plan to do."

"Oh Sara, how could I bring up a child and teach it all about life? I haven't had a chance to find out about life myself. I need to go to school, get a job, and learn how to take care of myself."

Sara admitted silently that Hillary was absolutely right. She was literally still a teenager, and not a particularly mature one either for all of her eighteen years.

"I simply can't face my family with this. They have very narrow views on petting and sexual looseness before marriage. I just can't disappoint them. Just a few months ago I overheard my parents talking about the sister of Cam's best friend, Fred Beeman. His sister, Mandy, got into this same...situation, but in her case it wasn't even her fault. She was raped. My parents actually forbade Cam to remain friends with Fred any longer. You see? I have to have an abortion... and I have to do it so that Cam won't get suspicious and work himself up into a rage against Skyler.

"Cam doesn't seem that type, not the 'get even' sort of person."

"I know, he comes off as being placid, but if he feels deep down about something, he'll almost ignite...and in this case might end up in trouble because of me. Will you help me? Oh, please God, you've got to help me!"

"Hillary, how can I help you kill a living human being? It's against my beliefs. I'll willingly help you find a place, a home, to have your baby."

Hillary began to sob again. "I was so sure you were my friend...I..."

They turned the corner onto Perrot Street and then in just a short block turned again to head back in the direction of their rooms. The first block of the street was heavily wooded and quite private so Sara stopped a second time to ask, "How long have you known?"

"Just a few days." Hillary groped in her pocket for another paper hanky.

"Then there's still a chance that you'll abort naturally."

"Do you think so?" For a moment Hillary looked hopeful. "I've heard that sometimes hot baths can accelerate the process...but we only have showers in our rooms." An idea struck her. "Maybe I could use the hot tub over at the Holiday Inn. But if the hot tub doesn't work, you'll help me won't you?"

Sara shook her head.

"You've got to!" Hillary shrieked, not caring whether she was overheard or not. "You're my only friend here at the fort." She bent over holding her face between both hands, and Sara watched her shoulders vibrating from the hysterical sobs. Then Hillary lifted her head and between her teeth whispered dramatically, "If you don't, I'll kill myself rather than go through with it, and that will be worse than killing a fetus!"

"Oh Hillary! You wouldn't do a dreadful thing like that. The Bible tells us that all life is sacred and that means your life as well as the baby's."

Between sobs and noisy sniffling sounds from her nose, which she constantly jabbed at with her paper hanky, Hillary stoutly proclaimed, "Yes, I would! I will! I can't face my family. They will freeze me out of their lives forever. It's better to die than be an outcast."

"But their attitude is totally wrong, and maybe your family will come to understand that in time. For heaven's sake, this isn't the mid-east where daughters are stoned for being raped or...easily persuaded!" Sara took the sobbing girl in her arms again and held her tightly.

What a ghastly situation, Sara thought. She desperately wanted to help Hillary. She felt as fiercely protective towards her as she would have felt over a younger sister if she had had one. Should she tell her about her own pregnancy? It would certainly point out that if she, Sara, had the confidence to carry on in spite of the coming baby, then Hillary could somehow gather the strength to do the same. Sara discarded that idea immediately. Hillary was younger than she by several years, and her character hadn't had a chance to develop...much less gain a firm dedication to a cause such as pro-life. Also, if she told Hillary about her own predicament, Hillary might inadvertently leak the information so that Jonathan would learn the truth too soon. Somehow secrets never stay secret among folks who work closely together and have become almost like family.

Sara didn't believe that Hillary would actually harm herself. True, at the moment she was hysterical, irrational, but after she calmed down, she would think better of her threat to kill herself. "Promise not to harm yourself?"

"I'll go right over to the Holiday Inn first thing in the morning and ask about the hot tub. No, I'll do it right now."

"You'll probably have to pay a fee for the use."

"That's the least of my worries. I'll wait one more week, then if this thing doesn't abort naturally, I'll..."

"No, Hillary, don't even think of such a thing." Sara decided that she would have to keep a close eye on Hillary. Immediately afterwards she realized that she couldn't watch Hillary every minute of the day and night. It just wasn't possible. She considered telling Cam to watch Hillary and then wondered if he actually would try to beat-up on Skyler. In her heart she hoped Skyler would suffer. He was a womanizer. He should be throttled or have his testicles removed. She turned her head away so that Hillary couldn't guess at the murderous thoughts running through her head. Not that Hillary in her present state of panic would even notice such nuances of expression. Sara told herself sarcastically, "What a staunch Christian you are with all your *get even* ideas?"

They had completed their walk, almost a rectangle on the sidewalk and road and now had returned to within a half-block of their rooms. Sara noted that Hillary was trying to put on a cheerful face in case they should meet up with other employees living at the motel. "Let's eat out tonight," Sara suggested. "It will cheer us up."

Hillary nodded, still sniffling and wiping at her eyes. Yes, Sara reminded herself, Hillary was still just a child. Somewhere in all that birthing material that she had collected, Sara had read that there was far more danger in a teenage pregnancy. Wondering why, she vowed to hunt for the passage and read it again.

"Let's go for pizza and beer...lots of beer."

"Pizza, sure."

"I've never seen you drink. Are you a teetotaler or something really weird?"

"Yes," Sara laughed. "I'm something really weird. You probably shouldn't drink anything alcoholic either. It isn't good for the baby."

"I couldn't care less. And anyway it's not a baby. It's nothing but a blob right now."

Sara doesn't attempt to argue with Hillary over the point. What good would it do at this particular moment when Hillary is ready to fly into a hundred jagged pieces like an exploding light bulb. Perhaps as time goes on and Hillary becomes calmer and acclimated to the idea of being pregnant, Sara can slowly influence her to think more kindly towards the innocent bit of living tissue in her womb.

CHAPTER FIFTEEN

S ara hears Jonathan's distinctive voice even before she actually sees him. He must be talking to someone standing just outside the row house kitchen. His voice always brings about such mixed emotions: a sensation of serenity, of comfort and…something else…a tiny thrill that she tries to ignore. She remembered his touch when he rescued her from Skyler down in the tunnel. Previous to that incident, she had carefully blocked-off her true feelings. She had disciplined herself to think of him only as a friend. Yet now, when Jonathan steps inside the door carrying his tripod and cameras, she finds all her senses standing at full alert. There is a sudden leap of excitement. She hopes she doesn't look as addled as she feels.

"Could you, Sara and Ansel, take time from your work to pose beside the fireplace so that I can take a picture?" Seeing Ansel nod, he opened the hinged section of the counter and set his tripod down, apparently to aim through the opening at an angle.

He began to pull out the legs of his tripod as he spoke and then checked the level. "Ansel, if you could pretend to be stirring something in that large pot hanging over the fire, and perhaps Sara could hold the lid or maybe the poker to tend the fire."

Sara wiped her wet hands on the towel hanging from a rope strung between two square nails and moved over to the fireplace. Ansel smoothed down her striped apron and straightened her mob cap; then lifted down a huge spoon from the black metal bar of hooks that spanned the whole width of the stone fireplace just above the opening. Jonathan moved his tripod a foot to the left to incorporate both women into the picture. When satisfied with the focus, he took four shots.

"Thanks ladies. Sara," he asked, "can I borrow you for an outdoor photo? Ansel, you don't mind do you if I take Sara away for fifteen or twenty minutes?"

"No," Ansel answered with a shrug, wondering what good it would have done if she had objected.

"Bring that makuk," Jonathan pointed towards a shelf above the pastry table.

Sara reached for the birch bark container and followed Jonathan out the door. He led her down the Rue Dauphin, better known as the Kings Way, through the Water Gate, and a few yards east along the beach where he stopped.

"What's this all about?" Sara asked.

"I need a photo for an article I've written for a magazine called History Today. I hope you don't mind being taken away from your work."

Sara smiled. "Definitely not."

"I want this photo to look spontaneous. I'll use the digital cam effect and then freeze the picture. Just walk towards me holding the birch bark container under your arm as though you had just come back from picking berries, then when I say, 'slow', you walk slower, almost to a stop, and I'll snap the picture."

"Where should I be looking?"

"Turn your face partially towards the water. The breeze is just strong enough to move your skirt and your hair, and the camera will catch that effect. All right, begin your walk."

Sara walked slowly towards Jonathan looking off beyond the sun-dappled water to the distant shore until she heard him call out "slower now," followed by "stop." "Good, that's great. One more time, please."

Sara went back to the starting point and repeated her walk.

"Now for this next shot, could you appear as though you were about to enter the Water Gate. Let's do it twice just to make certain that one of the takes will be usable."

When they have finished, Jonathan placed the camera back in its case to protect it from the lightly blowing sand and left the tripod standing. From his pocket he pulled out two power bars and handed one to Sara. "Your reward."

Sara giggled, "Yes, we animals do have to have our rewards or else we just don't perform very well."

"That's exactly what I figured." Jonathan smiled and settled himself down, long legs crossed, on the warm sand and unwrapped his bar. Sara followed suit. It was sunny and pleasant by the shore this morning. In spite of a breeze, the water was fairly calm, moving slowly and fingering the shore gently as though touching something too tender to risk hurting.

Because of her chewed-off, blunted fingernails, Sara had difficulty removing the paper from her bar.

"Here." Jonathan took the bar away from her and quickly ripped off the paper. Like a scolding parent, he said, "See what happens when you bite your nails?" When they finished, Jonathan took their bar wrappers, rolled them up, and tucked them inside his jacket pocket. "I don't want to add to the junk already left here on the beach by the tourists." Sara nodded in approval. Then he abruptly changed the subject, "No more scary encounters down in the exhibit under the Trader's Quarters?"

"No. I'm sorry I caused such a ruckus. When my brother visited here on the Fourth, he reminded me about that time when those boys kidnapped me. He claimed that it happened right here in this fort."

"Probably it was in the old exhibit, the one that had dioramas and led down from beneath the Soldiers' Barracks before it was redone."

Sara nodded. "I had partially forgotten the incident or maybe wanted to forget."

"That's natural. Now that you've faced up to it, you probably won't feel so jumpy when you find yourself in narrow places, hallways or tunnels."

"I'd better get back to the kitchen." Sara started to rise, but he put out his hand to restrain her so she sat down again.

"Sara, I could use a model and an assistant on a day trip I'm taking to Drummond Island next Monday to photograph their relatively new museum building. Any chance of getting you to forfeit your day off to pose for me? It's a nice scenic drive and the island is interesting, though we wouldn't have time to see a great deal of it. Have you ever been there?"

"No, but I know there was a British Fort there long ago. Surely you could photograph whomever happens to be in the museum at the time."

"I could, but I know that a picture of someone in authentic costume is more likely to be accepted by history buffs than someone dressed in contemporary clothes, which are often shorts, bare midriff and a pierced nose. Also," he smiled, "I'm offering a free lunch as part of my incentive package."

"Sounds like one of those corporate executive offers." Feigning seriousness, Sara asked, "Is a new car thrown in as part of the deal?"

Jonathan shook his head. "Let me put this offer in another way." The tone of his voice, the voice that had so attracted her to him several weeks ago at their first introduction, had changed from the light banter of a few minutes ago to a soft persuasion. "I would really like to have you come...as much for your company as for your assistance."

She hesitated before answering. How easy it would be to succumb to his persuasion. Should she allow herself to become further involved, even in a friendly way, with Jonathan without telling him the truth... that she was expecting another man's child? Her conscience warned her that telling him was clearly the honest thing to do. But surely she couldn't do it right here, where even now she could see a group of thirty chattering tourists streaming through the Water Gate, kicking up the sand, on their way to view the cannon firing demonstration?

In truth she found Jonathan's offer tempting partly because she preferred to be with someone on her day off rather than be closeted alone with her personal problems weighing heavily on her. Such flimsy reasoning! Doubtless her subconscious mind was being devious and concocting any excuse to be around Jonathan because he already strongly appealed to her. But, she rationalized, surely one single day could do no great harm, at least not to him. To herself? Well, that was different. She knew how much easier it was to forego a treat right from the beginning rather than have to give it up later.

She thought of the pleasure of spending nearly eight hours with someone she admired; of course afterwards the whole day would have to be coldly blotted out from her mind like heavy slashes of a black felt pen. She silenced her conscience by making a vow: I'll positively keep our association from becoming too personal.

"Well? You seem to be going over an entire list of pros and cons in your head before answering. I was hoping the decision would be relatively simple...that my esteemed self would be a great inducement to say, yes." He laughed good naturedly, deprecatingly.

"All right." She knew she sounded reluctant and tried to cover her negative reaction with a smile. "What time?"

"I'll pick you up at nine o'clock on Monday morning. You don't have to wear your costume. Just bring it along. There will be a place to change inside the museum when we get there."

Sara nodded. "I must get back." This time she arose quickly from the sand and headed straight for the Water Gate before he could stop her. To appease her conscience, she again promised that she positively would tell Jonathan about the baby during the trip to Drummond Island.

CHAPTER SIXTEEN

Guilt rides Sara's conscience every day and even more so on Monday just before the excursion to Drummond Island with Jonathan. Twice she thinks of phoning him to renege, but in order to do so she must ask Pat for his cell phone number and that might invite curiosity. Also, she convinces herself that she will be letting Jonathan down if she cancels. He will then have to find someone else to pose for his photos, and it might be too late. She has no excuse for going back on her word, except maybe the one of sickness, yet that is no longer valid. She feels great and assumes that she appears exceptionally healthy.

Sara intuits a lot about her conscience and its deceitful twists and turns in attempting to justify itself. "Your excuse," she admits, "for not telling Jonathan the truth *before* going on the outing is simply that you want to soak in as much of his presence as long as you can and fool yourself into make-believing it could be permanent."

She notes, as she peers in the bathroom mirror, the slight filling out of her cheeks and how her dark hair, longer now, detracts from her too thin neck. She stands on tiptoe trying to visualize more of her body in the short mirror. Her stomach looks perceptibly rounded now when undressed, but not visibly protruding enough when dressed to give her condition away unless someone scrutinizes her carefully. "Finally," she declares to herself, "I'm into that blooming stage of pregnancy that I've read about."

❖ ❖ ❖

Jonathan had parked his gray Honda Van outside her door at nine o'clock on Monday morning, patiently waiting. Sara wore the only jeans that fit her properly, the beige ones, a red checked cotton blouse and her wheat-colored sweater. She thought the sweater, left unbuttoned, partially disguised the beginnings of her rounded tummy. She carried her costume over her arm.

"Will my shoes show up in the pictures?" she asked Jonathan, looking down at her Vaneili shoes, her most expensive purchase from back in her Chicago days.

As Jonathan opened the back door of the van, he looked down at her square-toed black shoes with two-inch heels. "Very likely, at least in some of the photos."

Sara laid her costume on the back seat and then went back inside her room for the flat-heeled black slippers and black stockings that she had always worn with the costume.

Jonathan drove slowly over the bridge at the required forty-five miles per hour. As they reached the first pair of suspension towers, Sara peered out the window and through the bridge railing to watch a freighter pass below. As the long narrow freighter slipped underneath the bridge, she could see the rectangular hatch covers and the long metal arm of the self-unloading apparatus. When she twisted in her seat and looked back towards the shore, she could clearly spot the colorful flags gaily waving from the fort's gun platforms.

Jonathan seemed very familiar with the area between St. Ignace and DeTour where they were to board the ferryboat for Drummond Island. Now and again he mentioned points of interest such as the little town of Hessel that hosted the yearly Boat Show.

"Then we must be close to the Snow Islands."

"Yes, coming up soon. The Islands are just off Cedarville, the next town."

"I went with my family on a little tubby boat to the Snow Islands. That was years ago. I vaguely remember it." She did recall how her father, as usual interested in history, had told her that most of the places on the map had French or Indian names because those were the people first in the area. "I think we boarded the boat on Mackinac Island."

"Those smaller boats aren't running regularly any longer. On special occasions the ferry boats from Mac Village take passengers."

Along the highway on the eastern side of the town of Cedarville, Jonathan pointed out a boat museum. "They restore old boats that are given to them or that they find abandoned. That's something I enjoy doing very much, saving and restoring old things."

"Just boats?" Sara could tell by the keen sound in his voice that this subject of restoring things was of prime interest to him.

"No, also furniture; mostly things of historical significance."

"People, too?" Sara had no idea why she had tried to insert a touch of humor; the question was so utterly senseless. But she noted that Jonathan smiled.

"I think God restores people better than I ever could." Then he told her about the time when he was twelve or fifteen and he, much to his parent's consternation, had brought home a completely unknown couple for dinner because they had lost their wallet while visiting on Mackinac Island. "That was just before everyone carried credit cards.

"What a kind thing to do." That act seemed so in keeping with what she already knew about Jonathan's personality.

"Not very thoughtful of my mother who had no idea company was coming to dinner. Even after all these years, she never misses a chance to rib me about the incident."

After Cedarville it was another twenty-four or five miles to DeTour Village and neither one of them talked a great deal. Sara didn't feel it necessity to fill the miles with chatter; nor did Jonathan evidently. It was peaceful to sit and enjoy the scenery instead of having to do the actual driving. Occasionally she caught glimpses of Lake Huron through the lush forest of trees. Suddenly the woods disappeared and an ugly mountain of stone slabs arose on the side of the road. "What's that huge pile of rock? It's enormous."

"It's a dolomite stock pile. I guess they make ceramic tile from dolomite... other things too. There's a quarry here and on Drummond Island where we're going, and another ugly pile beside the shore. Not a very pretty sight. To me, having that commercial eyesore so visible spoils the romantic notion of an island as an escape from the world."

"I can see a lighthouse over there."

"That's the lighthouse to the entrance of DeTour passage. It's one of the channels into the locks that takes the boats up into Lake Superior."

As usual Sara began to feel hungry long before lunchtime. She no longer needed her crackers to stem the nausea, but still needed some food to hold back the faintness she often felt an hour or so before mealtime. This time she had come prepared by bringing two apples. "Would you like an apple?"

Jonathan glanced at her quickly, then back to his driving. "No thanks. Didn't you have any breakfast?"

"Oh yes, but I get terribly hungry anyway."

"None for me, but go ahead, chonk away on your apple. We'll have lunch over on the island after we do the photography. I know a delicatessen that's got every food imaginable."

"A delicatessen? It's the last thing I would expect to find on a small island in the north woods."

"They have everything from clams to caviar and pickles in a barrel."

After arriving in the small village of DeTour, they promptly joined a line of cars waiting for the ferry. The boat ride itself was very short, barely twenty minutes from loading to unloading. Most people, just as Jonathan and Sara did, stayed inside their cars. Anyway, the ferry wasn't made for sightseeing. It was simply a double-ended barge where cars parked bumper to bumper, and with a pilot house constructed over one side of the hull. It looked unseaworthy to Sara. Over the bulkhead, she could see their approach to Drummond Island and the mountain of stone that Jonathan had mentioned earlier. He was right.

The dreadful sun-parched pile of stone did spoil one's notion of an island as a magical place to leave the prosaic world behind.

Once off the ferry, Jonathan took a road opposite the stone pile. It seemed to Sara a long distance from the ferry to the village, but the winding road could not have been more than ten miles or so.

"Just a bit further now." Jonathan finally turned down a street that led towards the water. He made a second turn and there on the left side of the road was the museum. It was made of newly varnished logs and looked quite ungainly from the outside. The inside of the building was vast, like a barn, and not partitioned off into sections. Sara whispered to Jonathan as they entered, "Isn't it too dark for photos?"

"I'll have to use the flash, but maybe we can also shoot some pictures from the outside."

Jonathan shook hands with a woman at the desk and introduced Sara. "Mrs. Meacham; Sara Kolenda. Mrs. Meacham grew up on this island and has most of its history right in her head." Mrs. Meacham appeared flattered by the remark.

Mrs. Meacham pointed to the women's restroom at the far side of the long room. "You can change into your costume over there if you like, but bring your purse back here and I'll tuck it in my desk drawer. There aren't likely to be many people visiting this early in the day, if any, but let's play it safe."

Sara nodded and took her costume into the restroom to change. She hung her jeans, blouse and sweater on the only hook available and changed into her full skirt, blouse, laced bodice, mob cap, black stockings and shoes. When she walked across the wooden floor to the opposite side, she could see that Jonathan had already set up his tripod near the stone fireplace.

"All set?" he asked in a kindly tone. "I want you to stand with your back to that side of the fireplace. By the way, remember how you mentioned the British Fort here on the island?" Sara nodded. "These stones came from the fireplace in that fort."

"Nothing else left... no stockade?"

"No, it's all gone now and the land is privately owned."

Sara posed by the fireplace and then again in an old chair next to a spinning wheel. Mrs. Meacham showed her the proper way to hold the spindle of natural fiber as her foot pretended to work the treadle.

Several pictures were taken and Sara began to rise from the chair when one of the front legs made a warning sound of wood splintering followed by a loud crack as the leg completely parted from the rocker portion. "Oh!" Sara gasped, trying to regain her balance, and suddenly found herself on the floor. Immediately, before she could pick herself up, she felt Jonathan's arms lifting her to her feet. His dark eyes seemed full of genuine concern. Was that so, or was she just imagining the special caring signals in his eyes?

"Are you hurt?" One arm was still around her waist.

Sara shook her head, wishing his arm would remain where it was. "Is the chair an antique?"

"It was old, but not a valuable antique. Don't worry about it." Mrs. Meacham soothed, "and it can be repaired. See, where the glue came unglued?"

Sara and Jonathan stood facing each other longer than necessary as though they were reading whole history pages in each other's faces. Sara wondered if Mrs. Meacham noticed the overly long pause.

Jonathan finally stepped away and became busy refocusing his camera on Mrs. Meacham standing near her desk. While he was occupied with that, Sara tried to wrest her mind off Jonathan and her pleasant reaction to his touch. She refocused her attention on a cork board which displayed some of the black and white photos of the early settlers who had first come to this island. Then she spotted the large marine chart showing all the tiny islands between Drummond Island and St. Joseph's Island in Canada. As soon as she got a chance, she asked Mrs. Meacham, "Are there any vacant islands left?"

"Oh yes, two or three at least."

"How do people living on the islands manage about groceries?"

"Well, most of them come right here to the village for supplies once a week so naturally they have to have boats. In winter those boats are stored over there at the boat yard that you can see across the street. Some of the smaller islands have no electricity at all and are quite primitive...oil lamps and outdoor privies; people on other islands have their own generators."

Jonathan took several more shots outside the building, two with Sara standing beside the museum sign on the front lawn. Afterwards she went back inside the building to change again into her jeans and shirt, to collect her purse, and bid goodbye to Mrs. Meacham. Just as she and Jonathan drove away, a car full of people arrived in the parking lot to visit the museum.

Several miles down the road, Jonathan turned into what looked like a private driveway beside a house. Was it a mistake, Sara wondered? Then she spotted the delicatessen further along behind the house. Way out here in the woods seemed an odd place to find a delicatessen. The whole place didn't look very upscale to Sara, but she was so hungry and faint that she would have eaten leather shoe-string soup as some lost traders from the long ago past had to do when caught in the wilderness without food.

Inside the door of the delicatessen, Sara was mollified. The walls and aisles were crammed with every imaginable item from New York cheesecake, flown-in she was told, to gourmet jams...even the barrel of pickles previously mentioned by Jonathan. She was suddenly overwhelmed with too many choices. There was a variety of salads and natural cheeses and five or six kinds of breads and a walk-in cooler where she was told to step inside and pick out her own juice or whatever she wanted. Finally, she settled on a vegetarian-filled cheese bread roll, and a milk shake. Jonathan ordered a polish sausage sandwich and coffee, specially roasted. Then he asked for two Kosher pickles from the pickle barrel.

They sat outside at a picnic table to eat. The food tasted wonderful. "How about some dessert afterwards?" Jonathan suggested.

"Sorry, can't. Even this is more than I usually handle. I should have asked for half a sandwich."

From across the picnic table, Jonathan watched Sara with amusement. He liked the enthusiastic way she attempted to engage her mouth over the humped sandwich roll. Then he laughed outright when the alfalfa strands began to drop down from her mouth like falling whiskers.

"Guess I'll have to fork it in as if I were eating a stack of hay."

"Wait, I'll get a fork." He headed for the store before Sara could rise from the picnic table bench. When he returned he was carrying forks and two plates of cheesecake.

"Oh, I really can't eat that much."

"Something tells me you can eat it later then. Inside they'll Saran wrap it for you."

"Thank you for a wonderful lunch, Jonathan, but you'll turn me into a blubber ball."

"It's part of the plan."

"What do you mean?" Immediately Sara is alert.

"To feed you so much that you become a form of pliable dough, and I can mold you into liking me."

"Methinks you are joshing. Anyway, I already like you."

"Good. I'm making progress. You seldom mention much about yourself. Got any constant companions?"

"Yes, Hillary. Or was that a subtle way of asking about boyfriends?"

"Yes."

She can tell by the timbre of his voice that he is no longer kidding. "None at the moment."

"But one in Chicago that you wanted to get away from."

"Past history."

"Not allowed?"

She shook her head. "New slate."

"Thanks for coming today. I like your company. Perhaps we can do this again?"

"You mean, more photos?"

"No, I mean dinner out...a genuine date."

"Oh, I don't think..."

"Just dinner, Friday? It's therapeutic. It will make 'new history' for your new slate. You need rehabilitating."

"And naturally restoring old things is your hobby."

"Young things too." He smiled beatifically.

His voice was so persuasive, so positive that he was drawing her in the right direction. She almost felt an actual tug...wanted to take the path he aimed to draw her down...wanted, like a silly child reaching out for a toy that she couldn't possibly have. His arms were, figuratively speaking, open. If only she were free to fall. If only... "I'll think about the dinner."

"Fine." Now he grinned, momentarily satisfied. "I'll give you until the end of our trip today to think about it."

Ashamed of her weak-willed evasion...of not telling him about the baby, Sara looked down at her paper plate and reaffirmed to herself the promise she had made to her conscience: I will tell Jonathan the truth about the baby by the end of this day.

They finished lunch and Jonathan took her leftover sandwich and the cheesecake back into the delicatessen for a Saran wrap. When he returned he said, "I want to show you another part of Drummond Island before we go back. Do you mind?' Sara shook her head. Any prolonging of the trip was an excuse to extend the pleasure of being around Jonathan. It might very well be the last occasion when they would ever spend time alone together.

Jonathan drove back to the main road and headed south, then switched to a dirt road that ended up in a protected cove with a beach of sand interrupted at intervals by giant rocks. Here, the water was translucent...pristine.

"It's a beautiful spot." Sara's eyes followed along the empty shore. "Do we have time to walk on the beach?"

"Certainly. That's what I intended."

"Strange how nature dumped these rocks along the shore almost artistically. How did you find this secluded cove?"

"Actually it's not that secluded. I once knew someone who had a cottage along that other shore." Jonathan gestured in the opposite direction from where they were walking. "Look carefully through the trees and you'll see several cottages. I wouldn't mind having a 'getaway' shack here myself."

"Or perhaps on one of those little remote islands between Drummond and Canada?"

"Yes, one of those too. I see we both hunger for privacy and getting back to nature."

"Yes, privacy, but not back to privies."

He chuckled, "I agree on that point as well." They strolled companionably along the shore until the beach turned into a tangle of brush and trees growing close to the water's edge and they were forced to turn back again. As a memento, Sara picked up several snail shells and tucked them in her jean pocket. Again, she was keenly aware of Jonathan's closeness though they weren't actually touching. They stopped to rest on a huge rock that nature had indented to fit almost perfectly to their backsides.

Sara prompts herself: right here in this serene spot, is the opportune time to tell Jonathan about the baby, but she hates to spoil this perfect day. No, be truthful, she tells herself; you're an out and out coward. You like the way he looks at you with pensive dark eyes and dread to think of them changing into "judging eyes." She also likes the way their tastes, hers and Jonathan's, mesh so well. It's similar to the way a piece of puzzle has been die cast to fit another portion of the same puzzle.

She is beginning to care about Jonathan too much and that makes her feel even guiltier about her cowardliness. She knows, as the minutes slip by, that once again she will put off telling him about the baby. Possibly the appropriate time will be just as they arrive back in Mac Village late this afternoon. She sighs openly and notices Jonathan looking at her. Obviously, there will never be a right time.

It was past five o'clock by Sara's watch when they crossed the bridge once again and arrived back in Mac Village. Her heart began to beat at a faster rate and she felt beads of moisture prickle her forehead. For the last five miles she has been rehearsing in her head exactly how to tell Jonathan that she is pregnant. How to begin? Jonathan, I can never go out with you on a date because it wouldn't be fair to you. . .or should she first tell him how much she has enjoyed the day and then drop the bomb?

They turned into the alleyway in back of the office and in front of Sara's room. She felt weak and shaky in anticipation of her announcement but made herself begin her confession: "Jonathan this has been a splendid day, thank you, but I can't..." when he interrupted."

"No, thank *you* for posing for me. I am the one to be grateful."

At that moment Pat came hurrying out the back door of the office and tapped lightly on the window of the car. "Jonathan, there's a phone call for you from your mother."

Jonathan turned off the ignition and headed for the office calling back over his shoulder to Sara, "Friday, about seven."

Sara didn't answer, just took a deep breath to calm herself. She didn't know if she was relieved by the interruption or disappointed that the traumatic moment of confessing was still to be faced. She reached into the back seat with shaking hands, picked up her costume, shoes, and the food Jonathan had had wrapped for her at the delicatessen, and unlocked the door of her room. Inside, she stood with her back to the door and spoke out loud, "Sara, you're such a lousy weakling...a shirker...coward!"

Yet being a coward wasn't typical of her. Always she had been able to confront people in a forthright manner, telling them plainly, and not always diplomatically, of their failings; and sometimes confront herself just as brutally when she had been lacking in some manner. But this time there was vacillation...irresolution. The reason was transparent enough: she couldn't bear to end things between herself and Jonathan. But nothing has really begun. "Oh yes it has," she told herself in a quivering voice, "it definitely has."

CHAPTER SEVENTEEN

*J*ust as Sara is trying on a skirt for her dinner date with Jonathan, and discovering how tightly it fits, revealing more of her tummy than it should, there's a heavy pounding on her door. It's Hillary, and she bursts into a paroxysm of tears even before Sara has shut the door behind her.

"It's been nearly a whole week! I've soaked and soaked in that hot tub over at the Holiday Inn. Nothing seems to drown that...thing. Maybe I should drown both of us. I'm sick every morning! I can't go on like this. Please, please, help me, Sara!"

Hillary is in such a hysterical state that Sara realizes she can't forsake her to go out to dinner with Jonathan. "Here, lie down on my bed while I do a quick errand, then we'll talk it all out." Hastily she runs the cold water in the sink and wrings out a washcloth to put on Hillary's swollen eyes. "Be right back."

Sara knocks on Jonathan's door. When he opens it, she notes that he has been about to button up a clean white shirt in preparation for their dinner date. He has already changed out of his usual khakis into a gray pair of slacks. Surprise shows on his face at the interruption, but his brown eyes immediately reflect concern.

"I have to cancel our dinner. I'm sorry, but Hillary is ill and I simply can't leave her all alone."

"Isn't her brother around?"

"It's not the same, but no, I haven't seen him around. Please forgive me." She starts to leave when he puts out a hand as though to stop her.

"Is there anything I can do…make a run to Cheboygan for medicine or something?"

Sara shakes her head indicating no, and hurries back to her own room where Hillary is waiting. Between gulps and tears Hillary asks, "Did you have a date with someone?"

"Just a casual dinner with Jonathan. It can wait." Yes, she thinks with relief, so can my confession to him about the baby. Hillary has given her a temporary reprieve. Sara takes the washcloth from Hillary's forehead and runs it under the coldwater tap again, rings it out, and then resettles the cloth back on Hillary's swollen eyes, "Let's have some of my chamomile tea. I'll go fix it."

"First promise that you'll help me," Hillary begs. Sara almost melts from the intensity of her pleading eyes. "In every way I can, but I can't take you to an abortionist."

"But you've got to! You're the only one I can count on!" Hillary's whole face explodes again into a shuddering eruption of tears. "If you don't, I'll kill myself!"

"No, I don't think you will do such a foolish thing. Having a baby is not the end of the world. I know this because…" She catches herself just in time before blurting out anything further. "Be right back with the tea."

Over in the community kitchen, she boils the water in the microwave, pours it over the tea bags, finds a tray and hurries back to her room with the two cups. When she opens the door, Hillary is no longer lying down on the bed. She glances into the bathroom. Empty. Quickly Sara sets the tray down and dashes over to Hillary's room. The door is unlocked, but Hillary isn't there either. Then she tries Cam's room, but he seems to be out and the door is locked. "Oh my God!" Sara says out loud. "What if she really means to harm herself?"

She hurries across the street and through the back gate into the park grounds. She looks up the path but sees no one. The door to the changing cabin is locked, as is the Priest's Gate. She runs towards the beach and then, seeing no one there either, tries the heavy double doors of the Water Gate. They are bolted shut on the inside. Back she runs to the Land Gate. It's partially ajar. Maybe the security guard has just gone inside, or maybe Hillary left it open. Sara slips through the door, calling out, "Hillary are you here somewhere?" Then she shouts across the empty parade ground, "Hillary!"

"Who?" A man answers as he comes into sight from around the corner of the nearest row house.

"My friend, Hillary."

"No one's here. I've just checked all the buildings."

"Thanks." Sara runs back across the street to knock on Hillary's door once again. There's no answer, and when she slips the door open, the room is still empty. For a brief moment she considers asking Jonathan to help her find Hillary, but quickly discards the idea. He will ask too many questions, probe too deeply; his doctor's training might lead him into guessing too much about her own situation before she has a chance to tell him.

Over in the parking lot she notices that Cam's maroon colored Fiesta is missing, but that's hardly significant since Cam himself could have taken the car. She knows however, that Hillary also possesses a set of keys to the car so she could have taken it. Sara decides to cruise around the streets a bit looking for Hillary, though she realizes how hopeless that could be in spite of Mac Village being a small area. She picks up her canvas shoulder bag and the car keys from her own room but leaves her door unlocked.

Sara doubts that Hillary in her misery will head for the shopping areas, so instead she turns her aging Suberu west in the direction of the school and the library. It's the same vicinity where they had walked just a week ago when Hillary had first divulged her nocturnal escapades with Skyler. Sara tries all the streets between the main avenue and the water. She even cruises slowly along the narrow lane behind the cottages that are spread along the bay. No Hillary.

Not knowing where else to look, Sara decides to head for the swimming beach, though why Hillary would go way out there at this time of the evening, she can't possibly imagine. Then seconds later, she recalls one of Hillary's sobbing remarks, "'Nothing seems to drown that thing…maybe I should drown myself!'"

Sara speeds west towards the swimming beach. Probably the idea is foolish. Doubtless Hillary has gone off somewhere with Cam, though it's unlike her not to leave a note. Sara realizes she is going way over the speed limit, which is just forty-five, but she has this terrible urge to hurry after wasting so much time driving around aimlessly. If Hillary is bent on drowning herself, she has gotten a good half-hour head start. After the road has turned south and then west again, Sara can see straight ahead the beach now immersed in the warm buff-colored glow from the lowering sun.

Even though the evening is warm and lovely, there is just one car in the parking lot. It's a Fiesta like Cam's. Quickly she parks, avoiding the deeper sand ruts, and dashes out between the high sand dunes onto the wide beach.

Squinting against the strong slanted rays of the western sun, Sara peers out across the water. Approximately where the second sand bar ends, a figure is wading outwards through the water. The water reaches up to the level of the person's waist. It's definitely a woman. She appears clothed, not wearing a swimming suit. A sweater has been thrown down on the damp sand by the edge of the water. Immediately, Sara recognizes the sweater. It's Hillary's. Sara yanks off her sneakers without untying them and runs into the water, not caring whether her jeans get soaked or not.

"Hillary! Hillary!" she yells. "Come back. Stop!" She splashes out to the first sand bar, which comes barely to her knees, and keeps on trudging, half jumping, half leaping through the water. "Please, oh, please make her stop," she chants out loud. If Hillary continues into deeper water, she knows she can't rescue her. She herself isn't that strong a swimmer, and right now she isn't in very good condition for any kind of physical exertion.

Sara can see that the water is now up to Hillary's chest, and that she appears to be getting ready to start swimming straight out into the deeper, colder blue-gray water. Sara cups her hands around her mouth hoping her voice will carry far enough. "Hillary, come back! I'll help you."

Hillary stops and turns her head but not her body. Sara now stands motionless in water up to her thighs. The air is warm, but the water is cold, and quickly turning her bare feet into sticks that can no longer feel the ripples of sand underneath them.

"How do I know?" Hillary shouts back at her.

"I promise." Sara makes the sign over her heart, then watches as Hillary turns back around and looks out into the inky, deeper water.

"Please, Hillary," she calls. "Don't do this terrible thing." Again, Hillary turns around. This time her whole body is facing the shore. Slowly, very slowly, she moves back in the direction of the second sand bar where Sara stands visibly shivering in the cold water. They meet, and Sara puts her arms around Hillary and together they remain for a moment as though consoling each other. Sara has begun to shake even more violently, not just from the cold water. . .also from the stress. . . the close call with suicide.

"Come-on-n-n-n, Hillary," Sara urges in a stuttering voice. "We're both soaking wet and freezing. Did you bring a towel?"

"Oh yeah, sure! Every time I decide to drown myself, I always remember to bring a towel." They both break down laughing and giggled hysterically all the way up the beach to the parking lot. By now Sara is shivering so violently that her teeth click whenever she tries to talk.

Hillary begs, "When we get back and get into dry clothes, will you come to my room, and help me make some plans?" Sara nods, wondering exactly how to go about finding a nearby abortion clinic. Perhaps first, Hillary will have to get phone numbers and addresses of clinics. Then she, Sara, will have to find a way to drive her to the nearest clinic on her day off. They will have to be very discrete, very careful not to let Cam or anyone else get wind of the situation. Oh, how she doesn't want to do this terrible thing! Tears of frustration flood her eyes as she drives back to her room. Maybe it's sheer exhaustion, but she can't stop shaking. Already it's been a long day, and she tires more easily now.

"See you in a few minutes," Sara promises Hillary as she heads for her own room where she struggles out of her wet jeans that plaster her body so tightly that her rounded stomach is clearly visible. She hopes Hillary, too concerned with her own situation, hasn't noticed.

Hastily, Sara gulps down the tea, now cold, which she had prepared earlier for Hillary but had left in her own room. During the last mouthful, she feels a soft throb in her abdomen, and she touches the area with her hand. "Just letting me know you're around? Isn't it a little early to feel you kicking?" Maybe the throb had been the result of her strenuous activity, her churning frantically through the water to reach Hillary. She will have to take it easy and rest more often. "Sorry about that little chum." Already, she and the baby have had some nice long one-sided talks together. "So how do I address you? Until I get a sonogram, I won't know whether to discuss baseball or dresses."

There was a light tap on her door. "Come-in," she calls, thinking it is Hillary.

Jonathan steps inside and looks around. Not seeing anyone else, he asks with an indulgent smile on his face, "Were you talking to yourself?"

Sara doesn't know quite how to answer. Had he heard her use the word, *sonogram*, or had he only heard a mumble of unintelligible words? "Yes, just talking to myself."

"How is Hillary?"

"Better now, but I promised to spend the rest of the evening with her. I am really sorry about tonight." She glances over her shoulder hoping he won't notice her wet T-shirt and jeans hanging over the shower rod just inside the bathroom.

"We'll have dinner some other time. I have to be out of town part of next week, but let's get together on some evening when I return." He looks at her with concern. "You look exhausted. Are you taking care of yourself?"

Sara nods. "Yes, I'm fine. Thanks." She *is* almost fine and so grateful to have someone like Jonathan show concern for her. Sometimes she feels so alone, so bereft of affection.

Jonathan realizes that he is hovering too much because Sara is behaving like someone in deep thought who can't quite switch back to the present. Yes, that's a good example of how Sara often seems to him, as though she is in limbo between her past life in Chicago and this new one and needs to be jiggled awake albeit in a very careful, solicitous manner or she might be traumatized. Other times she simply seems bewildered…as though some problem floods her life right over the riverbank of her mind.

"Call me, if you need help with Hillary."

"Thank you, I will." Sara smiles at him as she slowly, softly closes the door. She doesn't want him to misinterpret her need to hurry back to Hillary as shutting him out of her life too abruptly.

❖ ❖ ❖

Hillary had spent several of her off-work hours at the library using the out-of-town phone books to find an abortion clinic. The computer would have been much faster, but the available ones at the library were often in use. Besides, they were located out in the open where strangers could read over one's shoulder. She had found a book on pregnancy and copied out portions of it on scraps of paper and ends of envelopes. She didn't dare sign the book out. The librarian might notice the title of the book and begin to wonder why a teenager was reading it unless she had gotten herself into deep trouble. After all, Mac Village was basically very small when not swelled with summer tourists. It was a place where gossip could start as a small twist of yarn at the beginning of one street and roll up into a whopper of a ball by the time it reached the last narrow dirt road.

"Listen to this," Hillary said when she and Sara met the following evening. She began to read from her notes. "A lot of guilt is often laid on a woman by those who advocate the rights of about 300,000 eggs in the ovary. The basic question is, are we killing life. What is a person? A person is someone who possesses a personality. The embryo and the fetus in the uterus have none of these characteristics. They are not unique. They cannot think, they cannot feel."

Sara counters: "They could still have a spirit. It isn't something that can be measured by science."

Hillary's expression is doubtful. "There's more," She continues reading from her notes written in a scrawl that overflows right to the edges of the scrap paper. "'We terminate life whenever we cut grass or eat beef, when we send soldiers off to war, and when we don't give a needy country foreign aid.' There. I don't feel badly about having an abortion at all after reading those things. But I *am* a little scared."

Sara doesn't respond immediately. The material Hillary has just quoted from the book is full of beliefs radically different from her own. At first, after hearing Hillary read her notes out loud, Sara had wanted to flood her with opposing arguments. She felt it necessary to stand up for her own helpless unborn child. Then, her affection for Hillary took precedence over any disagreement, and she temporarily blotted out her own ideas in order to calm Hillary's fears over the actual abortion procedure. "I've heard that it's quite painless. . .only a bit uncomfortable."

Later, back in her room, Sara is surprised to realize that her own arguments against abortion have mellowed somewhat; no longer are they a bonfire crackling hotly as they had been during the protest meetings back in Urbana and Chicago. The arguments are now just a low glow, although nowhere near dying out either.

Hillary's predicament brings to mind her own early days of uncertainty. . .her nausea each morning and helplessness when she first discovers that she is pregnant. Yet, in her own situation, there has never been a doubt in her mind; her baby already has a living spirit and a right to be born.

Sara confessed to herself, "Hillary's problem has forced me to look at the broader view. . .the view someone else has to face in their distress." Pro-choice was not a brand new idea to her, not at all. It's just that Hillary's predicament was "closer to home," and the argument of individual choice had been brought sharply into focus. She had now felt Hillary's head on her shoulder. . .heard her sobs. . . her plea for help. It was no longer the plight of some anonymous person walking across the street to the door of the abortion clinic. Hillary was a friend who literally pleaded and clutched at her hand.

Now Sara understood the other side of the abortion question... understood it up close. "But...it's not going to alter my own situation or my mind. I still believe that that tiny morsel of humanity growing inside has a right to be born. I'm on your side, babe." Sara patted her tummy.

CHAPTER EIGHTEEN

*A*s Jonathan passed the Northwest Row House, he could smell the pungent aroma of wood smoke, possibly wood from an apple tree. He recalled that there had been some recent pruning of apple trees at Discovery Park, some of which might have been hauled into the fort for use in the kitchens. Through the kitchen window he saw Sara about to struggle with a heavy log to feed the fire, and observed that Ansel wasn't in the kitchen at the moment to help. He wasn't at all sure if Ansel would have deigned to help lift the log even if she were present. He turned around and stepped through the open window.

"Here, let me." He took the log from Sara's hands and laid it carefully down onto the hot ashes. "What's cooking this morning?"

"Baking," Sara corrects him. "Cherry pie. It should be baked in about an hour if I tend this fire properly."

"Ansel makes great pies."

"Indeed, she does." Sara feels a little awkward. She hasn't seen Jonathan for a week, and she hopes he won't bring up the subject of the dinner date last Friday that she had cancelled because of the crisis with Hillary.

"How are you getting along?" he asks instead.

"Just fine. My parents are coming next week."

"I hope you'll introduce me to them."

"I will, of course, if you happen to be around. I assume they'll be part of an encampment...another Rogers' Rangers group."

"I understand from talking with Pat that Hillary isn't able to come to work today. Anything to do with the illness she had on the night of our dinner date?" Sara didn't answer at first, so he continues to probe. "Exactly what is wrong?"

Sara hates the fibbing, especially to Jonathan. "Something to do with her stomach," she finally answers and bends her head down to close the cover of the wood box. At least that statement isn't a complete lie. Hillary's morning sickness is certainly related to having an upset stomach. On her own ten-minute break she plans to hurry back across the street to Hillary's room to see if she needs anything, that is, if Ansel is physically able to take-over feeding logs onto the fire.

Jonathan touches Sara's arm to regain her attention. "You and I haven't had our dinner date yet. I'll be out of town for two or three days next week, but perhaps the weekend just after your parents have come and gone would be an opportune time?"

Sara nods, avoiding his eyes. This time, if they finally do go out to dinner together, she must not allow herself to squirm out of divulging the truth. Not again. She must confess to Jonathan about her baby. But right now, she tries to think of a way to bend the conversation away from herself.

"You never told me where you live when teaching at Western Michigan University?" All she knows about him is that he lives with his mother on Mackinac Island in summer and that he likes crackers in his soup. She wants to know more and more personal details about his life even though she has absolutely no right to one single morsel of information. She notes by the expression on Jonathan's face that he seems pleased that she's curious enough about him to ask questions.

"I have a house near the university. Actually, it's located closer to Kalamazoo College than to Western Michigan University. The house used to belong to my parents, but my mother now spends her winters in Florida and only makes a brief stop at her former home. Anything else you want to know? I'll be happy to tell you, but will the information be reciprocated?"

"Not necessarily," she teases. Does it seem like she's leading him on? Yes, of course, it must. Actually, she yearns to know much more about this man who has such great humor and naturalness, whose voice plays on her feelings with the emotional impact of a cello. Sometimes he makes her feel so comfortable, like the ease of someone she has been acquainted with for years. Other times, his physical presence nullifies her usual common sense like a compass needle swinging wildly away from north. At those times she fears she behaves like an utter bubblehead.

In spite of their aborted dinner plans, she can tell that Jonathan continues good-naturedly to believe in their eventual coming together, and she feels ashamed over her vacillating. From now on there must be no more stalling if she is to keep any pride in her own integrity. And when she does tell him about the baby? That will certainly be the end of their association. Why would any man want to date another man's pregnant girl friend? Absentmindedly, she closes her eyes.

"Something wrong?"

"No," she fibs for the second time, "except that I forgot to return that university catalog you loaned me. Perhaps if I drop it off at your room or at the office at lunch time?"

"The office will be fine. There's no hurry, except I may need it as soon as university registration begins. Will you be registering for the fall semester?" She sighs and shakes her head. "No funds?" he asks, guessing at the truth.

"That and other reasons. When we get together next time, I'll explain." Yes, she has a lot of explaining to do. How she wishes she could escape the truth. She can just imagine the sparkle of interest in Jonathan's eyes switching off...bulb blown...and she will instantly be in the shadows, figuratively speaking. All will be over; their association will become history...ancient history. His uncritical, naive belief in her, the sharing of his prize bits and pieces of historical knowledge that he thinks she might find interesting as well as his joking, teasing manner...all will stop. Maybe he won't even acknowledge her presence in the same room or out among a group of people. No, that idea is

ridiculous. She refutes it immediately. Jonathan isn't like that. He's not an uncaring person.

Skyler suddenly makes an appearance at the kitchen window and doesn't notice Jonathan who is just leaving by the door. "Hey, Sara, did you make any pies for me today?"

"Never for you, Skyler."

Jonathan turns back into the room. "Looking for a handout?"

"Oh, I didn't see you, Dr. Reidel."

"Now that you have..." Jonathan raised his dark eyebrows, a discrete hint for Skyler to buzz off. "Does that guy hang around here often?"

"Quite often."

"I'll ask Van Hecker to speak to him."

Sara nods in approval. As far as she is concerned, Skyler deserves any reprimand thrown at him plus castration.

❖ ❖ ❖

Later, during her morning break, Sara hurries through the Priest's Gate and down the path to cross the street, no longer suspiciously checking parked cars nearby now that so many other things are on her mind. She's anxious to see how Hillary is feeling. There really isn't much she can do to help Hillary except sympathize with her over her nausea and urge her to nibble on crackers.

Yet there is more in her attempt to comfort Hillary than just to stem her nausea. She knows from first hand experience exactly how important it is to have a friend to talk to and be guided through this first period of pregnancy. She remembered how she had cried, wishing she had someone to confide in, when she first arrived in Mac Village. In spite of her so-called "spunky" reputation, she had felt utterly alone as morning after morning of sickness plagued her.

She taps lightly on Hillary's door and then peeks inside. Hillary has fallen asleep. Gently she tries to wake her so that she won't miss anymore of her work schedule this morning. If Hillary doesn't show up at all, the suspicions will grow; she has already missed two whole mornings. "Hey, rise up even if you don't feel like shining," she urges, trying to keep her tone lighthearted.

"Oh, I didn't mean to fall back to sleep."

"Feeling better?"

"Maybe. Thanks for waking me. I'll get dressed." Hillary sat up slowly, a test to see if she was still nauseated.

"I have to hurry back to the kitchen," Sara explains. "See you later, around suppertime, when I get back from Cheboygan. I'll buy you some more crackers."

"Thanks. Something different this time?" Hillary begs in a plaintive little girl's voice. Sara nods, but quickly adds before closing the door, "I think plain soda crackers are the ones that work best against nausea."

❖ ❖ ❖

At four o'clock, Sara shed her apron and prepared to leave the row house kitchen. She had a four forty-five appointment with the obstetrician in Cheboygan. She hoped Ansel wouldn't think up any excuses to delay her at the last minute. All the baking had been finished as well as the cleaning up. Even the floor had been swept. Then at the last minute, Ansel did add one more chore.

"I want the windows washed with vinegar and wadded-up newspapers. It's a way early settlers cleaned their windows," she claims. "I read about it in a book."

"But they didn't have newspapers around the fort way back then to wad-up," Sara countered. Anyway, she was certain that the windows were cleaned by the maintenance workers so she firmly told Ansel, "I really don't have time right now. I have a doctor appointment. You try the new method to see if it really works and then tell me about it tomorrow." Ansel appears surprised that Sara has for the first time defied one of her orders, but she says nothing more about it.

❖ ❖ ❖

Since no cars were allowed on Mackinac Island, Jonathan typically kept his Honda Van in the parking lot in St. Ignace, the town at the other end of the bridge or sometimes in the lot next to the cabin rooms across the street from the fort so that he would have ready access to transportation when the need arose, as it did this afternoon.

He had been informed earlier in the week that a married couple of French Canadian heritage living in Cheboygan had decided to turn over to the Park Department a firearm that had been passed down in the family from generation to generation. It was a military rifle from the early 1800's period or so he had been told. He needed to check out its authenticity.

After informing Pat where he was heading in case someone was looking for him, he started for Cheboygan late in the afternoon. Learning where he was going, Pat asked him to stop at the office supply store on his way for some forms she needed but had not yet received.

Jonathan had just concluded his appointment with Mr. and Mrs. Rolleau regarding the long thin rifle, a very well-kept artifact, and was heading for Walmart when he spotted Sara's dark blue car in front of him. He was sure it was her car because it was a Subaru with a very rusty rear rocker panel on the right side. The final give-away was the Illinois license plate.

Suddenly, before he could respond, Sara's car turned into the hospital parking lot. He pulled over, and when the traffic thinned, reversed to the entrance of the parking lot, and drove in. Perhaps she was going to visit a patient in the hospital. Then he spotted Sara walking from her parked car into the line of doctor's offices along one side of the hospital. He recalled her saying, "It's nothing catching," followed by a laugh when he had asked her if she had an illness. It might not be catching, he thought, but if she was still going to see a doctor, her illness must be either serious or long running like tuberculosis or perhaps cancer.

Just outside of the offices was a sign that listed the doctors: Pediatrics, Dermatology, Gynecology and Obstetrics, and also Gastroenterology. Unless he followed Sara and looked into each individual waiting room, he would have no idea which one she had entered. He chided himself, "You have absolutely no right to spy on her." Still, he couldn't help feeling concern over her.

"But why?" he questions himself out loud. "Because Sara is different." He didn't know exactly why he was sure of this. Was it because of the calm firmness behind the hazel eyes? Not placid though. Once in a while he could see a perverse humor emerge. Maybe it was a warning signal or a sign of stubbornness? At other times she seemed deeply occupied as though she had a lot of sobering things to think about and didn't want to be side-tracked by incidentals.

"What could be physically wrong with her?" he asks the empty car. "Strange," he muses, "She looks particularly healthy now that she has put on a little weight."

Jonathan drove out of the parking lot and back into the traffic. He needed to finish his errands at Walmart and then pick up the office forms Pat wanted before the store closed. An hour later on his way back past the hospital parking lot, he noted that Sara's car was no longer there.

CHAPTER NINETEEN

Sara is looking forward to seeing her parents even though the visit is coming a few weeks earlier than she would like it to happen. Finally she is going to tell them about the baby, though waiting until she gets even further along in her pregnancy seems more prudent. The longer she waits to tell her parents, the less pressure, if any, from them to talk her into having an abortion. It figures there are always some things you have to hold back from your parents when trying to leave the home nest behind, but this news about the baby isn't one of them. Now she's ready and looking forward to getting her secret out into the open. What a relief it will be. She hates this feeling of being sneaky.

It's now the second week of August and getting closer to the end of the work season here at Fort Mac, so it doesn't really matter who knows about her pregnant condition; certainly it doesn't matter if Ansel, Pat, or most people know. Jonathan is the exception. That Jonathan should hear the news trickling down through the fort grapevine is unthinkable. Sara feels very deeply about this. After all of his kindnesses and her own close feelings, she wants the news to come straight from her. Yet, he hasn't been in or around the fort for several days, so how can she tell him?

Sara spreads out the wood ashes in the fireplace before jabbing at the hot lumps with tongs to help them cool down and completely die out before closing the kitchen for the day. She looks up at the window, which is closed today because it has rained a bit earlier, and sees her mother's round face peering through the window. Her black and gray hair is more tightly curled than usual because of the damp weather. Next, her father's face joins that of her mother, and Sara joyfully hurries out the door to meet them.

Ansel is not around at the moment, so Sara feels less constrained and lingers cozily over the hugs and kisses with her parents. She clings overly long to her mother's shorter figure, and afterwards her mother holds Sara at arms length and looks carefully into Sara's eyes, as though to ascertain if something unusual is causing the longer, almost clinging hug. Seeing nothing to alarm her, she wastes no time in catching Sara up on the local news from Oakland.

Sara hasn't seen her parents since last Christmas, so her smiling mother has saved up a lot of chit-chat about relatives: a cousin who has gotten married, hometown friends Sara has known since grade school such as Penny, and Brian's newest girlfriend...even the dog's broken leg.

"Poor old Suzy," Sara exclaims over the dog. "I have news for you too," she begins but is over ridden by her mother's lilting voice blurting out her biggest news of all.

It must be something really exciting, Sara thinks, because she can see her mother's face blossoming pink as the words burst out. Sara also notices that her father's longish face is broadening into a grin.

"Your father and I are going to England to live for a whole school year. Just imagine!"

Sara is stunned but neither one of her parents notice how her smile, previously genuine, quickly switches to a fake, camera-ready, smile. "But when Brian was here, he told me the board had chosen someone else?"

"Yes," her father gives a shake to his folded umbrella, "but Harrison has some health problems, so I'm going instead. I'm to exchange places with a history teacher in a school in Manchester, England, and he's to come over here and fill my place in the Oakland Public School. I'll teach American History over there in England, and he'll teach British History over here."

"That's...that's wonderful!" Sara finally stammers out, feeling a loss of energy as though her legs are going to fold up unexpectedly.

She sinks down on the nearby ladder-back chair beside the china cupboard.

Sara has been supposing all along that she will live in Oakland, have her baby in Oakland, and have her mother at her side the whole time. After all, childbirth is something her mother has been through twice before so naturally she should in theory be able to pass on all her knowledge, even show her how to care for the baby afterwards. But that isn't all she has been depending upon. She also needs a place to live that will cost her nothing.

Disappointed after hearing the bad news, Sara feels all her former resolve draining away. It had been carefully built up, like sturdy weaving, from the time she first realized she was pregnant. Now that her courage has raveled, she feels herself falling with no net below. Her courage seems to sink in folds upon itself, in a heap. She wants to hide herself away until the impact of the bad news can be assimilated. Who will help her now?

"That's amazing news, wonderful," she repeats in a flat voice. Neither her father nor her mother seem to notice her low-key response since they are both so caught up in telling her their big news.

"We are even exchanging houses," her mother goes on clarifying the situation. "Mr. Morris and his wife will live in our house, and we will live in theirs. It all works out so beautifully." Her mother is ebullient. The thrill and chirp of excitement in her voice is something Sara hasn't heard for years.

Sara realizes immediately that she must not spoil the splendid occasion for her mother. She mustn't even consider smothering that happiness with her own news about the baby. No, even though her yearning to tell is almost insurmountable. She must not even hint to her mother of the thrill of holding a tiny newborn grandchild, as it gurgles and yawns, in her arms.

"Yes," Sara nods. "It works out neatly for you. When do you leave?"

"Before the end of this month. Less than two weeks from now… on the…" Her father looks at his watch calendar. "The twenty-first.

What are your plans, honey? Have you made arrangements to return to school for your Master's Degree?"

"I guess I have no plans at the moment." That is certainly the truth, but it leaves out the biggest truth of all…the pending birth of her baby. What *will* she do now? She has counted heavily upon the free room and board at home…and also, she admits, her mother to fill-in as occasional baby sitter. Sara can't completely control the sudden disappointment that has shot down her plans. Everything feels as though it's pressing hard on her chest. She realizes that some of her misery must be showing on her face.

"Not feeling well?" her mother asks.

"Just a little tired from being on my feet."

Her father chuckles, "That's never stopped you before. No one could ever get you to stop and rest. Whatever happened to our energetic, undaunted, daughter?"

Sara smiles weakly. She wants to blurt out: I'm having a baby. I have a right to feel tired! Of course she doesn't say that. She can't now. It might spoil all the marvelous plans her parents have. They deserve a change in their lives after all the years of sameness…after bringing up two children. Often they have talked about traveling, but she knows they find it difficult to stretch a high school teacher's salary to cover such a luxury.

Sara changes the subject. "So, are you going to be with the re-enactors this coming weekend here at the fort?"

"Actually no," her father answers. "We're going on to the Apostle Islands in Wisconsin tomorrow. There's to be a camp gathering over there on Madeline Island. Want to come? Your mother brought some of your old costumes for you to wear, just in case."

"Thanks, but I can't leave here. I've already used my day-off this week; it was last Monday. Will I see you again before you leave for England?"

"Well, only if you can make the trip down to Oakland in the next two weeks. We have a lot of packing to do…not just for the trip, but packing up personal possessions like photographs and also things in your room and Brie's that we wouldn't want our guests from England to use."

"Oh." Sara immediately thinks of the outgrown stuffed animals in her room with which she might entertain her infant as he or she grows older. "There are a couple of things from my room that I wouldn't mind having with me, but I would have to drive down in one day and return here the next morning."

"What a long drive," her mother exclaims. "We could box up whatever you want and mail it to you." Her mother's face begins to wrinkle up in concern, "Isn't this job over and finished in September? Where will you go then...back to Chicago? Didn't you tell us in a letter that you had a serious boyfriend who was a graduate student there?"

"We broke up." Sara's statement came as close to the truth as she dared.

"I'm sorry, honey."

"Oh, it's for the best." But maybe not best for the baby, she adds to herself.

A few minutes later, Ansel returns, and Sara introduces her to her mother and father. When her mother goes off to the rest rooms outside the stockade walls, Sara walks a few steps away from the kitchen with her father.

"What will you do, Sara, when this tourist spot closes for the winter?"

"I'll find something."

"I know you want to go back to school. If we were going to be here, you could live at home and take a few classes at Western Michigan."

"It's ok, Dad. I can't afford the tuition this fall anyway. Maybe next year." Or, she admits to herself morosely, maybe never.

"I wonder if you couldn't be a substitute teacher somewhere since you already have one degree...maybe in some private school perhaps. I could help you with room rent. How about it?" He watches her face crumple up ready to cry. "Oh now, Irish lassies don't cry." He pats Sara on the back.

After a gulp to hold back the tears, she sniffles, "Don't forget, I'm only part Irish. I'm also part Polish like you."

Her father nods and offers a paper hanky to Sara. "But you look Irish like your mother, and you have her Irish nature."

Her parents had this ongoing flap about their origins that was part quarrel and part teasing. They had repeated it umpteen times throughout Sara's growing up years until it had become a boring routine. Her father would claim that Sara got her spunk from her mother who like so many Irish people became riled up at the least little loss of independence. Then her mother would counter: Sara gets her stubborn streak from you, her Polish father, because the country of Poland has been overrun so many times by foreigners that the Poles have passive-resistance down to a fine art form. Then, her mother would conclude in a huffy voice: "Passive resistance is just another name for stubbornness." And so the stale script continued to repeat itself.

Pensively, her father said, "I don't feel right about leaving the country and not knowing who will take care of you."

Sara sniffs again. "I'm old enough to take care of myself."

"Yes, but occasionally you still need help. Try to get on the list of teacher-helpers for the fall term from the School Board. It's worth a try. I'll send you money each month to help out with the rent until you get a job." He put his arm tightly around her and let her cry.

"Oh, Dad, thank you." She sniffles. "You're a dear, but you mustn't feel obligated."

"You're a smart girl, and I don't want you to waste your life just doing temporary jobs like this one."

Sara wipes her eyes and gives her father another hug. "I must get back to work. I'll see you later."

Her father nods. "Yes. Right now I'm going into that new exhibit, the Soldiers' Barracks before it closes. Mother and I will pick you up a little after seven at your room and take you out to dinner. In the meantime, think of a good place to eat. By the way, I like the way you've let your hair grow." He gives her dark hair a final brush with his hand and then strides away. Sara watches him as he greets

Phil Van Hecker standing beside the barrack's door and engages him in conversation. Ten minutes from now her father may still be there talking to Phil. Her dad was like that...friendly as a puppy dog...always ready to talk to new people, and of course absorb more historical facts. Too bad he and Jonathan couldn't get together. They could have endless discussions since they have so much in common.

CHAPTER TWENTY

*I*n the office, Pat was bending over the right shoulder of her part time helper, Mrs. Pettrie, teaching her the office computer system when Jonathan entered. Immediately, Pat stepped over to the counter to see how she could help him.

"Hello, Pat. I just came in to tell you that I'll be down in Lansing part of next week. You have my cell phone number if anything important comes up."

"Do you want me to inform people where you have gone?"

"Sure; it's no secret. There's an archaeological meeting there on Monday and Tuesday. I don't leave until Sunday afternoon, and I'll be back fairly early in the afternoon on Wednesday." He heard the office screen door slam and turned to see Phil Van Hecker moving up to the counter in heavily booted feet. Phil's face carried his accustomed frown of worry; in fact, if he had been without it, he would cease to have been Van Hecker.

"Pat, Hillary's sick again. Who do you think should fill-in on the children's games, Prother or Kolenda?"

"Ask Linette," Pat suggested. "She's already done it many times before." Phil nodded and slammed back out the door again.

Pat sighed. "That's twice this week."

"What's wrong with Hillary?" Jonathan asked.

Pat looked down at the counter and shrugged. "I don't know. Hillary is usually fine by ten o'clock."

"And she's not the only one." Ansel spoke up slyly after unexpectedly entering the hallway through the back door of the office. "Exactly the same thing happened with Sara when she first came at the beginning of the summer." Ansel smiled sweetly and dropped her poison bomb, "Morning sickness, probably."

Pat immediately flipped her hand at Ansel trying to pass a "shut-up" signal to her. "Just gossip going the rounds, I presume."

Jonathan pretended that he didn't follow the conversation. He became very busy reading the papers in his hand, but his mind had already made the right connections...the leap between "morning sickness" and pregnancy. But Sara too? He quickly removed himself from the office and stood just outside the back door. He didn't want the expression on his face to reveal his deep concern. Probably Ansel had hoped to see disappointment or shock on his face. He sat down on the plastic chair outside his room for a moment to digest the gossip.

He recalled that day over a week ago when he had followed Sara's car to the series of doctors' offices located next to the hospital in Cheboygan; he had wondered at the time which doctor she was going to visit. Now he could pretty well guess, that is, if Ansel's gossipy tidbit was more than just a rumor. Naturally, Sara would be reluctant to tell him what was wrong. Again, he recalled her in the restaurant saying with a laugh, "It's not catching."

If Ansel's diagnosis was accurate and Sara was indeed pregnant, it certainly explained why she kept treating their dinner date like a dance, one step forward and two steps sideways, even though it was perfectly obvious to him that their attraction for each other was mutual. Her pregnancy, if true, must be the reason why she was always reluctant to make firm dates with him even though they were just casual dinner dates. Still thinking of Sara, he unlocked his room door, entered, and dropped his briefcase on the bed.

Pregnant. Well, wouldn't that also explain why she had left Chicago and Northwestern? Obviously she had wanted nothing more to do with the father of her child. Perhaps it had even been a case of date rape, or the guy had run out on her? Those were just two possibilities. His mind went on concocting all sorts of scenarios as he washed his hands in the tiny bathroom.

Deep disappointment overcame him...that proverbial sinking stomach feeling. Surely, he quizzed himself, he had not planned on anything more permanent to their relationship than just a summer friendship...or had he? Yes. Now he admitted it to himself. He had felt something a lot stronger stirring in him when he was with Sara than mere friendship. He was reluctant to put an exact name to the feelings that seemed to draw him ever closer to her.

Now what, he asked himself? How do I behave towards her when we next meet in the fort? But more importantly, what would Sara do? Live at home, have a baby, and never get a chance to go back to school for her Master's Degree? What a waste of her potential. No, he reasoned further. She was still very young, early twenties, so that left plenty of time after the birth for her to return to school. That is, if her folks or someone gave her a boost.

His mind was a vortex, churning up like the water he saw behind the ferryboat he rode back and forth several times a week. He wondered why she didn't have an abortion. Don't jump to conclusions, he warned himself as he changed his shirt. Wasn't it also possible that she actually wanted the baby...maybe didn't even believe in abortion? According to the newspapers he had been reading lately, there was more and more agitation going on against abortion clinics. He had seen the news and TV photos of huge groups of hecklers causing security problems in front of the clinics.

Should he confront Sara with his new knowledge? No, of course not. Too embarrassing for her. He wondered if she would ever get around to telling him about the baby. About seven-fifteen, he left his room with the intention of heading in the direction of the parking lot. Just outside Sara's room a few doors away, a strange man and a woman stood. "Can I help you find someone or direct you?" he asked in his usual helpful manner.

"Thanks but we're waiting for Sara. She's our daughter."

"Mr. and Mrs. Kolenda?" Sara's father nodded and held out his hand to shake.

"I'm Jonathan Reidel." Just then Sara came out of her room, locked her door and turned around.

"Oh," she smiled at Jonathan, " you've met my parents. Good. I was hoping you could meet." Jonathan nodded gravely, not looking at her directly. Sara prompted her parents, "Tell him about your exciting news. They're going to England for a whole year."

Her father took over the conversation. "I'm to be an exchange teacher. I understand from Sara that you, like myself, are also a teacher, a professor, during the school year."

"Yes, and during the summer I'm Curator of History for both forts and Discovery Park. When are you leaving for Europe?"

"On the last day of August," Sara's mother announced cheerfully.

"And Sara is going with you?" Jonathan asked.

"Oh no," Sara answered for herself, "I'm staying here until the end of the season."

Jonathan noticed for the first time that Sara was wearing a loose shirt over her jeans. The current fashion in blouses made every woman look pregnant and could easily cover up any fullness in the tummy. But hadn't she worn all her blouses tucked neatly inside her jeans when she first arrived here? In the back of his mind he had hoped all along that Ansel had been spreading malicious chitchat only to satisfy her jealousy. But now he had to admit that Sara looked more robust, healthier, than when she first came in the spring. He thought back and recalled her fainting spell, which had occurred over in the vegetable garden right in the middle of the ankle-high corn. That had been soon after her arrival at the fort, hadn't it? Reluctantly, he confirmed to himself, that yes, it was definitely possible: Sara might be pregnant.

He stood there quietly listening, his mind only partly on Sara's parents who were explaining details about the exchange teaching job; but mostly his thoughts were on Sara herself. If her parents were to be gone and the family house put to use by the exchange teacher's family from England, Sara would have absolutely no place to live during the last months of her pregnancy. That could be tough unless she was able to make alternate plans. Evidently Sara didn't consider him a close enough friend in whom to confide; she had purposely held back the news about the baby. Soon he excused himself from the family gathering and walked off in the direction of the parking lot. He supposed it was none of his business, but he couldn't keep his mind off of Sara's predicament.

❖ ❖ ❖

That evening after returning from dinner and saying a tearful "good bye" to her parents who were leaving early in the morning, Sara sits for a long time on the edge of her bed mulling over her future. "How will I ever cope? I have no place to stay and no one to stay with and only a promise from my father that he will send me rent money. But of course a promise from my dad is as good as—what was his favorite saying—'as good as money in the bank'? But no amount of money will fill the emptiness of having a baby all by myself without Mom or Dad or someone to care about what happens to me."

As she takes her shower, the water mixes with tears and runs down her rounded belly. She thinks of her friend, Fay, in Urbana. "Will she take me back in again? It's a bit much to ask." Anyway, Fay's apartment isn't that large and certainly not big enough for two adults *and* a crying baby. Maybe she should have done exactly what Hillary is going to do. End the pregnancy. "Absurd!" she exclaims out loud, accidentally swallowing a huge mouthful of water. Here I go again, she thinks, seeing both sides of a question too clearly: the side against ending the life of a living being, and the side for the wonderful freedom that an abortion could bring. She lifts her face to the stream of water mixed with more tears. "Anyway, it's too late. I had so counted upon living at home with Mom and Dad."

She wraps a towel around her wet hair and continues discussing her lonely situation. "Presuming on my parents for help like that was probably unfair of me but what else could I have done?" The answer comes immediately, the easy one: find Larry and marry him. At one time she had cared enough for him to contemplate making their live-in situation legal. She pounds her fist against the white metal wall of the shower producing a deafening *chung-chung* noise. "I don't want to marry him." After knowing Jonathan, how could I care for Larry... especially after the terrible things he and Dars have done? Isn't it better to deprive the baby of a father than to give it a father who can never live down the stigma of being a *criminal*?

CHAPTER TWENTY-ONE

*A*nsel stood on the other side of the office counter while Pat shuffled through the envelopes in the file box looking for her paycheck.

"Find it?" Ansel leaned further across the counter trying to peer into the box. "As you were flipping through, I noticed that Sara's check was still there. Why hasn't she picked it up?"

"Also Hillary's. She and Hillary have driven down state. It's Sara's day off, so she drove Hillary to some interview or other at one of the universities."

"You mean Michigan State, I assume. Any more signs of Sara on the subject of. . ."

"No." Pat cut her short. She had guessed the subject and didn't want anyone to overhear the word "pregnancy."

Ansel looked around to make sure they were alone and spotted Mrs. Pettri sorting newspaper clippings on a folding table in the room behind the office. She lowered her voice so that it wouldn't carry that far. "I overheard Sara and her brother talking—that was over a month ago—back on the Fourth of July when he came to visit. He told her that she had certainly gained weight."

"So?"

"Well, I know how you feel about Jonathan."

"So?"

"Don't get huffy. I'm on your side. You know, Jonathan never fails to stop in the row house kitchen and talk to Sara whenever he comes over from Mackinac Island. I could clue him in on the truth about her. He seemed so absorbed in his papers the other day that he might not have heard what I said about Sara being pregnant."

"You know, Ansel, if Jonathan doesn't care for me, then finding something scandalous about Sara is not going to make him love me instead."

"Just trying to help."

Pat abruptly handed Ansel the envelope with her paycheck inside.

Ansel grabbed it and walked out the door without even a "thank you."

❖ ❖ ❖

Sara had certainly expected to do all of the driving on the way back from Lansing following Hillary's procedure at the abortion clinic but not both directions. As it turned out Hillary was so keyed-up, so nervous about the pending medical procedure, that she wasn't a reliable driver even for the beginning of the trip down to Lansing. First she drove too fast, and then her mind wandered to the point of slowing the car to a crawl on the four-lane highway. Sara had to remind her to use the directional signals when she passed another car and even to stop tailgating. In the end it was far less stressful if she herself did the remainder of the three and a half hours of driving.

The city of Lansing and its streets were completely strange to Sara, and Hillary wasn't much help at reading the street map either. Eventually, after stopping twice to ask directions, they found the clinic. It was located on an urban street of small, mixed, ethnic stores: Italian, Thai, and Mexican food restaurants and grocery stores. Sara passed the clinic and turned right into a neighborhood of small houses before stopping to park.

"Why didn't you park closer to the clinic?" Hillary asked. "There were lots of empty spaces."

"Just a precaution. I noticed a small group of people protesting against abortion just across the street from the clinic, and we don't want any of them to take notice of the car and maybe follow us afterwards." Also, Sara's quick glance had spotted only one policeman standing near the protestors and one security guard standing across the street at the door of the clinic.

Sara parked two blocks away in front of a small, poorly cared for bungalow with missing patches of siding. She and Hillary walked back to the clinic. As they approached the clinic, which was wedged between a small bakery and a deli, Sara pulled her visor cap further down on her head hoping not to be recognized. She knew of cases where protesters were bused-in from Detroit or Chicago. In fact, she had once been one of them.

Sara counted only five or six hecklers standing across the street. It was a relief to see so few. One woman was holding up a baby doll covered with red paint to represent blood.

"Why are those people so mean?" Hillary asked.

Sara's answer was an indecipherable, "Ummm."

Inside the waiting room, Hillary had to fill out a form stating any childhood illnesses she had gone through, any medications she was currently taking and everything she knew about her past health. After completing the forms, the nurse told Hillary, "Come with me, please."

"Can I bring my friend?" The nurse nodded.

Sara shook her head. She didn't want to hear about the dreadful procedure. She already knew what took place, or thought she did. She shook her head again.

"Please?" Hillary begged, showing signs of panic.

Sara knew that under similar scary circumstances she would want a friend to be with her, so she relented and followed Hillary and the nurse.

Inside a small room, which looked much like the room in any doctor's medical practice, Hillary's routine vitals were taken: temperature, blood pressure, and also a urine sample was requested. Hillary made a face of disgust, but took the small cup into the bathroom nearby. When she returned, the nurse took the cup and sent them back to the waiting room.

The waiting seemed interminable, nearly an hour in which Hillary whispered nervously to Sara almost nonstop, trying to keep her mind off of the pending medical procedure. Finally, Hillary's name was called. Back inside the little room where they had previously been, the nurse explained the abortion procedure itself, which would last only ten or fifteen minutes. Sara could see the relief on Hillary's face.

"Will I be put to sleep?" Hillary asked, and quickly added, "I'd like to be put to sleep."

"No," the nurse smiled, understanding how frightened most patients were. "You'll be awake, but you will get a local anesthetic, lidocaine. Since you have been pregnant such a short time, the vacuuming procedure is the appropriate one for you. Afterwards we'll make you comfortable in a lounge chair for about thirty minutes, and then you will be discharged. It's a very simple procedure and chances are you won't feel a thing outside of a few pin pricks and the coldness of the metal speculum as it's inserted into the vagina to widen it so that the hollow plastic tube can be inserted, and the contents of the uterine cavity be removed by suction."

Sara felt a cramp in her chest as she heard the procedure so vividly described. She realized her breathing was coming in short, quick breaths and tried to take deeper, longer ones.

"Will there be bleeding?" Hillary asked, with a quiver in her voice.

"Yes, just as you bleed during one of your monthly periods, and you might feel a bit crampy. We'll talk about that afterwards. Are you ready?"

Hillary seemed agitated, but at least she wasn't crying. She reached out her hand and tugged at Sara's. "Please come with me," she begged, looking at Sara.

The nurse shook her head. "We prefer to keep that area completely sterile. Your friend can be with you right afterwards while you are in the recovery lounge." Hillary looked at Sara with pleading eyes even as she followed the nurse out of the room.

"I'll be right out here waiting," Sara called after her. She reached out her arm as though to yank Hillary back, then let it drop. It would do no good to stop Hillary and make her go through all the decision making process again.

❖ ❖ ❖

To get her mind off the procedure just described by the nurse, Sara paces back and forth in the waiting room. She feels agitated; if she could only run away from this frightening place. Others in the room are looking at her...probably her pacing is disturbing them, so she sits down. *I shouldn't be here at all.* The breathing in her chest gets tighter. It doesn't go away even when she breathes out in small bursts to relieve the hypertension. Will the stress she feels harm her baby? She picks up a magazine, but her tense fingers accidentally rip a corner of the cover. For several minutes she just sits there shivering, feeling a rawness in her stomach as though she herself might bleed at any moment.

All Sara can think about is that a tiny living human being is being sucked from its safe, natural world, the womb, and then actually thrown away like garbage. She attempts to soothe herself with the idea that the procedure will actually save one life, Hillary's, as well as cost one. There you go again, she angrily chides herself. You keep seeing multiple sides to the same issue. Is nothing in this world ever clearly marked with tags certifying right or wrong? She snidely asks herself: do you, Sara-the-saint, know when that tiny blob of matter becomes a human being? Can you prove exactly when God inserts a spirit into the living nerves, bones, and flesh? Is it done from the beginning at conception or is it wafted into the baby just before it is born? Or is there no such thing as a "spirit" at all, just brain synapses? She slaps the magazine down on the table, stands up, and begins to pace all over again.

Less than a half hour later, the nurse beckons to her. "You can be with your friend now." In answer to Sara's questioning look, she adds, "She's just fine."

Sara follows the nurse into a pleasant lounge that is equipped with several couches, end tables, and green houseplants in large pots. Hillary and one other woman are in there recovering. The other woman, older than Hillary, is resting on a cot. She occasionally groans as though with heavy cramps, but Hillary is half sitting up, quite alert. She looks a bit wan, but smiles at Sara and whispers, "Boy, am I glad that's over!"

"Me too. How do you feel?"

"Not bad, actually…a bit weak in my legs. The nurse told me the only things to watch out for are excessive bleeding and infection. If either of those should happen, I'm to go straight to a hospital." Hillary continues in a whisper, "I think that woman must have had a different kind of abortion."

Sara nods. She has heard about the Saline method, which takes longer to cause abortion.

"I can hardly wait to leave."

Me too, Sara thinks, but doesn't say it out loud. "How bad is the bleeding? Did they give you any extra pads for protection, or do we need to stop at a drugstore?"

"Enough for now, I think. I brought some with me in my overnight case, and they also gave me some."

❖　❖　❖

When they left the clinic around five-thirty, Sara noticed that the anti-abortion crowd across the street had grown to about twenty people. Again, she pulled her cap down as far as she could over her forehead, hoping that none of the protesters were people who had seen her before. As they walked down the street away from the clinic, three people, two men and a woman, separated themselves from the group and began to stalk them. Sara glanced quickly back at them to see if they were carrying any type of containers. She remembered how Dars had thrown red food coloring to represent blood all over a young woman back in Chicago. It was just one of his less dirty tricks. Sara took Hillary's arm and tried to hurry her along. She steered her down a block parallel to the one where they had parked the car.

"Hey! This isn't the way." Hillary looked around and stopped.

"No, but we're being followed."

"So what. I feel kinda wobbly. I don't feel like walking too far."

"Not much further." Sara led her down an alley and then cut between two houses. It was a clear invasion of property, but no one came out to stop them. "This is just a shorter way to the car." Again, she quietly urged, "Not much further." They came out just a half block from the car, and the three protesters were not in sight. Sara almost pushed Hillary inside the car and then quickly pulled away from the curb.

She had driven just one block when suddenly two men appeared, one on each side of the car. They began running along beside the car shouting, "Kid killer, kid killer!" Sara speeded up.

Hillary screamed at Sara, "What are you doing? You're heading right back to the clinic where there are even more protesters!"

"There's a policeman there too." Sara hoped his presence would provide enough incentive for the two men to stop harassing them. When Sara turned the corner into the street near the clinic entrance, the policeman blew his whistle at the two men chasing Sara's car and immediately spoke into his cell phone for backup.

"They're not stopping!" Hillary began to cry, as she hunkered down in the back seat.

"Don't panic," Sara said but found it difficult to quell the breathlessness in her own voice. In her rearview mirror she saw a police car pull out from a street near the clinic and heard the up-rising blare of its siren. The squad car pulled up even with the runners and the men stopped chasing. Sara sighed with relief.

A few minutes later, after Hillary had recovered some of her nerve, she said admiringly, "It's almost as if you had had practice dodging protesters. Sara didn't respond to the praise. If Hillary had been fully aware of some of Sara's anti-abortion experiences back in Chicago, she probably wouldn't have trusted her at all.

She and Hillary were planning to stay overnight in a nearby Motel 6, cheap but clean. It was just a precaution. Sara had insisted upon it. "If you should have excessive bleeding or cramps, we'll be near the clinic or a hospital where it can be handled." There was no hospital at all in Mac Village. At first Hillary had wanted to head straight back to the cabins at the fort; now she was relieved to lie down on the flowered bedspread in the motel room and take a nap. Rather than go outside to eat, Sara had promised to order-in Chinese food from a nearby restaurant.

CHAPTER TWENTY-TWO

*I*t was misty on the return trip, and the Subaru's older windshield
wipers only partially cleared Sara's view of the road. Their loud
thump repeated a beat in her ears that added to the monotony of
driving the four-lane highway. Hillary was lying down in the back
seat of the car with her knees bent, in a sort of scrunched up fetal
position.

"We're almost there," Sara called back to Hillary as she took the
last exit from the highway into Mac Village. "You'd better sit up now
if you can, just in case someone is watching us. They might get the
wrong impression by seeing you slumped in the back seat."

"All right," Hillary answered faintly, and Sara could see in the
rear view mirror that she was slowly forcing herself into a sitting
position. Just two blocks further, and Sara drew the car up behind
the office and in front of Hillary's room. "You're going to lie down
the rest of the day, aren't you? You'll have to be on your feet almost
all of tomorrow."

"Yeah, right." Hillary closed the rear car door but stuck her head
back inside the front window. Tears were once again forming in her
eyes. "Thanking you enough would be impossible, so I won't try, but
if there's ever, ever, anything, I mean anything, that I can do for you,
just ask."

Sara reached her hand out and touched Hillary's face where tears
had begun to wet her cheeks. "That time may come," she smiled
sadly, "who knows." To herself she admitted, oh yes, that time will
certainly come, but there will be nothing you or anyone else can do

to help. In a lighter spirit, Sara quipped, "You could shower me with bags of gold."

"It shall be as you wish, Princess," Hillary smiled wanly.

After parking the car around the corner in the lot, Sara told herself that she deserved a nap. She felt exhausted not just from the long tedious drive on the throughway, but from the emotional tension caused by the abortion event itself. She longed to go to her room and lie down, but at the last minute decided that it would be prudent to first pick up her paycheck before the office closed for the afternoon.

As she entered the office, Sara noticed a fan on the counter gyrating back and forth with a small sound like a kitten's purr at the end of each swing.

"I guess it's been uncomfortable and sticky up here, too." She said conversationally to Pat who nodded as she riffled through the box for Sara's check.

"Sara, how did Hillary's interview go?"

"I think well. Better ask Hillary." Once again she has had to circumvent the truth.

Though Sara had been expecting a confrontation all summer, Pat had never mentioned seeing the pregnancy book carelessly left peeking out from under Sara's bed. That had happened soon after her arrival at the stockade. Pat had certainly seen enough of the title on the cover of the book to be suspicious of Sara's condition, yet ten weeks later she still had not mentioned it. Sara guessed that Pat, being a genuinely thoughtful person, a fair person, had simply ignored the implications. Sara recalled the time when Pat had made sure she had something to eat on that embarrassing afternoon when she had fainted in the vegetable garden over in the stockade. All summer long Pat had made cakes for birthdays and holidays to share with the interpreters. Often she brought munchies and left them out on the counter in the office allowing everyone to help themselves. No one ever went hungry.

The phone rang, and Pat picked it up with Sara's paycheck still in her hand. Sara watched the expression on Pat's face change from politeness to concern. When she put the receiver down, she quickly jotted something on the pad of paper nearby. "I need a favor," she said looking squarely at Sara.

Sara yearned to go to her room and flop wearily on her bed, but Pat seldom asked favors of anyone. In fact just seconds before, she, herself, had been adding up the favors Pat had done for everyone throughout the summer.

"Could you take this message over to Linette in the fort? I know you still have the remainder of the day off, but I need to stick right here by the phone since Mrs. Pettri has already gone, and my cell phone is on the blink."

"Of course. I'll go right over." Sara held out her hand for the message and her check.

As she handed them over, Pat cautioned, "The message is urgent. Linette's mother is very ill...a stroke."

❖ ❖ ❖

Jonathan takes a few notes at the archeological meeting in Lansing, shakes hands with some old friends whom he seldom gets to see, and makes a few new contacts in the field. Archaeology isn't his main interest, but just the same he needs to keep abreast of any new findings in the field. Henderson, the chief archeologist from the Mackinac Island Fort is also present at the meeting. Jonathan finds it difficult to keep his mind on some of the lectures, especially the unsubstantiated report regarding the finding of a runic stone in the upper peninsula of Michigan that was supposedly carved by the Vikings. Instead of paying more attention as he should be doing, his thoughts keep wandering back to his keen disappointment after hearing the rumor from Ansel that Sara is pregnant.

He assumes that his disillusionment regarding Sara partly stems from that old fashioned, primitive and selfish idea of wanting to have a woman all to one's self, untainted and tightly sealed like a brand new bottle of bourbon. However, he's not so unsophisticated that he doesn't realize that men and woman these days often live together before marriage, or that even if Sara weren't pregnant, she would have doubtless slept with at least one other man in her life by now.

Disappointment rides with him the remainder of the drive back to Mac Village. Without quite realizing it until now, he has all along visualized Sara as part of his future. He can't understand why he has allowed such nebulous plans to build up in his head undetected, but here they are. Now it will be difficult to reverse gears and cool down his ardor and his future hopes.

"Perhaps," he tells himself, "I can make myself think of Sara simply as a fellow human being in need and in no way closely connected to me." I can glean some satisfaction just from offering her friendship. He snorts out loud at the idea. "What makes me think I can be impersonal? What makes me think I can possibly keep my own emotions in harness?"

He recalls again the conversation he recently had with his mother as she was looking over his newest batch of photos from the fort in Mac Village.

"That's a good shot," she had said. "One of the interpreters?"

"Sara." He had intoned softly. Then his mother had also viewed the enlargement of just Sara's face and shoulders and smiled. He knew she suspected right away that he had enlarged the photo for his own use not for the historical archives.

"Now that's an excellent shot. Is she as nice looking as she appears in this blowup?" He had inclined his head, meaning yes.

Nice looking was his mother's highest compliment. Seldom did she use the word "pretty" or "beautiful." Those were words she kept exclusively for her favorite garden flowers. He supposed she saw the perfection of her flowers, her lilies or her huge dahlias, and particularly her roses as rating the top honors. It wasn't that his mother was totally parsimonious with her compliments, but she was just naturally careful with all her judgments including the spending of her money. That trait of not going emotionally overboard was likely inherited from her conservative Scottish's parents. She kept her highest praise for her flowers because, and this she had quoted once, "…a breeze can turn a flower's head but praise cannot spoil it."

Jonathan smiles to himself as he now remembers the teasing remark his mother had made after viewing Sara's picture.

"Is she one of your orphans?"

"Not yet, mother. Afraid I'll bring her home to dinner?"

"Bring her. She looks a bit wistful, in need of cheering up."

"Maybe I'll do that," he had answered at the time; but now... well, best to forget it, he tells himself. He forces his mind back to the present again and sighs as he steers the car onto the four-lane highway heading back to Mac Village.

Jonathan speculates out loud, "If the rumor proves true, who will help Sara through the coming birth?" She hasn't mentioned any other relatives besides her brother. Probably she has counted heavily on her parents for support but now, when the time comes for the baby to be born, they will be far away across the ocean. Maybe he can no longer date Sara, but surely it's still permissible to feel compassion towards a fellow human being.

Some of his shock over hearing about Sara's pregnancy has dissipated by the time he has driven part way back to Mac Village. Driving along the interstate highway, the solution to his problem about how he should treat Sara, never gets any clearer than the mist on the car windshield. Eventually his mind moves away from sheer disappointment and switches into a gear where he can consider what he, or maybe someone else, can do to assist Sara through her birthing period since her own parents can't. The help must be of a special sort, the kind that will not be interpreted as interfering, or even worse, as charity.

The thought never crosses his mind that he should completely abandon Sara now that he knows something about her that will eliminate her as a future girlfriend. His mind just doesn't work that way. It always works more in a "salvaging" mode, a sort of pick up the pieces and put them together again method. "Now, be careful," he admonishes himself, "she's not one of your artifacts or a piece of furniture to be glued back together. She's far more important than that. What does he mean, he asks himself? That in spite of a flaw, a broken leg, or a spindle to be replaced, Sara is worth renovating? You dunce! Not like that either. She's a wonderful living being with ambitions, wounded feelings, and undoubtedly regrets." Oh how he wishes he could know her more intimately, feel her body close to his as he had done on that boat ride back from Mackinac Island when they had huddled together under his windbreaker. Finally, when he is on the last five miles of his drive back from Lansing and the mist has thickened, almost to a low lying fog, he faces the truth, "I suppose I'm just looking for excuses to keep on seeing her in the guise of being the Good Samaritan."

Jonathan approaches Mac Village around three o'clock and notes how the mist over the land is actually solid fog out over the water. It totally obliterates the tops of the bridge towers, which are usually clearly visible from at least five miles outside of town. As he takes the exit ramp heading for Mac Fort, he resumes his thoughts about Sara. He surmises that some women in Sara's situation might latch onto any man as a last ditch effort to get a father for their child. He shakes his head. Not for a minute does he think Sara is a scheming type of person. If a husband had been all she wanted, an instant father for her baby, she would have kept their dinner dates and tried to inveigle him into marriage.

It's tantalizing to wonder what goes on behind Sara's remarkable calmness when she has so many hurdles to confront. She seems so self-contained. Is it her faith that gives her the courage to work her way through the momentous experience of giving birth all alone? Or... does she have someone, an aunt or perhaps that Chicago boyfriend whom she knows can help her at the crucial time?

❖ ❖ ❖

Sara carries the telephone message, which Pat has carefully folded, and walks across the street to look for Linette. After going through the first gate and walking past the garage belonging to the Natural Resources, she looks out in the direction of the water. She can barely see where the low sand dunes and the water separate. The fog, like a living creature, is crawling across the beach and creeping up the eighteen-foot walls of the stockade leaving only the spiky tops faintly visible. The moving fog gives Sara the sensation of crossing an osmotic line into another world. She closes her eyes and imagines she is about to enter the historic fort of the 1770's. From the parade ground she hears shouts and drum rolls, the same sounds that might have resounded throughout the fort back in the seventeen hundreds.

As she hurries up the path to the Land Gate, Sara hears several warning fog whistles. First, three deep blasts from a passing freighter, then three higher pitched ones, from a smaller boat. By now she can see no further than the corner blockhouse, and even that begins to shimmer and disappear. The whole point of land is quickly being swallowed up without a sound, without even a struggle, by swirls of fog. She is tempted by curiosity to divert from the path and dash down to the shore to become immersed, to disappear into the eerie phenomenon…maybe even to fade entirely away into another dimension. "Don't you wish," she mutters, as she forces her mind back to the present.

Sara found Linette in the Trader's Store in the Southwest Row House talking to Phil Van Hecker. Linette read the note quickly and told Phil that her mother had suffered a stroke. Without further explanation she hurried out the south door and down the Kings Way to the Land Gate and disappeared.

"Now who will I get to take her place in the wedding ceremony?" Phil grumbled. "It's Hillary's day off."

"Mine too." Sara started for the door.

"But you're right here. Surely you can take just a half hour to help us out?"

Sara shook her head. "Sorry, I can't."

Phil's voice began to rise. "Why not? It's not much to ask of you in an emergency."

"What's going on?" Jonathan asked as he entered the Trader's Store. His attention had been drawn by Phil's voice, which sounded unusually strident.

In the tones of a woman wringing her hands, Phil argued, "I want Sara to take Linette's place as the bride in the French Wedding. Linette's mother has had a stroke, and Linette had to leave suddenly, and it's Hillary's day off. Sara is right here handy but she refuses to help out…"

"...Sara, can I speak to you a for a minute?" By the gesture of his head and his softly spoken words, Jonathan invited her across the narrow pathway and through the wide church doors.

Just inside the church door, Sara whispered to Jonathan, "The dress won't fit me any longer...I've put on a lot of weight." Suddenly she realizes that this is an opportune time to tell Jonathan the truth and get the dreaded confession over with. No longer hiding it from him will be such a relief to her conscience. "The dress won't fit because...because...I'm pregnant."

"Yes, I know," he whispered in return. There was an empty pause before he added, "I'm glad you decided to tell me. Wait here; I'll be right back."

The stress of confronting Jonathan with the truth prompted Sara to start chewing on her fingernails in earnest. Next, a deep heaving began in her chest and sobs overcame her. Through the double doors she watched Jonathan approach Phil who was waiting in the doorway of the Traders Store. She heard Jonathan say, "It's almost the last event of the afternoon, so I suggest you skip the wedding and have the Voyageur's re-enactment a bit early. The weather isn't good anyway, and I see only six or seven tourists milling about."

While Jonathan's back is turned towards her as he speaks to Phil, Sara runs out the opposite door of the church and through the Priest's Gate. Outside the stockade she heads towards the shore and loses herself in the wavering fog. She drops down on the damp sand behind a wild juniper bush and sobs noisily, "Now Jonathan will have nothing more to do with me. He won't even want to admit knowing me. What man would after my confession?"

As she takes refuge down by the shore, Jonathan's sympathetic whisper echoes back to her, "I know."

"How long has he known about my pregnancy?" Not long, she guesses, or he would never have invited me out to dinner so recently. That was just last weekend. Sara hears footsteps and a voice calling. "Sara?" The stillness of the fog makes his voice sound hollow and far away. On her knees she bends lower behind the Juniper bush, her head touching the branches. She doesn't answer. Right now she can't face him. Later maybe. He calls her name twice more, and then she hears the sounds of his shoes scrunching through the damp sand and finally silence.

Now I'm completely on my own, she thinks…alone to face the future…to prop up my own low spirits. She knows how Jonathan's friendly interest in her has given her comfort…has bolstered her courage. His presence is something to lean against, even though she has no right.

Sara realizes that her tears aren't just over the loss of Jonathan's friendship, they're over everything…an avalanche of stresses: her fear of being tracked down by Larry, the loving help she can no longer count upon from her parents because it's suddenly been yanked out from under her, and now the end of Jonathan's attention. All along she has known, but refused to face the fact, that when he found out her secret, their association would end. End abruptly. Naturally she has no right to expect any further consideration from him.

Again, Sara puts her head down in her arms and makes no attempt to smother her crying now that Jonathan has gone. In her mind she lists the multiple roadblocks looming before her. "I'll have no job in a few more weeks and few prospects of one with my stomach clearly showing; I've nowhere near enough money saved up to pay for the hospital, the doctor, food, and baby equipment. Room and board in my parent's house has been the one solid thing I've been counting upon." Now she realizes how that fact has been the basis of her confidence right from the beginning. It has sustained her all through the summer, right up until the arrival of her folks and the shattering news over their trip to England.

Jonathan had said just now, *I know.* How? Maybe Pat? No, not Pat. She has been nothing but discrete all summer long. Yet Sara also knows instinctively that Pat is keenly interested in Jonathan and should, more likely, be the first one to tattle on her, possibly from jealousy.

Ah, jealousy…that sounds more like Ansel. She, more than anyone else, has been in a position to watch Sara closely and could notice any signs of morning sickness or detect fullness in Sara's breasts just before donning her voluminous white apron each morning. Yes, it is more credible to believe that Ansel is the tattler. From the first day she has shown prickliness, dislike. Yet what difference does it make who is the tattler? Everyone will soon know.

Sara sits on the clammy, cold sand for a long time before realizing how the dampness has worked up through her skirt to her bottom. She checks her watch. Hillary will be expecting her. She rises stiffly after crouching so long and brushes off the clinging sand as best she can, then walks, her body literally poking holes in the swirls of fog, towards the exit gate. She prays that she won't meet anyone she knows on the way. Somehow she has to adjust her face, wipe it clear of the tears and figuratively mask it up again before facing whomever or whatever is to come next. She arrives at the chain link gate next to the street and stops. Here the fog is slightly less dense. From sheer reflex she checks out the street and all the parked cars that the fog is covering with heavy beads of moisture. Feeling safe, she crosses the street to Hillary's room.

CHAPTER TWENTY-THREE

Jonathan checks out the beach once again in all directions looking for Sara, trying to penetrate the densely moving fog, which constantly betrays his sense of direction. Even the absence of the usual sound of lapping water confounds his senses. Where can Sara have disappeared to so quickly? Obviously he has upset her by claiming to know about her pregnancy before she could tell him herself, or does she consider it none of his business?

Maybe she never intended to tell him at all. But surely, he thinks, our friendship has developed into a relationship much closer than that of other fellow workers. Why wouldn't she tell me?

The significance of her condition continues to circle through his mind as it has all the way home from Lansing, yet it's just a few minutes ago that Sara herself openly confessed the reason why she could no longer fit into the costume for the wedding ceremony. Now the fact of her pregnancy is definitely confirmed. Now his mind must accept the truth.

"Stop kidding yourself," he mutters, as he tramps through the heavy wet sand and heads back in the direction of the Water Gate entrance. "You've let yourself become too focused on one girl this time, and that's not her fault, it's yours."

Exactly when had his interest in Sara blossomed beyond that of a casual companionship or a friendly sharing of historical trivia and a love of remote beaches and islands? A soft brush of sadness flows through him, as though he is being cheated out of some momentous event in his life. In actuality, he supposes he should be celebrating for not getting too tangled up in a complicated relationship. How is he to mediate two such opposing emotions in himself?

No longer will he visit Sara in the little row house kitchen, though the anticipation, the looking forward to, will not dissipate entirely. A residue will be left, a wishful thinking, about a relationship no longer possible. Already he feels a void. Back in the beginning when he first asked Sara out to dinner, he remembers how he had pressured her several times, and her reluctance to accept. Finally, against her better judgment, she capitulates. So whose fault are his dashed feelings? His own, he realizes.

Perhaps right from the beginning Sara's reciprocal interest in him has been a figment of his imagination? No, he's sure that she's not the type of girl to enter into relationships lightly. Anyway, my dating idea is certainly terminated.

Jonathan walks straight back through the fort and notices that Van Hecker has taken his advice about eliminating the church wedding. He hurries out the Land Gate and across the street to his car in the parking lot. As usual he is pressured for time due to a late afternoon meeting with other members of the staff and can't linger any longer. He has to catch the next boat to the island or he'll miss the meeting entirely. Standing beside his car in the parking lot, he suddenly decides to leave Sara a note and quickly scribbles a few words on a sheet torn from the notebook he always carries around with him. Then he backtracks to the rooms behind the office and slides the note under Sara's door.

❖ ❖ ❖

Hillary was snoozing on her bed but aroused herself just enough to mutter groggy answers to Sara's questions after she heard the door open and perceived that someone had entered.

"Have you checked on the bleeding?" Sara asked.

"It doesn't seem any worse. I just feel languid. Could you…would you mind bringing me some ice cream and a slice of pizza…if you're going out to dinner?"

Sara nodded her agreement but first walked over to the bed and touched Hillary's forehead, wondering if she was running a fever. Her skin felt cool. "I'll be back." Cautiously she opened Hillary's door, and glanced furtively in both directions, before quickly slipping out. She wasn't ready to face Jonathan again or anyone else right now, though she knew she would have to eventually. Instead of returning to her own room just a few feet away where Jonathan might confront her, she walked briskly around the corner to her parked car and drove off to the village.

❖ ❖ ❖

When Sara returned from the village with her arms loaded with food for herself and Hillary, the fog had moved further inland. The driftwood color of the cabins became merely a part of the fog itself, especially at the corners of the building where no lights penetrated. It occurred to her for a second time that she too might disappear into the fog like that Scottish village in the play, <u>Brigadoon,</u> and consequently all her problems would disappear as well. "Faint chance of that," she sighed, but nevertheless gave herself a momentary respite by letting the idea of escape linger in her head.

Now, it was far more difficult to distinguish objects in the foggy parking lot than when she first drove off to the village. Theoretically, the sun wasn't supposed to set until around eight-thirty this time of year, but in actuality no one had seen the sun all day long. The fog swirled eerily between the cars, first at eye level and then at knee level, a teasing of one's equilibrium. Sara locked the car and noted that she could see only the faint outlines of the cabin rooms, picked out by the small yellow bug lights attached under the eves.

Sara had just taken a few steps in the direction of the cabin rooms when she became aware of a tall figure standing at the corner of the parking lot. She thought it might be Jonathan, but then she noted the long hair and realized that it couldn't be. It was a stranger wearing eyeglasses with a small dark zippered bag resting at his feet. At first, she didn't feel any sense of alarm because her mind had become so encompassed in her own worries, especially the embarrassment of confessing her pregnancy to Jonathan. Since then, she had felt completely numb to everything else. Nothing could possibly be of any consequence next to the awful realization that Jonathan must be labeling her a "tease," or at the very least one of those girls looking for a husband to cover up their mistakes. Immediately after the fainting spell in the garden, when she first arrived at the fort, was when she should have informed him about her pregnancy and drawn a line there, never allowing their friendship to develop beyond formal parameters.

When Sara came close enough to see who was waiting at the edge of the parking lot, she let the container of pizza slip from her hand and land on the ground with a loud *thunk*.

"Hello, Sara. What a relief to find you again! Glad to see me?" Larry held out his arms.

Was this figure standing in fog an apparition? She fervently wished it were so. The shock of a ghost would be far preferable to an actual person...to Larry.

All summer long she had been skulking around corners of buildings inside the fort, carefully watching for strangers at the street crossing and dreading that eventually one would be Larry. In her thoughts she had anticipated over and over again the scene in which he might appear. She had been like Chicken Little all summer long expecting the sky to fall, and when it didn't, she felt supremely relieved and more confident. Now, unexpectedly, Larry was here. There was no way to escape.

Still in shock, Sara's legs refused to move forward, so she ignored Larry's arms and instead bent over to pick up the dropped pizza container. Her mind had already begun spinning out a form of prayer: please, oh please don't let him detect the baby. Finally, after fumbling, she retrieved the pizza box from the fog-dampened ground.

"I thought you had gone out of the country or something. I'm glad you're safe." And she was glad, but not glad enough to let him hug her. He dropped his arms.

"Food?" he asked eagerly.

"Yes, for my friend, Hillary. She's not feeling well. If you're hungry, I can get you some soup and crackers from the kitchen nearby."

"Yes, please. I'm terribly hungry. You see," Larry glanced around to make sure no one was close by. "I don't dare go inside restaurants too often. I might be spotted. Besides, my cash is running low."

Up closer Sara could see that Larry's blonde hair, once cropped short, had grown out thinly; obviously it needed washing. He wore a pair of thick-rimmed glasses, which she assumed were part of a disguise because he had never worn glasses in the past.

"Follow me." Sara unlocked her room door and scooped up the folded paper lying on the floor just inside. Quickly she pulled the curtains over the wide window facing the cement walkway that ran in front of each room. "I'll be right back after I deliver this food. Take a shower if you want to."

Larry voice pleaded, "Don't tell anyone about me."

"No, of course not."

Hillary was still dozing, so Sara gently touched her shoulder. "Here's your food. I'll be back in a while to check on you. OK?" Hillary nodded. Sara quickly read the note that had been pushed under her door.

"Who's the note from?" Hillary asked.

"Jonathan." Sara folded the note and stuck it in her pocket.

"Ah, ha! I always thought there might be something interesting going on between you two."

"Sorry to disappoint you. I'll check on you later." Sara hurried out the door before Hillary could stop her with further coy insinuations. In the community kitchen she opened a can of hearty pastrami soup and heated it in the microwave. Instead of crackers she spread some bread with peanut butter, thinking that it would be more nutritious. Also, in the refrigerator she found a chunk of cheddar cheese that was probably left over from one of Hillary's or Cam's food stashes; she had no qualms over filching it.

Again, she checked carefully in both directions before emerging from the kitchen with the loaded tray. Her precautions, she decided, were little needed. Jonathan had probably gone back to Mackinac Island by now, and other people were still out to dinner or hunkered down in their rooms on this damp, unpleasant evening.

When she returned to her room, she found Larry lying on her bed sleeping. She poked his shoulder to wake him up and gave him the tray of food. "What are your plans?" she asked.

"Can you give me a lift to DeTour?"

"Right now?"

"Yes, dark is best."

"It's also very foggy. What then, after that? Are you going to try to sneak into Canada?"

"Yes."

"But DeTour isn't Canada you know. It's the Upper Peninsula of Michigan. You would need to go further north than DeTour, maybe several miles further north and then take a boat across to St. Joseph Island to be in Canada. Even if you should make it, a stranger would be spotted rather quickly. Besides, how could you get even that far?"

"Borrow a boat somewhere."

"You mean steal." Sara saw Larry's quick nod. Sara recalled her visit to DeTour with Jonathan and how she had seen the long freighter, stadium length, passing by. She attempted to visualize the exact placement of St. Joseph Island on the marine chart she had seen that day in the museum when she and Jonathan had visited. St. Joseph wasn't really a legitimate island because it had a bridge connecting it to mainland Canada.

"I believe you need to go a lot further north than DeTour before trying to cross the main channel if you want to reach Canada. Do you realize that all the big freighters ply that channel? Though they're going slowly on their approach to the locks, they wouldn't be able to stop before making little match sticks out of a good size cruiser."

"I'll just have to chance it. I've taken plenty of other chances during the last several months. Maybe I could even find a small outboard motor. I'll figure that out later. My map says it's about fifty or sixty miles to DeTour, less than an hour's drive. Will you take me?"

"It's foggy out." Sara repeated and shivered.

"But will you take me? I suppose I could stay here all night and then let you drive me tomorrow, but then I'd have to hide out somewhere in the area until the following night."

Sara realized that the sooner she got Larry out and away from her, the less chance he would have of discovering her pregnancy. If he hung around until tomorrow, he might notice in the daylight how plump she had grown compared to the extremely thin profile he had known back in Chicago. Also, he might overhear Pat or Ansel discussing her pregnancy. Fog or no fog, she realized that it was far better to drive Larry to DeTour right away.

"I'll take you tonight. Excuse me for a minute." Sara went into the bathroom and again unfolded the note Jonathan had slid under her door. Again she read, "If I can be of help, let me know. I'm still your friend." Friend! She now knew, even if she hadn't confessed it to herself before, that she wanted Jonathan to be far more than just a *friend*. She felt her throat tighten up and a loud sob about to erupt, so she grabbed a towel from the rack and held it up over her mouth to choke off any sounds.

After gaining control, she asked herself, "What if I chuck everything right now and slip off to Canada with Larry? That way the baby will at least have a Father. It's the easiest solution to my problem, isn't it?" No, how stupid. She was forgetting about the real reason for Larry's disappearance back in Chicago. Larry was a wanted man.

She flushed the toilet, washed her hands, and decided to take some extra money along with her. It was money she had saved for the birth of her child. She could offer some to Larry. Money well spent if it guaranteed that he would never show up in her life again.

CHAPTER TWENTY-FOUR

Larry half drinks, half spoons his soup from the mug, devours the peanut butter on bread, the hunk of cheese, and then with a grin, squirrels away the apple in his pocket, "I might need this later more than now."

"I have one more errand to do before we can leave for DeTour. I need to tell Hillary's brother to look in on her while I'm gone."

"But you won't tell him where we're going, will you?"

"No, of course not. Be right back."

Luckily, there is a light showing from Cam's room, so Sara taps lightly on the window. The window tapping is the private signal the three of them use when they are in a hurry to make contact. Cameron comes promptly and opens the door. "Hi, what's up?"

"I'm going out this evening, and I wonder if you'll do me a favor and look in on your sister. She's not feeling well."

"Anything serious?"

"Just one of those monthly things, but there's some excess bleeding this time, which is a worry. Make sure she has no fever. There's a thermometer on the nightstand. So will you?"

"Of course. No problem."

"Thanks. See you." Sara makes sure that Cam has closed his door before she opens the door to her own room, which is located just twenty-five feet or so from his. He might accidentally spot Larry sitting on her bed next to the lighted lamp.

❖ ❖ ❖

The traffic on the bridge is moving more slowly than usual because of the fog. The flashing sign at the ramp entrance warns drivers to keep their speed down to twenty miles per hour. The fog siren on the bridge, meant to guide ships passing beneath its long center span, is a monotonous, high-pitched sound. Sara has heard it from her room near the stockade only once before during the summer. She drives carefully, noting how the tower lights on the bridge, which have been switched on earlier than usual because of the fog, beam down on the top of the blue car in front of her giving it a sickly green tint.

Larry has decided that it will be wiser for Sara to be the one to drive across the bridge since it will be her face that the man or woman in the toll booth at the other end will most likely notice and remember if any officials try to track him. Afterwards, they'll switch places and Larry can drive the remainder of the trip. It seems only fair for him to do most of the driving over to DeTour since she will have to drive the whole distance back by herself. After paying their four dollars at the toll booth, Sara turns into the parking lot of the information center and switches seats with Larry.

It's a relief to have Larry do the driving. She has already had a long, tiring day of driving from Lansing back to Mac Village. In the last two days she has gone through the stress of the abortion clinic, the worry over Hillary, and the biggest trauma of all: facing up to her moral responsibility of telling Jonathan about the baby. And now... Larry. Physically, she is drained. She leans back in the seat and closes her eyes.

The first part of the trip is on a four-lane highway, well lighted for several miles after crossing the bridge. The fog seems less noticeable here, but when they switch off onto the route following along the shore, there are fewer highway lights. The car headlights weakly try to penetrate the fog, which keeps swooping in erratic swirls like migrating birds. Sometimes one can't anticipate when the fog will move in a wave downwards and obliterate the road itself but give a clear unimpeded view above to the driver. Randomly, the fog will lift from the road but block out everything a few feet above the road. Larry drives slowly, sometimes no more than thirty miles per hour, so the fifty-six miles from St. Ignace to DeTour, which is supposed to take only an hour or less, actually takes an hour and three-quarters.

She and Larry converse very little with each other, so all through the miles Sara has time to think, though not too logically, about the pros and cons of going with Larry to Canada so that their child will grow up with his or her own father. Just suppose she precipitously decides to run away with Larry? She is confident that Larry will do his best to take good care of her and the infant if he can find work. But can he find work without being a Canadian citizen?

Sara thinks of all the negative comments, criticisms, and hurts she will avoid by disappearing. She can still keep in touch with her parents in England but disappear from everyone else's life, particularly Jonathan's. She chides herself, *so what if I don't have that dreamy, bell-ringing feeling for Larry that I have for Jonathan?* Larry is educated, smart, and has always made me feel secure in the past, that is, until he became too fanatical about abortion. Most of that fanaticism, she reminds herself, was due to the bad influence of Dars. Maybe security, not the weak-legged way I feel around Jonathan, is the more important thing to consider for the sake of the child. Isn't going with Larry right now, right tonight, a way to start a brand new life?

After passing near the town of Hessel, Sara breaks the silence. "Maybe I should go with you to Canada."

"No, no it's too dangerous. I might be caught, and there's no reason for you to have a bad record just because of me." There's a few minutes of silence before Larry continues, "If you felt so strongly about me, really loved me, why didn't you stay in Chicago where I could find you more easily?"

"I was afraid of being questioned by the FBI. Where is Dars?"

"I don't know. He went his way and I went mine. I didn't kill anyone, Sara."

"I didn't think you had, at least not on purpose. Why did you let Dars influence you so negatively? It was quite obvious to me that his ideas were far too radical."

"He convinced me that there was only one way to get the abortion laws changed and that was by raising the visibility of the pro-life group by doing something dramatic. Now I believe our actions gave the pro-lifers a thoroughly bad image and defeated our purpose. Even Dars didn't knowingly plan to kill anyone. It was just poor timing."

It occurs to Sara to tell him the conclusion she has recently come to: that each woman must make her own choice about her own body. She doesn't. Remembering how unforgiving he had been towards his sister, who had made her own choice of birth control by having her tubes tied, she doubts that Larry will ever bend his mind to accept the idea of free choice. Does she want to spend her life with someone whose mind is so narrowly fixed? She says nothing further about going with Larry to Canada.

The main street of DeTour is nearly empty even this early in the evening except for a restaurant-bar. Sara glances down the side street towards the water just a block away and can barely make out the dim outline of the ferryboat, probably the one she and Jonathan had taken to Drummond Island, moored at the dock. She thinks again about the lovely day she and Jonathan spent together, and then shoves the memory into an attic of her mind. In the future she must carefully obliterate such pleasant reminiscences.

They drive past a motel and the marina. Both are well-lighted but neither show visible human activity. Not a soul is in sight at either of them. All seems isolated by the fog, both sounds and colors. The DeTour streets appear completely empty, isolated from the world, except for a few cars parked outside a Dairy Queen and the nearby bar.

"Maybe this isn't such a hot idea coming at night," Larry says. "We stand out like the proverbial sore thumb in a small place like this now that the major part of the summer season is over."

"Just drive on as though we are on our way to visit someone in one of those cottages up ahead."

"What cottages? I don't see any."

"Up there around the curve is a road that runs just behind a long line of summer cottages. Yes, there's the road, I think, but we'd better get the map out first and check to see how far the road goes." Sara opened the glove compartment and brought out the state map and the flashlight. "Oh! This road eventually leads to route 48. We could have turned on route 48 way back before we reached DeTour and saved some driving."

"Now what?"

"Straight ahead. This should lead to route 48, and then we turn right. That dirt road behind the cottages along the shore might have gone through, but I'm not sure."

A half hour later they passed through two small towns and finally a sign pointing across the channel to Neebish Island.

"Those driveways all seem to lead to a cottage or a trailer home."

"How come you know all about them?"

"I was here years ago with my parents to visit friends. She reminds herself not to tell Larry about her recent visit to Drummond Island with Jonathan. "I can see lights in some of the cottages, but others appear dark."

"Why aren't they all dark and closed up? Didn't the fall session of school just begin?"

"Not for another week at least." Momentarily her mind wanders. Jonathan will be leaving soon to return to his teaching job at Western Michigan University, the same university she had hoped to attend. Sara visualizes the hill where the older section had started as a small teachers' college back in the dim past. Its three buildings with classical Doric pillars still stood, looking grand from a distance.

"Some folks," she tells Larry, picking up the thread of their conversation, "come back up to their cottages for the Labor Day weekend even after school begins. After that, lots of them, except for the year-round homes, do close their shutters for the winter."

"Suppose I get out at one of the driveways where the cottage is dark and reconnoiter. You keep driving on along the road so no one will be suspicious of the car stopping too long in one place. Then turn around further up and come back." Larry stops the car and Sara slides over into the driver's seat.

"Where did you put the flashlight?"

"Back in the glove compartment."

When Larry opens the compartment, a dim light goes on inside. After a moment of hesitation, he reaches for the flashlight, turns the beam fully into the compartment for a few seconds then closes the compartment with a snap. As Sara drives slowly away, she can see Larry making his way down between the trees, not on the driveway itself, but parallel to it. She notes how he uses the flashlight only intermittently to find his way. She tries to spot a mailbox or some marker so that on her return she will know where to find that exact same driveway, but there is very little to guide her. She drives further on and turns around about a quarter-mile up the road. When she returns to where she thinks Larry had gotten out of the car, she is able to spot him only by the blinking flashlight.

"No boat there. Nothing. The cottage is all shuttered up. Let's try another one further up the road."

Larry settles back into the passenger seat; Sara reverses into a driveway and turns the car around once more. Again they pick out a driveway where no cottage lights gleam through the trees. Larry gets out a second time and Sara drives on, repeating the former maneuver. Her mind slips back into thinking about her last weeks with Larry in Chicago soon after Dars, the unwelcome guest, had moved into the apartment.

Dars possessed sturdy short legs, a long torso, and dyed yellow hair, wooly as the winter coat of a sheep dog chained out in the yard in all kinds of weather. He wasn't very striking except for his unusual eyes, a glassy pale yellow with brown flecks. Sara imagined his eyes as chunks of dirty street ice.

Larry's rather boyish *I trust the world* philosophy had slowly become subsumed in the presence of Dars' dominant personality, blunt and less humane. Under Dars' influence, Larry grew more cynical, began to behave like a clone of Dars, or maybe like a blood brother. As he became more vehement in his criticism of the abortion clinics, the time and attention he had once focused on Sara was usurped by long, involved strategic meetings. Dars' tough-guy conversations were full of pessimistic predictions. "We've become as bloody as the Romans during their gladiator spectacles. The only difference is that the clinics do the killing before birth instead of later in a Coliseum."

Sara couldn't help but overhear some of the conversations between the two men since Dars' tenor voice was sometimes overly shrill, a fiddle in need of tuning.

"We'll never get anywhere with the abortion issue," Dars had intoned, "if we continue with those weak sit-ins. It's like putting a sling instead of a cast on a broken arm. Sometimes, though, the arm has to be broken again in order to heal correctly. What we have to do is reset people's minds, and the way to do that is to put deep fear into the clinics and the abortion doctors or we'll never get anywhere."

Soon after that conversation, Dars Nelson had moved on to stay somewhere else. Sara didn't know where and didn't care. *What a relief to have him gone!* Apparently, though, the damage caused by his influence on Larry had already been done.

Sara had found herself arguing with Larry in tones as sharp as Catherine in <u>The Taming of the Shrew.</u> She realized it too late. "The violent way Dars wants to do things will get you both put in jail, and it still won't change the abortion law one bit."

For the first time since they had met, Larry had snapped back angrily at her, "Got a better way?"

"Maybe you should work towards changing things politically."

"Sure, sure." Larry had laughed at her suggestion. "Takes too long. Besides, I don't have the connections…or the money. It takes money. Dars and I have plans that will bring the abortion issue to a blistering head, but I don't want you involved, which is the main reasons Dars moved out."

Now, months later, she remembers what she had advised: Be very careful, Larry. Don't let Dars talk you into doing anything violent. But he had. The violence had ended in a death. Now both Larry and Dars were fugitives.

Sara turns the car around and heads back to where she has dropped off Larry the second time. She tries to visualize a whole new life in Canada with Larry, a man who now, just after a few months, seems a complete stranger to her. Time can do things like that…

show up distinct differences. Each of them has changed. Larry now seems more focused on himself than her, probably from necessity...a need to survive. Did he ever really care about her? Perhaps he simply fell into cohabitation with her for the exact same reason she did... convenience. No, not true. She refutes that, remembering clearly his offer of marriage.

This time when she returns to pick up Larry in the car, he waves her past him a few hundred yards further. He opens the car door and whispers, "Douse the car lights. I found a canoe turned over behind this cottage and underneath it a broken paddle. It will have to do. Mind if I keep the flashlight?'

"No, keep it and this, too." She gropes in her purse and hands him part of the cash she has saved. This is her last chance to tell Larry about the baby. "There is something I haven't told you."

"Hurry then before someone notices the car."

"Never mind," she mumbles, suddenly changing her mind; it's not important. "Good Luck."

"Thanks. He gives her a gentle kiss on her forehead and a quick one on her lips and walks away. Then a few steps away, he returns to the car window. "If I make it to Canada, I'll send you a letter. I'll use a fake name. How does *Jake* sound? Then, if you should still want to join me, and I hope you will, dear Sara, you can come across the border in the conventional, legal way. Now drive away quickly before some neighbors get suspicious."

Larry waves his hand. It has been settled...at least in Larry's mind. The decision has been taken out of her hands, temporarily. "God, what a relief! Whatever was I contemplating?" she asks herself. Surely, following Larry, a fugitive, across the border would be disastrous. She drives a few car lengths and then flicks on the beams again. *Why did I keep the baby a secret? Didn't Larry have a right to know about his own child?*

"Because..." she tells the empty car, "because I've discovered that I love someone else."

As she drives down route 48 again, this time straight to route 134, Sara's stomach cries out for food, as it does so often these days. She wishes she could stop someplace for a snack. Also, she realizes how tired she is, and a cup of coffee might help to keep her alert. No, she tells herself, I mustn't stop. It might make local people aware of a stranger in the area, and when the canoe is found missing even though miles away from here, someone might remember an old blue Subaru with Illinois license plates in the parking lot. Reluctantly, she passes by a roadside diner and heads down the dark road. It's a bit spooky driving along the empty highway all alone at night. She turns the radio on for company.

A breeze has sprung up, and she notes with relief that some of the fog is dissipating. As she listens to the music on the car radio, she again feels exhaustion sweeping over her. It's been an emotional day with Larry turning up unexpectedly, a blurry apparition in the parking lot. "I'll be so glad to get back to my dinky little room to sleep." If she can sleep, that is. All her pent-up emotions have put her on high alert, throbbing and tormenting her mind. Tomorrow she will have to face Pat and Ansel and maybe even Jonathan again unless he has gone back to Mackinac Island.

Three-quarters of an hour later, she passes through the stop light, now flashing orange, at the intersection near Hessel. She tells herself that it's only ten or fifteen miles before reaching the four-lane highway leading onto the bridge. She feels the heaviness of sleep insisting on having its way. The drowsiness is so compelling that it acts like a drug over which she has no control. She fights it back by singing to the tune on the radio: Oh I be-lieve. . .yes-ter-day. Sud-den-ly I'm not half the woman I used to be. . . "No, I'm twice the woman," she laughs and isn't surprised when tears begin dribbling down her chin and on to her nylon windbreaker.

Desperate to fend off sleepiness, she talks to herself out loud. "Exactly what is there to look forward to?" she queries in an imitation of the stern third-degree type of voice she's heard Brian use as a lawyer. More and more, the idea of having the baby all alone without her parents nearby to sustain her seems formidable. "Is it possible, she wonders, to ask Brian to loan me some of the money to pay for the hospital and doctor expenses, yet keep it from Mom and Dad?" But she knows very well that she needs more than just money. What she longs for is someone by her side to care for her and help her through the birthing.

A patch of fog suddenly rises in front of the car, and she slows down to a crawl. Her eyes seek the white line on the right hand edge of the pavement to guide her but can't find it. Everything has vanished except a solid wall of gray fog. She swerves, thinking the white line must still be further to the right, but it isn't...just more and more gray fog. She feels the wheels running up over a small bank of piled dirt and then down again into a dip. The last thing she remembers is her head whacking against the steering wheel.

CHAPTER TWENTY-FIVE

Jonathan arrived late for the staff meeting at Grand Hotel on Mackinac Island. Anyway, his input was minimal since he couldn't keep his mind on the agenda after his failure to find Sara. She had simply vanished into the fog at the beach. Now he was also late for his mother's dinner, so he took one of the Grand Hotel hansoms, the reins held by a man in green livery complete with top hat, down the hill and through the village to his mother's house on Primrose Lane. As they passed the marina, Jonathan noted that the fog had obliterated most of the piers and moored boats.

"Sorry I'm late," he called out to his mother and dropped his briefcase on the gate-legged table in the hallway. In the kitchen he gave his mother a peck on her cheek as she bent to remove a casserole from the oven. "Those meetings always last longer than planned. Smells good."

"Nothing special, just baked pork chops and dressing, salad and dessert. Are you staying overnight?"

"Maybe not this time. I was going to but..." He sat down at the thick maple-topped table in the large kitchen and looked at his mother. "There may be a problem."

"What kind of a problem?" His mother knew her cues, and she knew her son. She was a sounding board for him, and once in a while he even listened to her opinions, but usually specific advice was not what he wanted. He only needed to verbally express his thoughts out loud in order to clarify his own mind.

"That girl, Sara, the one I spoke to you about once before?"

"The girl in the pictures?"

"Yes, that one. Well, it turns out that she's pregnant with no visible...no boyfriend, or none I know about. She apparently gave up a perfectly good job in Chicago to move away and take the lesser one over there at the fort...to get away from the man, I'm assuming, although I don't know that for a fact. That's just it. I didn't have any idea that she was pregnant until I overheard some gossip between two other women."

"Maybe that's all it was, gossip."

"I was hoping so...but no, it's true. She finally told me herself."

His mother noted the wrinkled brow, the nervous movements of her son's hands. She had already deduced that the girl, Sara, was a bit more important to Jon than just one of the many other employees at the stockade.

"This afternoon someone was needed to fill-in as the bride in the church wedding ceremony because Linette, the usual re-enactor, had to rush home to be with her sick mother. Hillary, the one who often substitutes as the bride, was ill, so Phil asked Sara to do it. Sara told him she couldn't. I took her aside to find out why. That's when she confessed that she could no longer fit into the costume because she was pregnant."

"What about her parents?"

"I'm almost positive she didn't tell them. They left for England just recently. Her father is exchanging positions with a high school teacher from Manchester, England. After the incident this afternoon when Sara confessed that she couldn't fit into the wedding dress any longer, she simply ran off before I could delve into the situation any further."

"And now you're feeling responsible. You did look for her?"

"Oh yes. I felt guilty because I told her that I already knew about her pregnancy. I was too blunt. I didn't take her feelings into consideration. Then I couldn't find her, and I didn't have time to look carefully. I had that staff meeting coming up and barely had time to catch the boat."

"I suppose she was hurt by your attitude or your lack of sympathy."

"She didn't give me a chance to show sympathy; she just ran off."

His mother reminded him, "Girls in Sara's situation are no longer cast out of society, so she shouldn't have been so upset over your knowing." This was not the age of coyness over physical functions either so why had this girl, Sara, seemed so devastated over confessing her condition to Jon? There was no shame in being pregnant. Just supposing, Edith posed the question to herself, Sara was nervous over having to confess her predicament to Jon because she cared for him. "What do you think she'll do, besides go off by herself and cry?"

"That's exactly what worries me."

"Is she the depressive sort? Might she do herself harm?"

"I don't really know. Up until now she's appeared quite confident, cheerful...but do I know her well enough to be certain? She could have been putting on a good face to fool me...to fool everyone."

"Sounds like she needs a friend right now. More casserole?"

He shook his head. He finished his pork chop and nervously stirred the dressing into his salad without eating any.

"So? There must be someone over there, someone who could talk to her frankly. How about Pat? She's an understanding person."

"Maybe. I might ask her. No dessert for me tonight, but I'll help with the dishes."

"Nonsense. I feel you pulling at the traces." Jonathan smiled at the old fashioned expression that she had inherited from her parents and they from theirs back in the horse and buggy days.

A few minutes later when Jon appeared at the bottom of the stairs with his zippered overnight bag in his hand, his mother showed no surprise, just handed over his briefcase. "I do hate to have you ride that ferry boat in this fog. Couldn't you phone Pat or someone to keep a watch on Sara without going over there yourself?"

"Don't worry; I'll be fine. Good supper. See you tomorrow."

❖ ❖ ❖

Even the faster boat made slow headway in the fog this evening. It seemed to Jonathan that it was doing more back and forth wallowing than forward movement. The boat sounded its piercing foghorn at the bow whenever the radar picked up a blip, and that was often since this was a busy ferry boat lane as well as an east-west route for freighters. At last they arrived at the breakwater in Mac Village and turned into the twisted channel and docked. The fog seemed even heavier over here. It silently swirled around distorting things that usually had a perfectly normal appearance. A street sign now appeared to be a man in a cape. A recreational vehicle coming down the street looked as huge as an army tank as it suddenly poked its hood through the wall of fog.

When Jonathan arrived in the parking lot near the cabins across from Mac Fort, it was already nine-o'clock. He looked around carefully for Sara's car, even walked twice between the rows of parked cars, but couldn't spot it anywhere. Perhaps she was still out to dinner even though it was well past the usual dinner hour. He walked quickly over to Sara's room and discovered that the window was dark. Nearby, he unlocked the door of his own room and turned on a light. For a while he tried to accomplish some paperwork but couldn't keep his mind focused on anything except Sara and where she might have fled to earlier when she was so upset. He felt responsible. Every twenty minutes or so, he stepped outside his room door to check for a light in Sara's room. By eleven-thirty she still hadn't returned, and in his anxiety he felt like pounding on every door in the place in order to discover what had happened to her.

The only light that remained on at this late hour was the one coming from Cameron's room, so Jonathan took a chance and knocked softly on his door. There was no immediate reply, so he knocked more insistently. He realized that his question about Sara would sound unreasonable to Cameron, and might start a whole chain of gossip, but he didn't care. He told himself that his need, bordering on the frantic now, was only to assure himself that Sara hadn't done something harmful to herself.

When the door opened, Cameron appeared in wrinkled old sweat pants, which he evidently used for pajamas. "Yeah?" Cameron's voice sounded fuzzy and tired. Jonathan could see that the bed was mussed up so Cameron had probably already gone to bed and fallen asleep with his light on.

"Sorry to bother you. Have you seen Sara?"

"Not since around..." Cameron yawned, "...seven or seven-thirty, I think. She came to my door and asked me to look in on my sister because she wasn't feeling very well."

In a modulated voice Jonathan tried to pry out more information. "Did she say where she was going?"

"No. Just that she was going out for the evening. I assumed she had a date. She's not back yet?"

"No. Thanks. Sorry to bother you so late."

"That's all right. If this is an emergency, I could wake up my sister. Sara might have told her where she was going."

"No. Please don't wake her. Goodnight."

But more and more it did feel like an emergency to Jonathan. Was he intuiting some real danger that Sara might have caused herself, or was his mind exaggerating the whole situation? If she were on a date with some guy, well, that signified a boyfriend, didn't it, and that in turn implied a guy she liked? When that idea struck his mind, he wasn't so much worried as annoyed. He went back to his room and read in bed for another hour hoping to hear the sound of footsteps walking past his room and then the unlocking of a door. It never happened.

CHAPTER TWENTY-SIX

When Sara first opens her eyes to the whiteness surrounding her, she thinks: ah, the fog is lighter now. Then she realizes that the whiteness is really hospital walls and hospital sheets, and a fleeting remembrance of the previous night returns to her. The throbbing pain in her forehead is making the details of the accident hard to gather into a thread of any logical sequence. She feels so sluggish. Trying to extract details of the accident from her brain is more like a taffy pull, a slow and sticky process. A middle-aged nurse appears beside the bed and takes her temperature through her ear.

"Ah, you're awake. You'll be happy to know that your baby is just fine. The doctor needed to take a sonogram to make sure the baby wasn't harmed by your little accident. Later, if he isn't satisfied, he may decide on further tests."

Hearing the word "sonogram," Sara immediately asked, "Is it a boy or a girl?"

"That's something you'll have to ask the doctor."

"Where am I?"

"St. Ignace Hospital and Health Center. They brought you in last night around eleven. You have a concussion and a large lump on your head plus a cut on your knee, but not much else. Doctor Humphrey from ER says you need to rest for twenty-four hours to make sure that both you and the baby are healthy."

"My car? Is it wrecked?"

Probably the police will tell you when they come in to ask questions about the accident. You were lucky. . .nasty fog last night. I even had a tough time getting here on time this morning since I live out in the country. It took me a half hour longer than usual."

"Why does my head hurt so much?"

"It's the concussion. I'll bring you something for your head. Can't give you anything too potent though because of the baby."

"I'll have to make a phone call. I'm expected at work today."

"Here. The phone's on the other side of the call button. Need a phone book too?"

Sara nods. "Thank you." She looks around her, more alert now, and discovers that the bed next to hers is empty, sheets pulled tightly. Out the window she can see parked cars and a greenhouse on one side of the parking lot. Beyond the parking lot is a glimpse of water. Her head feels so fuzzy that she slips back down under the covers and closes her eyes. When the nurse comes back into the room a few minutes later with the medication for her throbbing head, she rouses herself enough to take the pills, and then plops down again.

"Here's the phone book. You can raise the head of your bed a bit, but after your phone call you'd better get some rest." The nurse shows Sara how to adjust the bed to a sitting position.

Sara nods and hears the motor hum as the head portion slowly rises upwards. She has to force her eyes, bleary and tearful, to focus on the fine print in the phone book. She dials Pat's office number and explains in a shaky voice why she isn't able to show-up for work.

Pat sounds very solicitous and wants to know if there is anything she can do, so Sara tries to assure her that she is really feeling fine except for a severe headache and will surely be back at work by noon the following day. She says nothing about the baby, not knowing for sure if Pat knows about it or not, though someone, either Pat or Ansel, at the fort has certainly leaked the information to Jonathan. Anyway, it had been inevitable that he would find out sooner or later. She groans, replaying in her mind the scene in the church doorway when she had told him that she couldn't fit into the bride's costume and exactly why. She had felt remorse over the fact that she hadn't been the one to break the news to him before someone tattled. She had been ashamed and embarrassed as well. She had simply run.

Jonathan cared for her...she is sure, but probably no longer. No, now that he knows the truth, she must seem the deceitful sort...the type of woman who teases men. She closes her eyes again and it isn't until the baby kicks her several times before she rouses herself. "Quiet, little one. I don't feel up to a long talk with you just yet."

❖   ❖   ❖

The first thing Jonathan asked Pat the following morning when he entered the office at eight-thirty was, "Have you seen Sara by any chance?

Pat shook her head.

"Yesterday when I saw Sara, she was very upset." Jonathan was about to explain his statement when the phone rang, and he heard Pat ask if the person on the phone was "all right." Every neuron in Jonathan's head was alert. He listened carefully to the one-sided conversation that he felt certain must be concerning Sara. In his anxiety to know, he wanted to grab the phone from Pat's hand and demand, "Where are you? Why did you run away from me? Are you all right?" But he didn't. He laid his leather briefcase on the counter and waited, trying not to show his impatience.

Pat was saying, "If you need anything let me know." Then she hung up the phone and would have gone on with her work without further explanation.

"Well?" Jonathan asked in a voice that he hoped sounded unemotional, quite the reverse of his churned-up stomach. "Was that by any chance Sara calling to explain why she couldn't show up for work?"

"Yes. It seems that she was in a minor car accident last night because of the fog. She's in the hospital in St. Ignace. Apparently she has only a concussion. She was quite lucky."

Jonathan strove to maintain a calm voice, "Any more information?"

"No, except that she expects to be back at work around noon tomorrow. She's being kept overnight for observation."

His eyes met Pat's, assuming she would be surprised by his next question. "I wonder if she lost the baby?"

Pat showed no surprise whatsoever. "Sara didn't mention it. If she had had a miscarriage so late in her pregnancy, the hospital would keep her a little longer than a day wouldn't they?"

"Probably," he agreed, keeping his tone of voice flat and unemotional, which was becoming more and more difficult under the circumstances.

"Since you're going over to the stockade anyway, could you stop by the kitchen and tell Ansel the news about Sara?"

"Yes, I'll be glad to." He grabbed his briefcase from the counter and quickly left the office. As soon as he gained the door, he wanted to sprint to his car and take off across the bridge to the hospital in St. Ignace, but he didn't. He reminded himself that a smart man in his position would probably stay clear of a girl like Sara and her encumbrance. Out of sight of the office he quickened his pace, passed through all the gates, and strode across the parade ground to the Northwest Row House kitchen.

Ansel was sitting at the drop leaf table in the kitchen copying out recipes. Jonathan gave her the news about Sara.

Ansel just nodded her head and then mumbled something to herself.

"What did you say?"

"I thought it was a mistake to hire her in the first place."

"Indeed? Why is that?"

"You know why. She's pregnant."

He felt anger rising in his head and paused to take a deep breath in order to gain control over some of the words and recriminations he wanted to toss like dynamite sticks of meanness at Ansel. Finally, under control again, he spoke. "Yes, I know about the baby." Why does Ansel provoke him so? "Perhaps you should be a little more tolerant since you have no idea about the circumstances under which she became pregnant." He walked quickly out the door. He couldn't trust himself to listen to Ansel's criticisms of Sara and not retaliate in some unprofessional manner.

As he hastened away, Jonathan asked himself, why are you being so quick to judge Ansel? Even you don't know how Sara became pregnant. Why are you acting like such a fool? Inside his head he answered his own question: she's the only girl I've ever met who satisfies me on both an intellectual level and an emotional one. "Ha!" he muttered. "I suspect it's the emotional level that predominates. But the baby? With her parents gone, who would take care of Sara and her baby?

The infighting between his common sense and his soft feelings for Sara continued all the way to the hospital, and he asked himself over and over again, "Who will care for Sara?" He chided himself as he bounded down the wide hall in long strides, then told himself to slow down to a more reasonable pace. He stopped a nurse in the hallway and asked which room was Sara's.

"Mrs. Kolenda is in room one-o-three."

❖ ❖ ❖

Right after her light snack of broth, crackers, and milk, which is all Sara is allowed, she closes her eyes and feels like dozing off again when she hears a familiar voice asking for a room number. Even though she isn't standing on her legs, they immediately react as though she has been imbibing too much wine. It's fortunate, she thinks, that she's already lying down. She doesn't have to conjure up a mental picture of Jonathan, his smiling face simply flows over her like a warm shower even before he sets foot in the room.

Jonathan walks slowly over to the bed where Sara lies propped up in a half sitting position. Her hospital gown is far too large at the neck and her forehead appears as a huge swollen extrusion, nearly as black as her tousled nest of hair. She seems completely surprised to see him…has even opened her mouth to speak but remains silent.

"A fine mess," he grumbles in a scolding voice, but at the same time wishing he could kiss the bump on her forehead.

"Why are you so angry?"

He ignores the question. "Do you have any car insurance? Health insurance?"

"You sound exactly like my father." She sighs wearily but answers his question. "A little health coverage left over from my former job. No car insurance because the car is so old. Anyway, the accident was my fault, and I didn't hit any other car, just an embankment."

"Since it was foggy, I don't see why you should feel it was your fault."

Sara turns her face away towards the window and now he can see more clearly the huge area of black and blue extending down across the top of her nose. "I was also very sleepy and shouldn't have been driving."

"Where had you been that late at night?" Right away he knows the direct approach is the wrong one, but he can't stem his need to know. Why was she so careless as to be out driving in the fog anyway and after dark…and with whom? Why had she been so foolish as to put herself in danger? He wants to know everything.

Sara tells him the same made-up story she has already told the policeman. "I was taking a Chicago friend to visit some people in a cottage in Hessel."

"Anyone I know?"

"I doubt it, and I can't remember the name of the family she was visiting. I guess the bump on my head swept everything out of my mind. Maybe it will come back to me later." That also was the same thing she had told the policeman.

Abruptly, Jonathan changes the subject. "Pat tells me that the baby is quite all right. That's good news."

Now Sara openly smiles for the first time since his arrival in the room. "It's a girl, you know," she exclaims eagerly. "They had to take a sonogram to make sure the baby was all right, and I found out for the first time that it's a girl."

She seems so pleased by the news that he also feels a sense of delight. "I wish you hadn't run away from me the other day. I didn't mean to scare you away or hurt your feelings. In fact," now he hesitates, not knowing quite how to broach the subject, "I want you to know that I'm still your friend. I'd like to help you in any way I can."

Oh, she thinks, he feels sorry for me because of the accident, and that's probably the only reason. I'm to be like one of his orphans in need of help or a piece of furniture in need of refurbishing...someone to feel sorry for. "Thanks, but..." She is unable to keep the *sorry for myself* tears from welling up into her eyes and flowing down her cheeks.

"But?" He notes how she grabs at the corner of the bed sheet to wipe at her eyes, so he moves over to the bedside table nearby, pulls out a paper hanky from the box, and starts to wipe her tears for her. Sara jerks her swollen face away from him.

He doesn't want to induce any more sad tears, but there is something else he needs to know. After she has patted her own face and blown her nose, he asks, "Would the father of the baby have married you?"

Sara nods. "Yes."

"What kind of a person was he?"

"Very intelligent. He did something in biomedical engineering at Northwestern University."

"So you ran away. Where is he now, still back in Chicago?"

"I don't know where he is." It's the truth, but not the whole truth.

Something about the way she fails to look him straight in the eyes leaves Jonathan in doubt. She has abruptly closed her eyes and doesn't appear to be about to open them again. Also, he feels suspicious of her story about the accident. If she had just left a friend in Hessel, why was she so sleepy just a few miles farther down the road? Of course, the cause of the accident could easily be blamed exclusively on the fog...or is she covering up for someone? He is disappointed in her lack of forthrightness.

Sara rings for the nurse. "I need more pills for my headache," she explains to Jonathan.

He realizes that she doesn't have any idea how her evasive answers have hurt him, and he certainly can't tell her what his true feelings are towards her...probably never can. He tries once more to gain her confidence. "You can trust me, you know." He waits for her to open her eyes, but she doesn't. "I'm going now," he states lamely.

Sara doesn't raise her head or respond immediately but reaches over to ring again for the nurse. Jonathan walks slowly out of the room, stopping just outside of the doorway to mull over their conversation; if she doesn't trust me, how can I help her? Then he admonishes himself: don't take it all so personally. She's hurting right now. Anyway, what difference does it make whether she tells me the cut version or the whole cloth version of her accident? There's no point in agonizing over it. It's a closed door since we can no longer have any kind of close relationship.

Sara's throbbing head is making clear thinking impossible. Why doesn't the nurse come? She wants Jonathan to trust her, even though he can never be more than a friend, but she can't divulge where Larry is, not yet, not today. Larry needs time to escape safely to the mainland of Canada from Neebish Island. But she could explain to Jonathan about the abortion protests and related parts of her life... if those revelations will make him feel she is being more forthright... truthful. She opens her eyes. "Jonathan?" The room is empty.

CHAPTER TWENTY-SEVEN

The hospital book cart came around late in the afternoon and the lady wheeling the cart recommended an Ann Tyler book, which Sara is reading intermittently, attempting to get her mind off of her problems. This evening she feels overwhelmed by them, especially abandonment by her parents which she knows isn't the truth. Tears of self-pity begin to well up in her eyes. When she looks up, Pat is standing in the doorway of her room. Quickly Sara tries to blink away the moisture in her eyes before Pat notices. Immediately she wonders, how should I handle this situation, this visitor? Should I assume that Pat knows about the baby? Of course if Jonathan knows, so must Pat.

Sara notices that Pat has relaxed her dress code enough to wear slacks and a twin sweater set in blue. Her composure and neatness make Sara feel dumpy. Nervously, she smoothes out the bed sheets and runs her fingers through her hair.

"Hey there," Pat calls as she approaches the bed, "can I bring you something...such as a decent pair of pajamas?" Pat lays a recent Redbook magazine on the bedside table.

Sara laughs self consciously and once again tugs at the gaping neckline of the hospital gown, "Thanks, but I think I'll be out of here by tomorrow noon. I talked to Hillary on the phone, and she promised to help me bust out of here and drive me over to the police station to pick up my car."

"Is it badly damaged?"

"It still runs, I'm told. I'm sorry if my accident made the staff shorthanded."

"Accidents do happen. You couldn't help it. But when all the colleges resume a week from now, we'll really be in a bind at the fort. Hillary and Cam will be leaving, and Linette won't be coming back at all because of her mother's stroke. If someone can find a costume to fit, do you suppose you could take over Linette's job in the reenactment of the marriage ceremony in Ste. Annes?"

"What about the Northwest kitchen?"

'Ansel can handle the kitchen by herself. Also you could work straight through the month of September...if you haven't already made other plans, that is."

"Thanks. I'll think about staying. I doubt, though, if anyone can find a costume large enough in the bust and waist." Sara grins, "It's a growing problem."

"You aren't showing that much yet. If the waistline of the dress is a bit higher, almost Empire style, it will cover up most of the roundness in your tummy. No one will know the difference. When is the baby due?"

"Near the end of December or the first week in January." Sara relaxes now that the news about the baby is out in the open. She is so grateful for Pat's understanding that she suddenly burst out, "It's a girl!"

"You didn't know before?" Sara shakes her head and switches back to the former subject. "If you find a costume, I can alter it. I used to be quite good at redesigning my own clothes."

"Will do. Cam and Hillary are just outside waiting, so I'll wish you good night; I'll see you tomorrow."

"Thanks for coming to see me and for the magazine." Sara hesitates a moment before asking, "Do they know about the baby?"

"I don't think so." From the doorway, Pat waves a hand at Sara as she leaves.

Sara hears Pat's heels clicking down the hallway on her way past the waiting room. Seconds later, Hillary comes bouncing into the room with Cam following right behind. Hillary heads straight over to the bed. Her arms encompass Sara in a gigantic hug. "How do you feel?"

"Headachy, but otherwise fine. It's great to see you both."

"That's some bruise." Cam inspects Sara's forehead. "No wonder you have a headache. Is the bruise from the airbag in your car?" He hands Sara a bunch of daisies.

"My car is pre-airbag. Thanks for the flowers. Where did you pick these?"

"In that opening between the trees on the way to the swimming beach. You know the place...the one where I got poison ivy, but this time I was careful."

"Brought you something else, too." Hillary hands Sara a narrow white box.

Sara recognizes the small white box immediately. "Fudge. Very sweet of you...pun intended. Now each of you take several pieces. If I eat a whole half pound of fudge, there will be other ugly things sprouting on my face besides this mess." She points to the massive bruise on her forehead then opens the box. With the little plastic knife provided she cuts the fudge into pieces and passes the box to Hillary and Cam. Lastly, she takes one piece herself.

"Tell us about the accident," Hillary coaxes as she plunks herself down at the foot of the hospital bed.

Cam pulls up the single chair in the room. "What were you doing driving way over there on that road so late at night when it was foggy?"

"Just taking a friend to visit someone in Hessel." Sara sticks to the same story she invented to tell the police and Jonathan.

"That's weird. What friend? Anyone I know?"

Cam snorted derisively at his sister, "Everything is weird to you. Maybe it's none of our business. Ever think of that?"

Ignoring her brother, Hillary sputters, "Some friend...to ask you to drive at night in the fog..."

Cam interrupts his sister to tell Sara, "Last night around midnight, I woke up after hearing a loud knock on my door. It was

Jonathan wanting to know if I knew where you were. He appeared quite concerned."

"Oh?" A surge of warmth sweeps throughout Sara's body. Obviously Jonathan cares for her a little more than he lets on...more than she dares to hope for; or his concern could be chiefly for her abrupt disappearance right after her confession to him about the baby. Maybe he thought she was in such despair that she might do herself harm. Now that she has turned up safely in the hospital's care, his conscience will be clear.

Hillary wags her finger at Sara. "Is, 'oh' all you've got to say? You're holding out on me. There *is* something going on between you and Jonathan."

"No, not really," Sara answers wearily. She is beginning to feel overly tired, so when the nurse comes in to check the bag of fluid attached to the pole standing like a sentinel beside her bed and hints strongly that visiting hours are long past, Sara is relieved.

"Thanks for coming, you two...and for the gifts. I'll probably be back to work tomorrow. Are you still able to give me a lift? I think check-out time is around noon."

"Yup, glad to." Hillary gives Sara a kiss on her cheek avoiding the bruise.

Sara realizes how anxious Hillary is to be of assistance. She probably figures she'll never be able to repay Sara for standing by her during the abortion.

The nurse cautions Hillary and Cam: "That check-out time tomorrow isn't definite. Doctor Haskel has to decide whether to release her or not after he sees her in the morning."

"I'll phone the office tomorrow if the time is changed," Sara assures Hillary as she and her brother leave.

❖ ❖ ❖

Before eight o'clock in the morning Doctor Haskel arrives on his rounds and reviews the computer data on Sara, then confers with the nurse. Sara's headache is still severe at times, she hasn't slept well, and the baby is unusually restless, so the doctor insists that she stay one more night. Her relief manifests in a sigh. She can put off facing Ansel who doesn't like her, and others at the fort who may view her pregnancy situation with a sly snicker. For the first time since learning that she is pregnant, she feels cared for, secure and safe, although she isn't sure how the hospital bill will ever get paid. Now she can put-off facing up to people at least one more day.

Yet what am I so self-conscious about? She asks herself. There's no shame involved in having a baby...not even without a husband. Times are different than in my mother's day. Maybe I myself am the one being prudish, overly willing to wear a scarlet letter. "Why has my self-confidence become so shaky?"

About nine in the morning, she phones Pat and asks her to tell Hillary that she isn't going to need a ride today after all. A few minutes later the nurse brings Sara's midmorning glass of milk and lets out a shivery "Burr, it's cold in here this morning. They'll get the heat on soon, and then we'll all roast to death." After the nurse checks Sara's vitals once again, Sara is allowed to sit in a chair while the bed sheets are changed. A few minutes later, a woman from the lab arrives in her room to siphon another vial of blood for yet another test.

The morning drags along and Sara is given an escorted walk up the hallway and back, and then allowed to have a nap. The same pattern is repeated in the afternoon. Each time her vitals are taken, she wakes up. No wonder she is so tired. When she isn't sleeping, Sara tries to throw a lariat around her problems and gather them into some kind of decision about her future and that of her baby girl.

Sara wonders just how much she should confide to Jonathan about Larry and her past. Doubtless she and Jonathan have no future together; in fact, because of the baby they don't, but Jonathan, being the naturally caring person that he is, doesn't deserve to be stonewalled either. She wants to be forthright, to leave him with an honest picture of herself. She's anxious to correct the half-truths she told him yesterday.

She tells herself, when I see Jonathan again—if I do—I'll level with him. Larry must be safely in Canada by now, so I won't be scotching his chances of escaping by divulging where I took him on that foggy night of my accident.

"What if I never see Jonathan again?" she asks herself. "Then I'll..." She snaps on the TV, hoping to get her mind off of Jonathan and her uncertain future.

CHAPTER TWENTY-EIGHT

*A*round dinnertime Sara awakens, and her head feels more normal though the bruise has taken on an eggplant purple patina with sunset colors on the periphery. "Beautiful" she tells her image in the bathroom mirror. She is finally allowed to visit the bathroom without alerting a nurse to be nearby in case she becomes dizzy and falls. Maybe tonight or in the morning she will also be allowed to take a shower. She does her best to tidy her hair with the comb provided by the hospital. With a damp washcloth she works around the tender area of the bruise on her forehead.

Jonathan hasn't come to visit during the afternoon. Maybe he isn't planning to come again at all. Why should he? She closes her eyes remembering how she had evaded his questions about Larry with a lie. She tells herself gloomily, "He probably guessed that I was fibbing."

She has spent most of the evening sitting in an armchair beside the bed. When visiting hours are half over and Jonathan doesn't show up, she feels abandoned all over again...not that she has a right to expect him. By eight o'clock she is wallowing in disappointment, so she goes back to bed and slips down under the covers. She has a difficult time from keeping her mind from reopening her Chicago experiences...they're a full picture album. Sadly, she realizes that her past life images can never be shred or torn up like paper. The brain can never completely discard experiences. They remain there in her thoughts forever, stuck fast in her synapses. Her mind will always be affected by her memories, both good and bad. At least now that Larry has gone for good to Canada, some past events will begin to blur a bit as ink does on wet newsprint.

At first, after Larry had done his disappearing act back in Chicago, she had felt abandoned and cheated. Then she had faced-up to the truth: Larry had quite openly colluded with Dars and become a murderer. "At least circumstances wrenched me away from Larry before I became irrevocably mixed-up in his terrorist activities." Yes, but not detached quite soon enough. Now there was a baby.

On the Friday of their last week together, Larry went missing for one whole day without first telling her that he would be away. This was unusual. Larry almost always confided every move he made whether it was a trip to the grocery or a late evening working at the lab. He communicated by phone or by leaving notes on the kitchen refrigerator or on the bed pillow. By Saturday night Sara had begun to worry about him. Perhaps he had been in an accident or, more likely, been arrested. Much to her relief he returned late Sunday evening. "Where have you been?"

"It's better if you don't know."

Even after she had picked at him with further questions, Larry refused to divulge where he had been. But by the following evening she knew. In the Chicago Tribune and on the late TV newscast there was a special about an attempt to bomb an abortion clinic in Cleveland. It had failed.

At first she had gently probed to find out why Larry's former "live and let live" attitude had recently become buried under tons of cold, cement-like animosity. "Larry, you and I have always believed in saving life, not deliberately hurting other people to accomplish our ends. Remember how we discussed what Albert Schweitzer said? 'If a man loses reverence for any part of life, he will...'"

"'...lose his reverence for *all* life,' I know that quote by heart, but do you realize that a lot more baby blood is being thrown in the dumpsters behind clinics than adult blood? So if we waste some bastard abortionist's blood in our effort to eliminate abortions, well...it evens out doesn't it? In order to win a battle, there's bound to be a little spilled blood."

Sara had begun shaking her head even before he had finished with his diatribe. "That sounds like one of Dar's theories, not yours. Is he the one who went with you to Cleveland?" Larry didn't answer. "All this blood and guts talk doesn't sound like you at all. Maybe the abortion battle needs to be won by changing Roe versus Wade."

"Hopeless!"

At their next sit-in, where they lined up across the street from the abortion clinic in Skokie and were supposed to stay a certain number of feet away from the clinic, Larry crossed the line and knocked a policeman down. He was hauled off to jail. Sara went to the police station but was unable to get him released on bail. He was held twenty-four hours, and then Dars brought him home.

Two days after that incident she heard about the failed attempt to kidnap a doctor, not a clinic doctor, but a well-known and respected OB from Joliet. That night she asked Larry. "Did you have anything to do with this?" She pointed to the news item in the Tribune.

"Only the planning. Those simpletons screwed it up." Exactly one day later, Larry disappeared along with his blue zipper bag. Sara phoned Dars, but got no answer. She called the next day and the next. Finally she gave up. Obviously, Dars had gone into hiding along with Larry. When the news came out that a security man had been killed in a clinic in Detroit, and the FBI was beginning to questioning everyone, she immediately moved to the YWCA and the next day drove down to Urbana to stay with her friend, Fay.

As Sara relives the past, perspiration beads her forehead and trickles down her back. "Now stop it!" she admonishes herself out loud. She shivers convulsively and covers her wet, teary face with the hospital sheet when a voice penetrates her reminisces.

"Hiding from someone?" Jonathan thrusts a single tea rose under her nose, and Sara quickly sits up and grasps the hospital gown tightly at her neckline in one hand and takes the beautiful rose in the other hand.

"It's exquisite!" The delicate peach-colored bud is still tightly coiled, petals snuggly folding around each other like young cabbage leaves, or maybe lovers. She touches them with her nose. "Please thank your mother for me. I'm assuming it's from her garden?" Sara stuck the rose in her drinking glass and added more water from the plastic thermos.

"Roses are her specialty. I'm glad you appreciate it. She doesn't give them up easily, not even a single rose."

Sara looks seriously contrite. "You shouldn't have pressured her, not just for me because..."

"... I threatened to plow up her garden, cut off her hair, and steal her antique rocker." He watches as Sara bursts into laughter. He thinks how wonderful it is to see her smile so freely again. Then he sees her wince as the smile muscles in her eyes pull at her sore forehead.

"Actually, I'm fibbing. The rose came from a garden shop. I didn't have time to go home to the island. I told you all that nonsense in hopes of seeing you laugh again."

"Shame on you! To think an upright, serious history professor would fib so outrageously."

"When will they release you?"

"The doctor will let me out tomorrow just before lunch if my head continues to feel normal in the morning."

"And does it right now?" Jonathan tips her chin up to inspect the bruise. "Gorgeous colors...very abstract."

"My head has stopped pounding, and the baby has stopped wildly kicking me." Then quickly before Jonathan can interrupt or she loses courage, she adds, "I want to tell you where I went that night of the accident and some other things." Jonathan nods and sits down in the chair beside the bed.

Sara starts out her confession by telling him about the anti-abortion protests in Chicago and how it had come about that she shared the apartment with Larry. That was the hard part...telling him that she had shared a bed with another man. She wants to scrunch down in the bed even further and cover her face again, but she sits up straight. Next, she tells him about Dars and how the two men had bombed a clinic, and a security man had accidentally died.

"Did you know about it?"

"Before it happened? Oh, no. They kept it a secret. I only guessed it after both Dars and Larry disappeared, and the bombing incident appeared in the newspapers and on TV. Then I left Chicago and went to stay with a girlfriend in Urbana. When I discovered that I was pregnant I came up here to Mac Village."

"Did you ever consider an abortion?"

"No. Well, yes, when the morning queasiness seemed to go on and on, and I wondered if something was wrong with the baby." Then she added to herself, and after I met you. She pauses, afraid to take a peak at Jonathan's face to see how he is taking her confession.

"You remember when my parents visited the fort recently?" Her peripheral vision records Jonathon's nod. "I was just about to tell them about the baby when they broke the news that they were heading to England for the next nine months. My mother and father appeared so happy and excited about the trip that I couldn't spoil their plans. I didn't tell them.

"Three nights ago, Larry showed up in the parking lot and wanted me to take him up to DeTour or someplace where he could cross the channel into Canada to avoid being hunted by the FBI. I took him." Fearfully, Sara glances at Jonathan to see how he is reacting to all the revelations about her past and her recent deceit. His face looks stony, closed.

Jonathan asks, "Did you tell him about the baby?"

"No."

"Thanks for being straight with me."

"I didn't like fibbing to you."

"How about one more truth." Jonathan turns and looks intently into her face.

"What more is there to tell?" Sara feels drained, momentarily emptied of all her problematic past and so very, very tired.

"Did you love him?"

"Not enough."

"Did he want you to go with him?"

"Yes, but later, not in the canoe he had stolen. He wanted me to cross the border in the legal way and meet him somewhere if he made it across successfully."

"Will you?"

Sara never lets her eyes waver from Jonathan's face. She shakes her head.

"Not even to give your child a father?"

"I did consider it," she admits.

He glances away again. Best to disguise his reaction, since he has absolutely no right to feel one way or another about her decision. That Sara even considered going away with Larry, a fugitive, makes him simmer with unexpected anger. Or is he simply jealous that Sara would for one second contemplate choosing Larry as a father at all? With a great deal of effort he forces himself to appear neutral, the kind of stance a friend should take.

I've got a lot to digest, he thinks, and forces himself to remain calm when actually he wants to verbally rave at the man called Larry. Also, he is sorely tempted to spank Sara for her naïve manner of choosing a male friend and then slipping between the sheets with him. How could she have been so...easy? Yes, he is obviously jealous. Instead, he lets off steam by chastising Sara about something else. "Weren't you overly trusting to believe that an anti-abortion group would stick to non-violent actions?"

"Most of the people in the group were against violence, including Larry, until he became influenced by Dars. Are you going to inform the FBI about Larry?"

"I'll have to think more about it, but probably not unless the authorities should seek me out and directly ask questions about him."

Sara can sense the change between herself and Jonathan...actually feel the space expanding between them like galaxies rapidly moving further apart in the universe. Jonathan is not taking her admission the way she wishes he would. But why should he? Can she expect him to feel forgiving towards her for having slept with another man and then helping that man escape from the law? Oh how she dearly wishes circumstances could be different, so that Jonathan, the man she now believes she loves, will not be lost to her...but, of course, he *was* lost to her right from the beginning.

"Thanks, Sara, for setting the record straight. Now I must be going."

"Goodnight, Dr. Reidel." Somehow the more formal title seems appropriate now that she realizes how disappointed he must be in her character.

Jonathan snorts, "What's with the sudden formality? Goodnight, Sara." He doesn't wait for an answer, just walks out of the room.

Sara mentally follows Jonathan down the hallway. If only there could be some trail marker to lead them back to their former easy manner...their kidding and teasing...their special awareness of each other. It's too late now. But of course it has always been too late right from their very first meeting back in June. Until just a few minutes ago, she had stalled over telling Jonathan about Larry. Now she must reap the consequences, and deservedly so, of allowing herself to behave deceitfully.

What had she wanted when she first met Larry? A home...a nest to lay eggs in? Well, now she has the egg but no nest. She alone is to blame. Yet, in spite of that indisputable fact, she continues to feel sorry for herself. She curls up in the bed and hugs the pillow, wishing it were her mother's or her father's comfortable shoulder. Her whole situation seems so depressing. She covers her face with the bed sheet and quietly sobs.

The nurse will be in soon with her bevy of instruments and her bedtime glass of milk, so Sara once again begins to dab at her face to wipe away the evidence of her crying.

"Oh, I see we're in the dumps again. Your face is in danger of becoming waterlogged if you don't climb right out of that swamp. That's my advice." She gives Sara a pat on the shoulder. "That's a nice young man who keeps visiting you."

"Yes, he is." After the nurse leaves, she resumes her morose thoughts. "What will I do after leaving here? There is no one out there in the world to take care of me." Oh, she has a few distant aunts and uncles, but they aren't exactly family and not close enough to impose upon.

She keeps telling herself, you have to make some kind of plans for the baby's birth, and not keep putting it off. Perhaps one of those shelters, usually connected to a church, that give away baby equipment and sometimes even small amounts of money as well. I can try them, but won't they want information in return...possibly the father's name...a *wanted man's* name? No, I couldn't give them Larry's name.

Once again Sara considers borrowing money from Brian, her brother. He wouldn't want her moving into his apartment though, hanging around to scare off his current girlfriend. Right here, right now, in this hospital where the nurses monitor her, bring her food, and encourage her to get over the accident, is where she feels the protection she craves for herself and the baby. From now on, her life will never be as secure as it seems right now, right here.

CHAPTER TWENTY-NINE

$\mathcal{P}$at alerted Jonathan the next morning to a report from the security guard. Evidently he had discovered some minor disarray in the Trader's section of the row house in the southeast corner of the stockade.

"Could you check it out?" Pat asked, handing Jonathan an inventory of the contents of the Trader exhibit. "You'd probably know immediately if something were missing without even looking at this list, and I wouldn't."

"Sure. I'm going that direction anyway." A few minutes later Jonathan passed through the double doors of the Land Gate and veered off to the right where the Southeast Row House was located. He stepped inside the Trader's section and climbed over the Plexiglas barrier that kept the tourists from actually entering the exhibit.

Off hand he couldn't find anything missing; however, the rope bed was slightly askew as though someone had used it during the night. All anyone had to do to gain access to the bed was to climb over the railing that separated the viewers from the exhibit. It was easy enough to do since he, himself, had done exactly the same thing just minutes before. All the row houses were supposed to be locked after closing time. So how did someone get inside? Perhaps someone had already been inside hiding, and the security guard didn't check carefully before locking the door.

If someone had used the bed for sleeping, it was a mighty uncomfortable resting place since there were no springs in the bed. Also, it was shorter than contemporary beds. The average height of a man of the 1770's historic period was generally under six feet. The bed was made of intertwining rope, and there was no mattress and no bedding in the exhibit, although the pile of sample-size wool blankets was nearby, and some were unfolded, rumpled looking. There was also a stack of fur pelts that would make a good pillow, but they didn't look disturbed at all. Whoever slept there must have had a very rough night. In fact, sleeping out on the beach in the sand would have been preferable except for dampness and possibly sand fleas. Jonathan was about to double-check all the contents of the exhibit against the inventory list when Hillary came rushing up to the door. Just seconds before, Jonathan had been aware of the bell ringing from the wooden church just west of the parade ground, a signal for the marriage ceremony program to begin shortly.

Jonathan heard the sound of running feet and turned, surprised to see Hillary show-up in the doorway when he guessed she should be at the church as fill-in for Linette in the marriage reenactment. "Yes? What is it?" He noted that she was wearing the bride's costume. "You should be over at the church, shouldn't you?"

"Yes, Dr. Reidel, I'll hurry." Hillary fairly spit out her next words, "I promised to pick up Sara at noon at the hospital, but Mr. Van Hecker has rescheduled everything so I can't. Is there any chance that you or Pat...or someone could do it?"

"Yes."

"Thanks...oh, thanks heaps!"

He watched Hillary disappear from the door and sprint across the Kings Way to the church.

❖   ❖   ❖

By eleven o'clock all her hospital papers had been signed, and Sara was free to go. The hospital and doctor bills would catch up with her later. "But not late enough," she muttered sourly. While she was waiting for Hillary, she surveyed her attire wishing she had some clean clothes to wear.

She had washed her underpants and bra in the hospital sink and they had dried overnight, but the rest of her clothes were in the same state as they were the night of the accident. An ugly, bloody rip defaced one knee of the jeans, the ones she had bought just this summer. The blue shirt seemed in fairly clean condition, and she wore it loosely to cover up the top of her jeans, which she had left unbuttoned because the waist pressed uncomfortably against her stomach.

When Jonathan walked into her room instead of Hillary, she was momentarily speechless.

"Hillary's morning was rescheduled, so she couldn't come. I'm backup choice."

"Oh, I'm sorry. If I'd known, I could have taken a taxi over to pick up my car." She was about to apologize more profusely, but the nurse came into the room pushing a wheelchair. Sara carried her purse and the rosebud, its stem wrapped in a damp paper towel. As they walked down the hall, the nurse rattled off to Jonathan, probably thinking he was her husband or boyfriend, all the same admonitions Sara has heard before: watch for dizziness, too much sleepiness, cramps, bleeding, and of course severe headaches.

The nurse gave Sara an unexpected hug just before Jonathan opened the car door and helped Sara from the wheelchair into the car. As they drove away, Sara looked back and waved to the nurse who had been so solicitous during the last two days.

Sara feels her sense of security diminishing in relation to the distance Jonathan drives away from the hospital. The uncertainty of her future suddenly thuds down on her so heavily that she can barely draw a breath through her lungs. Tears begin rolling down her cheeks. She assures herself that Jonathan won't notice because his eyes will be only on his driving.

"Does everything seem that hopeless to you?" Against his better judgment, he wants to hold Sara and soothe her. He restrains himself.

"Sorry...didn't mean to be melodramatic." Sara quickly makes a swipe across her face with her hand, a figurative gesture to help herself gain control.

"You know, I don't believe you're quite ready to go back to work yet or even to drive your car. Why don't you let me drive you back to your room at the fort, and we can pick up your car tomorrow or the next day?" Before Sara can answer him, his cell phone begins bleating, and he pulls the car over to the curb in a residential area just a block from the water.

"Yes, Pat? I'll be over a bit later. I just picked up Sara from the hospital. Oh? Hold on, I'll tell her." He turns to face Sara. "Pat says some fellow with long blond hair and glasses has been asking for you."

Sara begins to tremble. "Larry," she whispers and makes a groaning sound as she bends forward holding her stomach.

In alarm, Jonathan pulls Sara over with his free arm to lean against him in the seat. Into the phone he asks, "What? No, you probably shouldn't have told him. I'll call you back in a few minutes." Jonathan quickly flips the phone shut and lets it slide down in the seat. Though the bucket seats prevent him from pulling Sara over any closer, he tries to hold her securely with one arm. "Do you have an actual pain or are you just scared? Should I take you back to the hospital?" Sara shakes her head.

"I assume that's the guy, Larry, you took somewhere north of DeTour the night you had the accident." Sara nods mutely. "What do you think he wants?"

"I don't know. Maybe he didn't make it across into Canada and..."

Sara was shaking so badly that Jonathan again considers turning the car around and rushing her back to the hospital whether she agrees or not. He tucks her head firmly under his chin and holds her as close as he can, hoping to calm her. "This guy, Larry, didn't make it into Canada so do you think he came back to get your help again? You don't have to see him."

"How can I not?" Sara lifts her chin slightly upwards to look into Jonathan's face, and his lips meet hers as easily as slipping a sheet of paper under a door. His kisses are gentle and full of unspoken tenderness.

Now you've done it, Jonathan tells himself. She has eagerly reciprocated and suddenly just kisses are no longer satisfying enough.

Now he wants to hold her on his lap, but once that happens there will be no way to stop himself from going further. He wants to probe... to explore every inch of her body...wants to be where he shouldn't. Oh lord! He has never felt such an overwhelming urge, but he isn't going to follow it. None of his hungry sexual desire is going to solve anything. He reminds himself that she has already been in that kind of situation—sex without commitment. Firmly, he tells himself to cool down. This wild need of his is just going to complicate Sara's problems. A calm basis, a stable mind is required to help her.

"I'm sorry," Jonathan's words stumbled out as he partially draws away, "I shouldn't take advantage of you while you're so upset and not well." To himself he snarls, what do you think you're doing? Nothing that I haven't wanted to do all summer, he answers himself. He looks down at the small white face with a lumpy forehead surrounded by dark hair and into the gray-green eyes and at last feels the rush of finally having her in his arms, though not the fulfillment he yearns. Now that he has started kissing her, it isn't easy to stop. It's like skidding on ice. He wishes they were off on some secluded country road instead of here in town where anyone looking out a window from one of the houses will get a free show, literally.

"Sara, I've wanted to do this all summer."

"And I wanted it to happen, but it wouldn't have been fair to you." She corrects the tense, "Isn't fair to you."

With reluctance, Sara moves her face downward out of reach of his lips. "We mustn't do this." Yet she keeps her head against his shoulder. She hates to let the moment pass, but she warns herself firmly: it must pass.

Jonathan sits quietly still holding her and thinking. Finally he asks, "Are you sure this Larry fellow didn't notice that you were pregnant the other night?"

"I doubt it. It was foggy and dark that evening when he came to the fort for help. I wore this same loose shirt and a sweater over it. No, I don't think he noticed; yet why else would he retrace his way to confront me? He's jeopardizing his chances of escaping out of the country." To herself she wonders, had he after all guessed that there was something different about me, something suspicious about my weight gain and healthy appearance? Back in her Chicago days when she had first met Larry, she had been a size six with pinched indentations beneath her cheekbones. "Oh!"

"What?"

"I left a prescription in the car glove compartment written on the gynecologist's note pad. Larry might have spotted it when he reached inside for the flashlight but thought nothing about its significance until after I dropped him off."

"Yes, that might be a possible reason for his returning. Perhaps if you stay away from your room a night or two longer, he'll simply think it's too dangerous for him to hang around, and he'll move on."

"But I can't afford to live anywhere else, even temporarily. Anyway, I would have to return eventually. Pat says they need the help. Cam and Hillary are leaving next week because of the beginning of fall semester at their universities. You'll be leaving, too."

"Yes, but you could go to Rose Cottage at least for tonight." Sara starts to ask where Rose Cottage is, but Jonathan is already groping with his free hand around in the seat for his cell phone, keeping the other hand firmly under her arm. She feels highly conscious of his hand held tightly just beneath her right breast. Jonathan rests the phone against the steering wheel and with his left hand punches in a number. After a moment someone answers.

"Mother? Jonathan. I'm here in St. Ignace. I need to bring home a guest to stay all night. Is it all right? Yes, Sara. She needs to recuperate. Thanks. Want me to stop for groceries?" He turns to Sara, "She's getting her list. Help me remember what she wants." He listens again and repeats out loud: "Oranges, chicken for stir fry, V-8 juice. Anything else? We'll catch the boat to the island right after the grocery shopping. See you." He turns back to Sara, smiling. "There, it's all taken care of."

"You didn't give your mother much chance to say, no."

"She's very adaptable. Besides, I've already told her about you."

❖ ❖ ❖

While Jonathan is in the grocery store, Sara remains in the car. She closes her eyes and basks in the warm aura of being cared for by Jonathan even if it's only temporary. So much has just taken place that she needs to absorb the implications...to relive the sensation of having Jonathan's hand under her breast. She mentally replays his kisses. Clearly they want each other, their sexual chemistry overcoming everything else...both of them forgetting reason. Later on, she warns herself, when Jonathan cools his ardor he will think things over and regret letting his common sense be overridden by sexual desires. I, however, will never regret the amazing sensations. No matter what happens from now on, I will look back and remember this day warmly...not just because of our strong physical attraction for each other but also because of the loving attention Jonathan is giving me when I feel so alone and so needy.

CHAPTER THIRTY

*T*he boat ride from St. Ignace to Mackinac Island was much shorter than the one from Mac Village to the island, only about fifteen minutes from dock to dock. Jonathan insisted that they sit below deck where Sara could be protected from the wind. They settled on a long empty bench seat near the stern, and Jonathan placed the grocery bag down between them on the bench, partly to discourage himself from fondling Sara as his urges kept compelling him. In any case he decided that he'd better rethink his precipitous behavior in the car. Now that he had let his feelings out of the cage— now that he had unleashed his intimate feelings—how could he logically return to his former position of being just a friend standing on the sidelines? One couldn't backup in a crowded tunnel either, nor completely retreat from an intimate kiss like theirs. Maybe it wasn't wise of him, but he felt no regrets over the warmth of his affection. Did Sara, he wondered?

Sara kept her head turned away from the aisle hoping no one would notice her ugly swollen forehead. Jonathan laid his arm across the back of the bench behind Sara, but he didn't try to touch her. All the same, she felt cosseted. Neither one of them make an attempt to talk over the roar of the twin engines, which were louder and more vibrating near the stern. It would have meant shouting to be heard.

Upon arriving on Mackinac Island, Jonathan left Sara briefly to search for a carriage taxi. He found one at the street end of the dock. "Andy, nice to see you. Can you take me to Rose Cottage?"

"Sure, Dr. Reidel. Hop up."

"Hold on. I have another passenger for you." Jonathan went back to collect Sara, help her up the high step into the taxi, and join her on the seat behind the driver. The two carriage horses were urged forward by Andy's voice, "Walk on."

"Andy, I thought you were driving the Island House Carriages."

"That was two years ago. Last year I switched back to taxi driving."

"How's the family?"

"Good. My wife works in the tourist bureau this summer, and Tessy, she's eighteen now, works in one of the fudge shops here on the main street. She goes to college this fall."

The taxi passed the long line of tour carriages lined up on the left side of the main street. Sara knew they were waiting for the next group of tourists to arrive off the boat from Mac Village. She watched a man carry two heavy buckets of water to the lead team of horses. As their taxi passed the park, Sara could see people sprawled on the lawn enjoying the noontime sun and eating their picnic lunches. The grass verge on the right next to the marina was filled with huge sails laid out to dry. About a block further on past Ste Anne's Church, the driver said, "Gee," and his horses swung to the right down a short dead-end lane in the direction of the water. Sara noted the sign: Primrose Lane.

"Thanks, Andy" Jonathan paid the driver, and Sara watched in awe as Andy commanded the horses by voice and slapping reigns in a series of backup and forward movements until the carriage had swung completely around in the narrow little lane. She turned and looked at Rose cottage; it appeared small and neat. The porch roof was festooned with hanging baskets of blue ageratum and red geraniums, and the tiny balcony above the front entrance was embellished with lacey wooden curlicues.

"It's a combination of Queen Anne and Cottage Stick style," Jonathan explained as they walked through the front door. "Both styles were prevalent here on the island around the 1890's and early nineteen hundreds."

Inside the narrow hallway, Sara hesitated, suddenly feeling a bit shy, but Jonathan urged her towards the rear and into the country-style kitchen where he set the groceries down on a maple-block table.

"This is my mother, Sara." Mrs. Reidel turned from the stove, and Sara noticed the voluminous apron almost as large as the one she herself wore as part of her interpreter's costume. Barely peeking out from underneath were blue cotton slacks. Immediately after greeting Sara, she took the rose from Sara's hand.

"Here, let me give it some water. You do look a bit battered and tired." She laughed, "I mean you, not the rose. Sit down, Sara."

"Thank you, Mrs. Reidel." Sara was glad she had saved the rose since flowers were important to Jonathan's mother.

"Not Mrs. Reidel; Edith will do very nicely." Sara watched her give Jonathan's shoulder a pat. Then she moved back to the stove to stir something, and while her back was turned, Jonathan pulled one of her strands of gray hair hanging loose on her neck. "Ouch. Behave, Jonathan. We have company."

"She'll get her share of teasing, too."

"Yes, well, of that I've no doubt." Edith poked the spoon at Jonathan in a mock sword thrust. "I'm quite willing to share your teasing. All right, lunch is ready. Hot Clam Chowder and egg salad sandwiches."

"Sounds good." Jonathan said, "but I have a late luncheon meeting at the Island House, so I'll be on my way. Don't run Sara around your garden too many times. She's supposed to rest. I'll be back for dinner, if you'll have me."

"Do I have a choice?" His mother shook her head and laughed.

In passing, Jonathan gently touched Sara's shoulder. "See you later. If you have any of those symptoms that the nurse mentioned: headache, cramps, or dizziness, be sure to tell my mother. We have a medical clinic here on the island for emergencies; it's one that my father helped to establish."

Sara felt dumped in a strange environment. Still, she realized that Jonathan had taken a great deal of time out from his work to rescue her. The word "grateful" could hardly express her genuine feelings, yet at the same time she was disappointed that he wasn't staying. She called after him in a formal voice, "Thank you for everything."

"Well, isn't that just like a man to run off before we've barely become acquainted. We'll have to manage on our own. First let's eat, then talk."

Sara wondered if Jonathan's mother would confront her with embarrassing questions...like "who is the father of your child?" She finished her soup and nibbled at her sandwich before the questions began.

"When is the baby due?"

"End of December or beginning of January."

"Well, those things are often indefinite...especially the first baby. Jonathan tells me that you received a huge letdown when you learned that your parents were going off to England. I presume you had planned to live with them and have the baby there. Now you must feel abandoned."

"Yes, a bit, though I had no right to expect their help." She was beginning to get sleepy again, and involuntarily her eyes blinked several times. Evidently Edith noticed because she said, "We can talk more later." I'll show you where you can rest."

Sara nodded, "First let me help with the dishes."

"No, not this time. Come along." Briskly she steered Sara to the stairs.

Sara admitted to herself, yes, it had been a traumatic morning.... learning about Larry's return...Jonathan's open admission of caring for her. Events seemed to be taking breathtaking loops of highs and lows. Now exhaustion had caught up with her, so she gladly followed Edith up the narrow stairs to the small guest room. She missed the security of her hospital bed and the nurse's care, but this small room looked cozy with its slanted ceiling making up one wall. The single window faced the small back yard and the garden.

"Now I have a good idea." Edith said. "Let me find a large T-shirt for you to wear to bed, and then I can wash those jeans for you."

"No, please..."

"...it's no problem because I haven't done this week's wash yet. Everything will be dry by the time you wake up. The blood of course won't come out around the knee, but you'll feel better with clean clothes." Edith disappeared into the next room and quickly returned with one of Jonathan's white T-shirts. "Here, try this. The bathroom is next door. Just put all your clothes in the hamper."

Sara brushed her teeth with the hospital toothbrush and the small tube of toothpaste they had given her, noting that it wouldn't last long, but by tomorrow she would have her own again. Oh, tomorrow! That's when she would have to go back to facing up to...whatever. The T-shirt reached halfway down to her bruised knee, the left one. It was the same knee that had been banged against the police van back in Chicago. She neatly folded her jeans and blue shirt and dropped them inside the hamper.

On her way back to the guest room, Sara took a quick glance into Jonathan's room. It seemed fairly large and meticulously neat except for the sprawl of books on the floor next to the bedside table. The room was almost totally lined with bookshelves except for the space taken up by the bed and the window that apparently faced the water. Returning to the guest room, she cuddled down in the bed under the heavy white matelasse spread and almost instantly fell asleep.

The next thing Sara was cognizant of was a light knock on her door.

"Sara? Jonathan was just on the phone and wanted me to check up on you. It seems that the nurse at the hospital advised him to make sure you weren't sleepy because of the concussion."

Sara stirred, but at first didn't recognize where she was until her eyes focused on Jonathan's mother standing beside the bed. "My head feels fine...no headache. Tell him I'm quite all right."

"Good. It's four-thirty. I'll put your clean clothes right here on this chair so you can get dressed. I want to show you my garden before I begin cooking supper."

"Thank you." As she dressed, Sara discovered that Mrs. Reidel had put a hot patch on the jeans to hold the two sides of the rip at the knee together, and though there were still some bloodstains, which now looked more like splashes of dried brown gravy, the jeans were at least more presentable than before. Sara reminded herself, "I'll have to make another visit to the Salvation Army Store, at least a size twelve this time." Maybe they even have some baby equipment. She had already made a list of all the things she would need, and it seemed overwhelming: crib, car seat, stroller, and on and on.

Edith's garden had raised beds, four in all, with a brick walk between each plot. The rose section lacked color this late in the season, but still a few pale yellow buds were left. The other areas held larkspur, pink cone flowers, hollyhocks, and a variety of mums One garden plot seemed confined to herbs: sage, thyme, mint and many others that Sara wasn't able to identify.

"This is lovely." Sara said, meaning it sincerely."

"Flowers are for people to enjoy and to raise their spirits. I'm going to cut some for our dinner table." First, Edith bent over and began snipping-off several wilted daisy heads, then looked up. "Here's Jon already."

"Hello, ladies." Jonathan circled his mother with his arms and gave her a squeeze.

"Is it that late? Time to get supper started." Edith quickly cut the last three roses, then disappeared through the back door with her bouquet.

"You look rested and your forehead has changed into lighter sunset colors." Jonathan looked down at Sara's neatly patched jeans. "I see my mother has been at work. She's good at fixing."

"She's been very kind. I slept all afternoon."

"Feel like a short walk down to the water?" Sara nodded and they strolled back through the garden and across a grassy area to the shore where the water splashed up against the wooden bulkheads.

"Did you go to the mainland? Has anyone seen Larry again?" Sara asked.

Jonathan nodded his head. "I checked it out again and it looked like some transient had been sleeping in the Trader's House. It could have been Larry, I suppose."

"He's going to hang around until I show up." Sara folded her arms tightly around her stomach as if to protect her baby. "He's going to stay and claim the baby as his."

Jonathan resisted the urge to hold her in his arms and comfort her. He could see how desperately she needed calming, but he was trying to prevent himself from becoming sexually aroused again. He barely succeeded. It was a losing battle. His hand gently turned her head and he gave her a kiss under her left ear. "If Larry finds you, surely you wouldn't go with him to Canada?"

"Shouldn't I?"

"No." Jonathan bites down hard on the word. "Not unless you love him enough to spend your life with him."

"No, I don't." Once she might have settled for Larry's constancy, his reliability. No longer.

"Dinner, you two," Edith called from the backdoor. "Stir Fry is best while it's hot."

CHAPTER THIRTY-ONE

*T*he dinner at Rose Cottage ends in a dessert of apricot pie, tangy and delicious. Soon after the dishes are washed and dried, Jonathan's mother suggests, "Let's take a walk up to the point. How about it, Sara, if you aren't too tired?"

"Some time this evening I'll need to catch up on reports," Jonathan explains, "but I'll go along to keep you ladies out of trouble."

"Pay no attention to his teasing. How about it, Sara?" Edith asks again.

Sara nodded her consent, though truthfully she felt more like going to bed early.

Jonathan leaned his computer against the oak newel post at the bottom of the stairs and joined them at the front door. They set off at a leisurely pace in an easterly direction. Near the point, a quarter mile from Rose Cottage, there were benches along the path, and Sara gratefully plunked herself down to rest.

"I expect you'll get your energy back in a few days, Sara. Just don't push yourself too hard," Edith advises kindly, though unthinkingly, since she was the one who urged Sara into taking the walk.

After watching the antics of the shore ducks and geese, they made their way back to Primrose Lane. Upon reaching the cottage, Jonathan suggested that Sara sleep-in the next morning while he checked on the repairs done to one of the exhibits inside the island fort. Then, right after lunch they could take the boat over to St. Ignace.

Sara nodded her agreement. In fact, she needed no urging to sleep late and delay her return to the mainland. She was looking for any excuse to avoid returning to Mac Fort. The longer she stayed away, the greater the chance that Larry would give up waiting for her and move on.

"At St. Ignace we'll stop at the State Police Barracks to find out where they've stashed your car. Right now I must get a bit of work done." Jonathan gave his mother a brief kiss on her forehead, and hugged Sara as he passed on his way to the stairs.

There was an old foot pedal organ in the parlor, and Sara asked if she could try playing it. Jonathan's mother nodded, "Of course you can, if it works at all. It's one of Jon's derelicts. He says he's saving it from being dumped. Personally I think he just can't bear to throw anything away...period."

"Like me." Sara whispers despairingly to herself, not meaning Edith to hear.

Edith glances up from her book. "That's different," she chuckles. "I suspect he thinks your legs are a bit more curvaceous than those on any piece of furniture."

Maybe, Sara disagrees silently. To test whether the antique stool is strong enough to hold her, she sits down carefully, noting that each clawed foot on the stool holds a glass ball in its clutches. She tries some of the simple hymns from a book leaning up against the fancy slanted music holder. The bellows of the organ leak air badly, and at one point make pitiful wailing sounds like a hurt animal. Exactly the way I feel sometimes, Sara agrees. I want to wail, not in pain, but for being trapped in this situation, this pregnancy. Otherwise, maybe I could be free to be part of Jonathan's life. She touches her stomach. Poor little babe...so wanted, yet so inconvenient. Finally she gives up trying to play the organ because she is growing too sleepy. She realizes that the antique clock on the mantel with a tin face chimes only eight times. It's still quite early.

"If you don't mind, I'll go off to bed now."

"You are excused. Obviously you are still feeling the trauma of the accident. Would you like something to read...something not too stimulating?" Sara nods. "Over there in that bookcase are some novels, and I particularly recommend those written by Anita Brookner or Edith Wharton. Both are excellent authors, but you won't be kept awake by dare-devil plots."

Sara picks out a book of short stories by Brookner and bids Edith, "Goodnight. Thank you for the clean laundry and mending. Thank you for everything."

"You're most welcome. Goodnight. There's an extra blanket in the closet if you need it."

An hour later Sara is still sitting up in bed half dozing with the book still open, when Edith taps on her door. She enters, carrying a glass of warm milk. "Doctor's orders."

Sara smiles groggily. "You mean Dr. Edith's orders."

"Right," Edith admits. She sets the cup down on the bedside table and checks to see if the window is open. "That window always sticks." She gives the bottom jamb a good smack with her fist, opens it a crack, and pulls the shade part way down.

"Thank you. I love the sound of the waves and the smell of water."

"Goodnight, Sara."

After Edith leaves the room, Sara firmly warns herself not to get too addicted to attention. Very soon she will be on her own again. When Edith and Jonathan think more thoroughly about getting mired in someone else's problems, their interest will surely fade, and they'll distance themselves, albeit in a kindly manner. Especially Jonathan. That's the way he operates, carefully, gently, so that he doesn't hurt people.

For now, she sips her milk slowly, savoring the care she is being given right here. Tomorrow she'll be on her own once again. She sets the empty cup on the bedside table and begins to settle down under the covers when she senses Jonathan's presence in the doorway of the room.

"Goodnight, Dear Sara." He comes over to the bed and places a light kiss on her forehead. It's a brotherly kiss, but what right does she have to expect anything more demonstrative when clearly she has been another man's woman, a pregnant one as well. Yet she wants so much more than just a brotherly peck on her forehead.

"Goodnight. Thanks for bringing me here. You've been so kind."

"Why so formal? It's easy being kind to someone like you." Gently, he tucks the covers up around her shoulders and leaves the room.

❖ ❖ ❖

Sara and Jonathan exchanged very little talk on the boat to St. Ignace the next noon, though Jonathan does ask her what she thinks of his mother and she enthusiastically responds, "She's wonderful. Is she always so upbeat?"

"Yes, just like me." He makes a clown's cheery face, then immediately becomes serious again. "Do you really feel able to drive?"

Sara assures him that she feels fine, though to herself she admits being nervous about getting back behind the wheel again. At the police station she signs for the release of her car, and they are directed to Harry's filling station.

Harry shakes his head as they all stand around staring at Sara's car, which looks like it has recently been in a junk car race and lost. The right front headlight is smashed inwards by the impact with the dirt bank, and a large portion of the grill is completely missing. As Sara gropes in her purse for her checkbook to pay the wrecker fee, Jonathan hands Harry some bills. He tells Sara, "You can reimburse me later."

Harry advises her to buy a new headlamp at Sears or Walmart and ask them to install it. "Until then, you can't do any driving after dark or you'll be fined."

"I'll follow you across the bridge," Jonathan tells Sara, "then if either the car or you break down, I can phone for help."

Harry waves to them as they drive off the lot.

Driving again feels strange and Sara almost panics. She assumes that anyone who has ever been in an accident probably feels just as nervous as she does. Staunchly, she grips the wheel, but too tightly and keeps over-correcting her steering. "I wonder," she asks herself, talking out loud, "if the wheels have been thrown out of kilter from the twisting action of the car hitting the bank of dirt…just another thing to spend money on until not a penny is left for the baby. It's all so hopeless."

She arrives in the parking lot at the fort feeling a little heady, but pleased with herself for persevering. Actually at one point in the middle of the bridge where the huge towers soared overhead, making her feel small and precarious, she had thought of ditching the car and running. Not that anyone is allowed to park a car on the bridge. No way. The Bridge Authority would likely assume she was going to either attempt suicide or maybe plant a bomb.

After making certain that Sara arrived safely in the parking lot at the cabins nearby, Jonathan waved to her and disappeared into the office while she unlocked her room to change into her costume. She drew her bangs down as far as she could to cover the ghoulish looking bump. No sense in scaring the tourists. "Now if it were Halloween, my purple bump would be stunningly appropriate."

At the row house kitchen, Ansel is polite but doesn't greet her with any enthusiasm or even ask questions about her accident. Sara notices that Ansel has taken down the dusty bunches of dried corn and onions from the rafters and tied up fresh ones. As usual, Sara does most of the toting of water and lifting of logs into the fireplace. The bending over makes her head feel slightly dizzy, so she braces herself with one hand against the stone chimney and drops each log almost directly down on the fire, which causes clouds of gray ash to rise up and outward into the room; after that, she needs to sweep up the ashes from the floor.

Nervously, Sara looks out the window of the row house kitchen. At any minute she expects to see Larry pop out from behind the church or the French Trader's House and this anticipation keeps her constantly on edge. Her pulse seems to be pinging at a more rapid rate.

Tourist participation is down this week but expected to soar next week, the week before Labor Day. Ansel isn't doing any baking this week or much cooking either, so carrying logs from the dwindling stack beside the Soldiers' Barracks to feed the fire is less burdensome than usual. Occasionally, Ansel even carries a log or two.

Ansel tells her, "The garden hasn't been touched since you've been away. So would you do it?" Sara knows that it isn't really a question. She still can't bend over without her head feeling slightly foggy, so she accomplishes only the hoeing part. "Maybe tomorrow I'll feel like stooping over to retrieve the loose weeds and toss them into a basket." The beans, attached to poles, are unbelievably tall...tall enough to hide behind if she should sight Larry while she's working in the garden. He will eventually show up, she's certain. When she finishes hoeing, she picks enough of the sturdy long beans for herself and some to give to Pat and Hillary.

Sara doesn't see Jonathan the next day. It's more or less as she's been pessimistically warning herself. With time to think over his intimate fondling of her in the car on the day of her release from the hospital, Jonathan now regrets his actions. As a consequence, he's trying to distance himself from her as gently as he can without being cruel.

"I understand perfectly," she tells him as though he is standing right there before her. "It's inevitable." Just thinking about her lonely situation causes shallowness in her breathing; each breath must be forced in and out like a bellows. In spite of the fact that she has no right to any attention from Jonathan, there is still that expecting... that waiting for something momentous to happen. It's as though a special concert that one has planned to attend is cancelled, but the tickets are still held in hand. There's an imprint somewhere in the mind's tangled wiring system that's difficult to change. A deep sense, obviously prompted by wishful thinking, tells her that her association with Jonathan is unresolved. Yet, logic strongly disagrees. Logic tells her that the end of their togetherness is imminent.

The second day after returning from Rose Cottage, she finds a brief note that had been slipped under her door. *See you this coming weekend. Jonathan.* Now she recalls that he did say something about helping with college registration. That explains his absence. She feels almost exhilarated. He has thought enough about her to let her know that he's going to be away for a few days. She tells herself that this attention is more than she deserves…in fact *more* than she should ever expect in the future. Just having him as a close friend will have to suffice. She feels a sob rising in her chest. "Friend." It's what she must get used to…and accept.

She writes a short note of thanks to Mrs. Reidel for her hospitality at Rose Cottage. Edith had made her feel comfortable with absolutely no uneasiness over harboring her, a stranger. Neither had there been any narrow-minded advice, not even a hint that she should sever her association with her son, Jon, even though she, Sara, was burdened with another man's child.

CHAPTER THIRTY-TWO

*D*uring the remainder of the week Sara allows her mind to think just far enough ahead to get her work done and no further. No more wandering in a maze of thoughts about Jonathan. Absolutely forbidden, she warns herself. She is able to get the headlight on her car fixed, but the car still looks ratty and the steering still tends to pull to the right. She is ashamed of the car's derelict appearance, but she can't afford to have the broken grill repaired or the fender popped out.

In her head she has written the letter to Brian over and over again asking him for his help. She dreads writing the actual letter, but she can't put it off any longer. Tomorrow for sure, she promises herself.

Four days from now is the annual Bridge Walk. She wonders if Jonathan will return and come over to the Northwest Row House kitchen to look for her, or will he begin the process of ignoring her that she's been expecting all along?

Larry hasn't shown up during the first two days after her return from Rose Cottage on the island, so she becomes less and less cautious. With relief, she decides, "I can relax. He has long ago moved on." Then, on Friday, Sara sees someone hovering just outside the window of the row house kitchen, and a sharp pain of stress springs into her stomach. She considers slipping out the north door and escaping, but Larry has already spotted her through the window.

He looks more than ever like a derelict, a street person. Besides his long hair and whiskers, he has a pulled seam in the shoulder of his jacket, and his visor cap is stained with sweat. It's very likely that he's the person rumored to have been sleeping in the trader's cabin.

His hair looks clean enough, though. Perhaps he bathes in the lake water just outside the fort after it closes in the evening and the beach is empty of people.

Rather than hold a conversation with Larry in front of Ansel, she steps outside the row house door. It's cooler this week so both windows to the kitchen are closed, and she hopes Ansel can't overhear their conversation.

"There you are!" Larry exclaims. " I've been waiting for you. Are you all right? That woman in the office said you'd been in a minor accident."

Sara pushes aside her bangs so that Larry can see the bluish colors still apparent on her forehead. "Why did you come back?"

"The prescription in the glove compartment hinted at... Well, I came back to tell you that I know you're pregnant. The baby...it must be mine. If you had told me, I'd have found some way to meet you in Canada right away, and we could have been married. We still can do that." He smiles eagerly, "though we may have to survive on your earnings for a while."

Sara prepares herself to fudge the truth, yet to lie coldly to Larry is not easy. He had been the kindly person who cared for her in the past, placing her comfort before his own. She still retains a loyalty towards him, yet not enough to follow him to Canada.

"I met another man after you left Chicago. I love him and want to marry him." That statement, as far as it goes, is no lie.

"I don't believe you! " Larry takes a step towards her. "You're just saying that to get rid of me. If it's my child I have a right to be its father! Is it? Answer me!" The scowl on his face was menacing as though he intended to take a swipe at her. Instead, he grabbed her by the shoulders and began to shake her until she saw everything swirling about her like fog on the night of the accident. She gasps and bends completely over. Disorientated; she staggers.

"Shall I call security?" a voice shouted.

In spite of her reeling head, Sara realized the blur standing in the doorway with a fireplace shovel raised in her hand must be Ansel.

Larry immediately released his hold on Sara and stepped back in surprise.

Sara managed to put a hand out, a signal for Ansel to stop. "Go, Larry, before someone turns you in." Sara meant "turn him in to the FBI" for what he and Dars had done in Detroit. Larry understood her meaning though Ansel could certainly not have. He turned and started to leave. "I don't believe you." He threw the words back over his shoulder. She watched him thread his way between the Soldiers' Barracks and the shuttered Blacksmith Shop and then disappear.

Sara drew up her apron to cover her face and continued to stand frozen to the same spot for several minutes. She could feel herself shaking. Ansel surprised her by gently touching her shoulder. "Thank you, Ansel; I appreciate what you just did."

"That guy had a shovel coming to him. God! I thought he was going to shake your head off." Ansel turned and stepped back into the doorway of the row house. "It's almost quitting time and that fog is rolling back in again. Why don't you leave early. I'll straighten up things here in the kitchen."

Sara nodded feebly, then made her way almost blindly to the Priest's Gate. All she wanted to do was lie down immediately so her head could feel better. But where? She stopped in front of the Priest's little house. It was the end of the day so most of the tourists had left. Why not rest here for a few minutes. Sara dropped down on the narrow bed and pulled the checked curtains across so no one would see her.

Her teeth are still chattering and her head continues to whirl. The mattress feels lumpy and smells mildewed too. Probably it was old. It doesn't matter. All she wants to do is lie still until her head feels clearer. In a few minutes, she tells herself, I'll go back to my room. Larry will surely have left the area by then.

❖ ❖ ❖

It was Hillary who found Sara sleeping in the Priest's House, and just in time. The security guard was nearing the end of his evening lockup routine. He had just reached the church doors and was about to finish up with the last row of houses located on the north quadrant of the fort including the Priest's House.

Hillary shook Sara gently. "Wake up, Sara."

"Oh, where am I?"

"You fell asleep in the Priest's House and the security guard is about to lock-up for the night.

"Oh, I never meant to fall asleep." Then she remembered what had happened: Larry had shaken her and she had felt completely disorientated. She reached for her shoes. "Guess I still feel tired."

"You need a keeper. Someone to look after you when Cam and I are gone. Hillary sat down beside her. How could you sleep on this lumpy mattress anyway?"

Sara decided not to tell Hillary about Larry. There was no need now. He was gone, probably for good. Her head felt better and her hands were no longer shaking. "Thanks for finding me in time. The windows are sealed so what would I have done if I had been locked inside?"

"Well," Hillary began to poke around, "there's a potty here in this lower cupboard."

"Saved!"

"Come-on, sleepyhead. Cam's waiting to go to dinner.'

CHAPTER THIRTY-THREE

"You'll write after we leave, won't you?" Hillary pleads. "It's our last week here at the fort." She, Cam, and Sara have met as usual in the community kitchen to share their dinners. Cam, too, claimed he'd like to know how Sara is getting along now that half of the employees in the fort were going back to college or university.

"Yes, I'll write; maybe you'll let me know if you actually learn to speak Spanish?" Sara teases, remembering Hillary's joke about the "wet floor" sign written in Spanish in the Burger King restaurant. Hillary had pretended to Cam that she understood Spanish and he'd fallen for it...even been extremely impressed by his sister's knowledge. He hadn't noticed on the bottom of the sign in smaller print the English words: *Wet Floor*

Both Hillary and Cam are planning to return to their same jobs in the stockade next summer, but Sara tells them that she'll come back only to visit. She doesn't explain why, though Hillary keeps picking at her to come clean about her mysterious plans.

In the evenings Sara is busy letting out the seams on a pale pink costume made of sateen material to wear as the bride in the re-enactment of the wedding ceremony in Ste. Anne's church. The costume is too plain for a wedding dress, so lace is being added to the neckline and also to the long tapered sleeves. Sewing by hand takes a lot of time and a lot of patience, something Sara doesn't have much of right now.

So far there's been no second return of Larry, so Sara becomes more carefree over being seen out in the open areas such as the parade ground. With relief she decides, "I can relax. He has long ago moved on.

❖ ❖ ❖

During her lunch break, Ansel hurried to the office looking for Pat. She heard Pat discussing something about sorting files with Mrs. Petri in the inner office. Ansel tapped nervously on the counter to get Pat's attention. When Pat finally came to the front desk. Ansel plunked down a newspaper on the counter. "Look at this!"

"So? It's yesterday's paper from the Canadian Soo."

"Look carefully at that picture. It's Sara's guy, isn't it?"

"What makes you think so? It's hard to tell who he is. He's so waterlogged."

"You wouldn't look too healthy either if you'd been hauled out of the water all shrunken-faced and covered with blood suckers. I'm sure it's Sara's guy."

Pat handed the newspaper back to Ansel. "How can you be positive that it's the same person or even a man?"

Ansel gave the picture a poke. "That's him all right; I'm sure. He's the guy who nearly shook her into another concussion."

"What if he's not, and you get her all upset for nothing? I've seen the fellow too, but this picture sure doesn't look much like him." Pat shivered and quickly read: *This unknown man was found floating between Neebish Island on the U.S. side and St. Joseph Island on the Canadian side of the border.*

"Others have tried that. The current's too swift."

"If you came over here to ask me to break the bad news to Sara; well, forget it."

"So who *is* going to tell her?"

Pat shook her head, then grabbed a yellow highlighter from a pencil holder and leaned across the counter and whispered in Ansel's ear so that Mrs. Petri wouldn't overhear the conversation: "Circle the article with this highlighter pen and leave the newspaper on your kitchen counter. Let her discover the news for herself. That way neither one of us will look like 'bad news mongers'."

"Yeah, at least you won't. Otherwise it's not a bad idea." Ansel left the office, letting the screen door slam with a bang.

❖ ❖ ❖

It was late afternoon when Sara hesitated long enough to read the highlighted article from the newspaper. She noticed how carefully Ansel had placed a rock on the newspaper to keep it from blowing off the counter every time a tourist opened a door and passed through. Obviously, people were meant to read it. Just anybody? Sara picked up the paper and noticed the picture of Larry immediately.

Ansel watched Sara quickly scan the article and waited for her to show some sign of acknowledging that the dead man was Larry, but Sara said nothing. She simply headed for the door taking the newspaper with her. She called back to Ansel, "I'll clean up the floor later."

Sara tries to tell herself that Larry's death, and there's no doubt that the drowned person is Larry, is a huge relief. But it isn't so easy to cancel feelings towards someone who has been a part of one's life for over a year. "Dead." She says it out loud and feels the chill of the freezing water rising around her.

Shouldn't she feel deep remorse...and a lot more guilt than she does? Surely it must be wrong to feel only chilled. All that remains seems to be out and out relief. She remembers the times in the past when she had felt such gratefulness for Larry's friendly help that she seriously considered marrying him. It wasn't that she had ever quite reached the point of wildly, sexually, coveting him. No, never.

She tries to get the sequence of events clear in her own mind: Dars had moved in to sleep on the sofa. Under the influence of Dars, Larry had allowed himself to become twisted in the wrong direction. Very soon even her mildest interest in sharing the bed with Larry had ceased...that was right after learning that he and Dars were using terrorist tactics against the abortion clinics. Then came the terrible event in Detroit, after which both men disappeared. Now, Larry was dead, and she ought to feel far more deeply over the loss.

What a relief to walk so freely down to her favorite spot by the shore and not constantly look behind her for Larry. She sits down for a few minutes to think over what it means to no longer have a stalker, real or imagined. Now she will never again have the worry and dread of his return...or the fear of his snatching the baby away from her after its birth.

Having to lie to Larry about the baby had at first given her a feeling of deep disgust for herself. After all, he is, was, the baby's father. Then she reminds herself, well, part of what I told him wasn't a lie. I did find someone else to love...Jonathan. Now Larry will never know where the truth ends and the lie begins. Nor will he know that her relationship with Jonathan can never develop beyond friendship. After a time, even that may fade out like paint mixed with too much thinner.

Oh, how she yearns for more than just being on the periphery of Jonathan's life. She literally pulsates when she thinks of him touching her on her breasts, her thighs...in all the delicate places waiting to be satisfied. But those sensual cravings are only a portion of what draws her to him like a magnet. There's his caring for people, his genuine thoughtfulness. Naturally, he can't be completely free of prejudice anymore than she. It occurs to her that one of his greatest imperfections, strictly from her own point of view of course, might be his inability to forgive a woman for a previous live-in arrangement.

"Dear Jonathan," she whispers the words softly, remembering his recent kindness in taking her to Rose Cottage to recuperate. She fears that eventually, after letting her past history with Larry properly soak into his mind, he will keep his distance even after finding out that Larry is now dead.

She has forgotten how long she has been sitting there by the shore when Ansel comes out of the Water Gate and looks down the beach in her direction.

"I'm over here," Sara calls.

"I'll close up. You can do the floor tomorrow."

"Thanks." More and more Ansel is acting like the friend Sara hoped she would become when she first arrived here back in June.

Instead of going back to her room, Sara turns further along the shore away from the Water Gate. Unfailingly, the water always draws her and soothes her. In fact the beach has always been her escape, even back in Chicago. Today, more than ever, she needs the privacy to gain perspective over Larry's death…over her own strange mixed feelings of relief and sorrow.

As she sits there on the shore, Sara begins to notice the remarkable change all about her. Above her the sun beams down warmly from a blue sky. Out across the water a cloud of fog unrolls, a heavy carpet of gray making its way slowly across the water towards her. First it envelops the bridge, but leaves the very tops of the towers peeking free. When she looks westerly up the shore, she can see the white feathery fingers of fog touching branches of the trees and high gables on the old cottages, yet the sun continues to beam down where she herself is sitting. Nature is being whimsical. She tells herself how much more appreciative she would be of the phenomenon except for her depression over her circumstances. Minutes later the fog withdraws, rolling itself up as neatly as if it had been a window shade.

She wishes there were someplace, a retreat, in which to vanish. It isn't the first time that she has longed for anonymity. How will she ever be able to blot out the closed eyes, the shrunken face, of Larry as he looks in death? She knows that it isn't going to keep his ghost from confronting her conscience over and over again.

As she reaches the street, she stops again and looks both ways. Then she remembers, "There is no longer any need to scurry around with Larry's shadow at my back…not ever again. The stopping, the constant checking; it's an ingrown habit," she tells herself. "Yet how can I be so callous as to completely wipe him out of my mind?" Remorse visits her again, and a few tears run down her face.

"Maybe I can quickly shuck my costume and drive off somewhere. A change of scenery sometimes helps. But what then? I can't stay away forever. I have a job, a job I need now more than ever."

CHAPTER THIRTY-FOUR

*A*round four-thirty, Jonathan has nearly reached Mac Village. He's tired, though it has been only a little over three hundred miles to Mac Village from Western Michigan University. He fights every mile as though each mile is a human adversary trying to keep him from reaching his destination. His real destination is Sara.

He pictures her as whole and lovely, even though her dark hair doesn't quite cover the huge black and blue mark on her forehead. Four days ago when he had left, the blue had lightened considerably, and acted more as a highlight to her gray-green eyes than as a blot on her face.

Her hair is longer than when she first arrived from Chicago back in June, but it still hangs straight except for the very ends, which now curve slightly and hug up to her slim neck. He feels heat generate throughout his body as he recalls that day in the car near the hospital when they each had been forced to reign-in their sexual needs after momentarily allowing them to slip out of hand.

Why hadn't he told her how important she was to him before? Why hadn't he spoken up firmly...given her the benefit of his advice against running off to Canada after Larry? Because at first, he had wanted her to make the right choice completely uninfluenced by him.

After her accident, Sara had seemed afraid of Larry...even wanted to avoid him entirely. But does she still feel that way or in the meantime has she changed her mind? Then exactly when she needed guidance the most to strengthen her resolve against following after Larry, he'd had to leave to fulfill his registration duties at the university. Since Sara had no cell phone, he had no contact with her except through Pat. Knowing intuitively how Pat felt about him, he was wary of using her as a go-between, except of course for fort business.

For all he knows, Sara may have changed her mind while he's been away and followed Larry to Canada. How was he to stop her? Of course, whether she goes to Canada with Larry or not is ultimately her decision, a rash, careless one, but none-the-less hers. Maybe she's past any influencing.

What if she's already done something foolish? He couldn't have stopped her since he isn't even there and hasn't been for over four days. "What if she still has too strong an allegiance to Larry...too strong to sever? After all, he cruelly reminds himself, she and Larry had lived as husband and wife.

Would she run off to Canada to live as a fugitive just because of some ill-formed, out-dated, sense of duty...her duty to the unborn child to make sure it had its natural father? Didn't she understand what an unstable future she would be leading the child into...as well as herself?

Now, belatedly, he has this terrible urgency to make sure she hasn't changed her mind and rushed off to Canada. His brain feels knotted by his effort to decide what is the proper way to persuade her, that is, if he isn't already too late. Openly, forthrightly, of course. It's the only way. This time he will speak up. He won't hold back. He doesn't want to let Sara drift away from him, not ever.

In his irritation at himself and his need for haste, he lets the car accelerate well above the speed limit. A State Trooper finally stops him on the highway near the town of Gaylord. Another delay; again, it's his fault.

Fifty-five miles later, he can see the bridge towers peeking above the trees, and he takes the exit closest to the fort. He pulls into the parking lot beside the cabins, but doesn't bother to lock the car doors. He hastens through the back gates of the fort to reach the Northwest Row House kitchen. There, he finds only Ansel. She is sweeping the ashes back into the cobblestone fireplace, getting everything straighten up in the kitchen before the end of the day.

Without turning completely around or waiting for Jonathan to ask, she says, "Sara had some bad news which upset her so I told her to leave early."

Thank God; at least Sara is here in the fort or somewhere nearby. He's relieved.

"That was kind of you, Ansel." Perhaps Ansel isn't quite as selfish as he presumes. That thought gives him an unexpected uplift towards humanity in general. But he doesn't dwell on it. He's in a hurry. "Can you tell me what the 'bad news' is?"

Ansel turns around to face him. "That guy, Larry, the one who hung around here asking about her…he's dead, drowned. He was trying to swim across into Canada."

"Where?"

"Between some U.S. Island and Canada. I can't remember the names of the islands. Anyway, Sara took the newspaper with her, a Canadian paper."

"Thanks, Ansel." He thinks he knows where Sara will run off to when she's upset, so he hurries to the Water Gate. In past times when Sara felt the need to calm herself, she had huddled down by the shore, her skirt ballooning out like one of his mother's blue hollyhocks. He looks carefully up and down the beach. She isn't there after all, only some children flinging pebbles at the gulls.

Just how upset is she over Larry's death? Everyone has a right to mourn the death of a friend; well, Larry was quite a bit more than just a friend. Sara and Larry were living as husband and wife. He supposes it isn't even proper to disturb Sara at a time like this. At least the death of Larry will unscramble Sara's mind enough so that she can now focus on one goal at a time. How thoughtless he is behaving in his haste to claim Sara's attention for himself. He reprimands himself. How unkind!

After looking throughout the fort for Sara, Jonathan begins to feel even more uneasy. Now that she has no reason to follow Larry, will she simply pack-up and disappear anyway? Will she run off without a final goodbye to anyone? Being upset and pregnant, many girls might do exactly that. Yet, he knows Sara's not the type to let people down. Pat is depending upon her now that so many employees have gone back to school.

He opens the office door and asks Pat if she's seen Sara. Pat shakes her head, so he then decides to exit out the back door of the office to check Sara's room, a thing he should have done immediately upon arriving, except he now realizes that he's behaving a bit addled.

❖ ❖ ❖

As Sara nears the corner of the office on her way to her room, she again pats her face to dry up the wet runnels on her cheeks. Her mind replays and replays a picture of Larry trying to buck the swift current to reach dry land. She clearly sees his sodden face as he floats on his back, hopelessly, ready to give up the struggle. Thank God his eyes are closed in the photograph. The newspaper picture brings on more tears. Again, she dabs at her face in case she should meet someone coming or going from the cabin rooms.

Avoiding the office, Sara turns the corner of the building and sees someone, a woman wearing a straw hat sitting in a plastic chair just outside her room door. The woman raises her head, and Sara recognizes Edith, Jonathan's mother. Perhaps Mrs. Reidel is waiting for her son to return since his room is just a few doors away.

"Hello, how are you?" Sara asks politely as she crosses the cement alleyway, and approaches Mrs. Reidel. "If you're looking for your son, he might be somewhere inside the fort." Sara gives her cheeks a final wipe to make sure she's left no trace of tears.

"No. It's really you I want to see. Pull up another chair. Take that one outside of Jon's room. He won't mind," Edith laughs, "anyway, he doesn't sit down that long at a time. I have a serious proposal to make to you."

Sara slides the white plastic chair closer to Mrs. Reidel, all the time trying to guess what brings her here. As far as she knows, this is the first time Jonathan's mother has visited the fort all summer.

In her usual forthright manner and without preamble, Edith begins, "When you finish the season working here, I want you to come over to Rose cottage on the island and stay with me until the baby comes, unless of course, you've already made alternate arrangements. It gets lonely over there on the island in the fall after Jon goes back to teaching, and I could use the company."

Sara gulps in astonishment. "You would do that for me?"

"What's so strange about that? I have an empty house and you need a place to stay. It's as simple as that."

"But you always go to Florida in the fall."

"So, I'll just go a little late. Jonathan tells me that he thinks you have limited funds and I doubt that you can find a job during your last few months of pregnancy. No doubt your parents will return in the spring and help you out."

Tears start to make new trails down Sara's face. Such kindness! She's at a loss to express her gratefulness...her astonishment at the generous offer. With no hanky available, Sara wipes her eyes with the corner of her long white apron. "Thank you, thank you...but maybe Jonathan won't feel the same way."

"Same way about what?" Jonathan demands as he quickly joins the two women. He has found Sara at last. What a relief!

"Mother, what have you been telling her that makes her cry?" It isn't like his mother to upset anyone, but Sara is in a fragile state right now. She has yet to recover from the car accident and now there's also Larry's death. He notices that Sara's eyes are still wet. He touches Sara gently on the shoulder. He tells his mother, "Sara's already faced one mountain today."

"So now I'm a mountain?" Edith laughs. "I assume she's crying because she's happy, not sad." Edith gives Jonathan a defiant look. "I've invited her to stay in my house over on the island for a while until the baby comes."

What a sweet mother he has...a prescient one too. She has unselfishly done what he himself has wanted to do ever since learning about the baby. Yet, he has let all sorts of mental roadblocks get in his way while his mother has no false boundaries to slow her down.

Jonathan chastises himself: At first I held back my love because of my prudishness…also my jealousy. What a slow pedestrian learner I am, he admits to himself. Not his mother, though; her unselfish idea of giving Sara a temporary home is typical of her kindness.

Long ago he had instinctively wanted to gather Sara in…to protect her. Yet, until just recently, he had believed Sara still held sentimental feelings for the baby's father even though he was on the *wanted* list for blowing up an abortion clinic. That Sara might still feel something for Larry, left Jonathan twisting in two directions: Just how much loyalty did she retain for Larry? Was the subject moot now that Larry was dead?

In the past few hours, he has nearly convinced himself that Sara, having gone through so many adverse experiences, might never want to have another close relationship…that of loving him. Would she need a great deal of time to recover from Larry's demise? He didn't want to wait.

Sara looks at Jonathan carefully. His concerned expression seems to reflect some doubts, yet when he looks at her, Sara discerns warmth and a spark of approval. "It's an excellent idea." He smiles. "May I come to visit once in a while, or is this to be exclusively a women's enclave?"

"You can visit if you behave yourself and don't upset the boat."

"Yes, boss Mother." Jonathan surmises that she's warning him against pressing Sara too soon about his own agenda, which she has easily guessed for some time.

Edith actually lets out a theatrical, "Humph. Of course, if you don't like the idea of sharing Rose Cottage, you can bunk over here in your icy, cold room when you come up here to ski from time to time." Edith flips her hand in the direction of his room nearby."

Now he smiles, pretending to go along with his mother's idea at least temporarily. Actually his mother's plan is an excellent one. Yet, he further considers: must I wait cooling my heels on the sidelines quite so long? Will I be traumatizing Sara if I expedite my own particular plan?

"A new beginning. Let's go out to dinner to celebrate...with your permission." He glances at his mother who nods her agreement. His plan will give him time to speak to Sara about her long time care, and he doesn't mean nursing care either, though there may be some of that as well before the baby is finally born. In a kindly voice, Jonathan asks Sara again, "Do you approve?"

"I'm so grateful." She bends and hugs Edith across the shoulders.

Jon notices how Sara's eyes, a luminous water-green, now seem enormous. Steady, he tells himself, or at least pretend to be patient. You've waited this long. "Then our dinner together will seal this propitious deal...your new temporary home, Sara."

His mother accurately interprets the smug smile on her son's face and decides that he has just made a huge concession, but only a temporary one, the significance of which is completely lost on Sara. At that moment Edith realizes how neatly her plans have almost, but not quite, coincided with Jonathan's. She isn't a bit surprised, and like an announcer on a "late breaking news story," waits for further developments.

Sara feels such a burst of thankfulness for Edith's rescue that she wants to cry out joyfully. Maybe she will do exactly that when she reaches the privacy of her own room with the shower running. Surely, she thinks, Jonathan will visit his mother on the island from time to time, so I won't be completely isolated from him; his visits are something I can look forward to, but I mustn't count too heavily upon anything more than just friendly interest.

"Before we go out to dinner," Edith remarks, "I need to freshen-up, and I assume Sara needs to change out of her costume." Jonathan hands his mother the key to his room but doesn't follow her. Inside, as Edith washes up, she figuratively pats herself on the back and would have in fact if her seventy-year old anatomy could allow such a contortion. Now that she has "turned up the heat" on Jonathan by offering Sara a place to live, she can almost guarantee that her son will take the reins out of her hands and gather Sara in his own inimitable way.

When Sara turns to enter her own room to change out of her costume, Jonathan firmly says, "Not so fast." He steps through the door along with her. "I want to have a word with you." His voice sounds stern.

There's something deeply serious in his voice, bringing Sara's eyes to focus on his face more intently. He is unsmiling. Perhaps he doesn't really like the idea of his mother's invitation after all, but tried to cover it up while Edith was around? Is he already regretting having let her accept? Still, she is positive that he feels more towards her than mere sisterly fondness, or did before he learned more of her past with Larry. Those sparks of sexual familiarity have tugged so strongly that she has had to struggle to resist them.

Sara feels Jonathan's hand on her back firmly pushing her into the room as he follows. He closes the door. She quickly looks around, thankful that she had earlier made the bed and not left a lot of clutter visible except for the stacks of boxes on the floor.

"Sara, my mother has her own agenda, but before she came along with her idea for your shelter, I had another plan."

"Oh? Then her invitation is going to interfere. I'm sorry. She should have checked it out with you first." Sara tells herself to remain calm and not let her disappointment show, but her little flame of courage flutters out quickly. She can actually feel the blood leaving her face. Her shoulders begin to shake…not noticeably to Jonathan, she hopes. There is no way she can keep her whole body from scrunching up in readiness for the severe blow that's surely going to come. Jon must already care for someone else.

Jonathan doesn't seem to notice her trembling. Instead, he draws her down to sit beside him on the striped bedspread. "There is something I want to tell you…or rather, ask you."

Here it comes; she stiffens and lowers her head so that Jonathan won't be able to detect her reaction to his news. She grabs a paper hanky from the nearby box as she tries to steel herself against whatever is coming; she wants to present a dignified stance. Instead, she begins to tremble all over. Why doesn't he get the agony over with?

"Sara, would you consider letting your little girl have a new father?

The question is not what she expects at all. It's wildly off-target. She looks up at Jonathan wishing he would clarify. She doesn't dare chance leaping into hopefulness only to face rejection. Does he mean himself? She answers cautiously, "Of course...if I love him enough."

"How about me? Could you love me...enough?"

"Jonathan! I have cared about you almost from..."

She isn't allowed to finish her sentence because Jonathan has tipped her body back on the bed until she is gazing straight up into his face. For a moment she can see the mischievous, happy gleam in his eyes and the curved-up shape of his generous lips until both come so close to her that everything becomes unfocused and she can't see anything. Ah, she thinks, I might not see, but I can feel everything and especially the fizzy, leaping sparks all the way from his mouth to my toes and not missing anything in between.

When he brings his penetrating kiss to a halt long enough for her to take a breath, she asks in a trembling voice, "Dear Jonathan, are you asking me to marry you?"

He nods. He lays his hand gently on her tummy. "The question is for both of you."

Sara's smile is bemused and full of love. "We both accept; me in person and the little girl by proxy."